CHARM SCHOOL

BEN REEDER

For Hemlok

Ben Reed

1

Cover art by **Angela Gulick Design.**

Website: angelagulickdesign.com

Published through Outlaw Lit.

Other books by Ben Reeder:

The Demon's Apprentice series:
The Demon's Apprentice
Page of Swords
Vision Quest

The Zompoc Survivor series:
Zompoc Survivor: Exodus
Zompoc Survivor: Inferno
Zompoc Survivor: Odyssey

Dedication:

Mikayela, Isabella, Emmett, Wyatt and Bennett: The best group of little grandmunchkins a man could ever ask for.

Acknowledgements:

One more done, Randi, that couldn't have happened without your unwavering support. And to Dora, my furry gray writing assistant, protégé to Musaba, who still maintains editorial control.

Special thanks go out to Angela Gulick, for making the last minute changes to the cover. As always, you never fail to amaze me and exceed every expectation.

Thank you to Marguerite Reed and Lawrence M. Schoen for getting me to NorWesCon and helping make it so productive, respectively. Congratulations, Marguerite!

For the awesome folks at Meta-Games Unlimited, thanks for letting me hang out and use your wifi.

Chapter 1

~ When a mortal says they want things to be 'fair,'
they really just want to win. ~ advice given to a young
demon.

Wizards aren't supposed to be whiny. But Dr. Corwyn was getting close to it. I could feel Shade's shoulders shake under my arm as she snickered quietly. Wanda was carefully looking at something on the far edge of the platform, but Mom looked like she wasn't about to spare his dignity. Even with dozens of people around us on the transit platform, her expression said she was ready to lay into him. Junkyard didn't offer an opinion. He was on an adventure, which was pretty much any time he wasn't at home or Dr. C's place. Any opportunity to mark a new part of the world as his was a good thing, as far as he was concerned.

"This is what I could afford," I growled in response to his latest complaint. In front of us was a teleportation platform, its triple rings dormant and upright. Around it was a series of runes, and the stone floor was inscribed with magickal symbols.

"Master Draeden offered to fly us up on his private jet," Dr. C said. "For free. We'd be there in a matter of hours, and we'd fly in comfort."

"No," I told him again. "I don't want to owe him any favors. And believe me, he'd think he was doing me a favor." Dr. C's lips pressed tight together as he looked at me, then he nodded.

"You're right about that," he said after a moment, his tone resigned. "You do know you're making it harder on yourself though, right?"

I nodded. "Yeah, I know you get sick when you teleport. I'll deal with it."

"Then so will I … again." I nodded, willing the memories of his troubles with teleportation back into the

5

box I'd built for them. Ahead of us, a group of Dwarves in gray business suits stepped onto the platform, handing tickets to the man at the opening in the waist high railing as they passed him.

"Last call for Denver Commons. Dennnnver Commons, transiting in three minutes. Last call!" As he finished, a woman in a flowing green dress came bustling up with two boys trailing from each hand.

"Denver Commons, that's us," she said as she let go of the boys' hands and dug in her purse. Moments later, she produced three tickets and thrust them at the man. He took them and gave them a quick glance, then nodded and gestured for her to go on. She grabbed the two boys by the hand again and stepped forward.

"Mom, do we have to take the transit platform?" one of the boys asked. "Barry always gets sick." The other boy was turning a little green around the edges, and the woman's eyes went wide.

"Oh, hell," the mother spat and rushed to the edge of the platform to grab something from a wooden box and hustled back to her sons. "I'm glad you reminded me." The Dwarves shuffled over a little as she returned and handed the less enthusiastic looking boy the paper bag she'd taken from the box. The man at the edge of the railing stepped back and went to a control panel by the upright rings.

"Transiting to Denver Commons," he called out as he manipulated the levers on the panel. "Stand clear of the platform! Stand clear of the yellow line." The nested rings started to spin with a metallic rasp, then the two inner rings rotated on their axis until they were horizontal, leaving a dark blue glow in their wake. A moment later, the inner most ring rotated along the second ring's axis, creating a third axis. The rings started to hum as the dark blue energy obscured the inside of the transit platform. Finally, the first ring stopped, with a rune glowing. The horizontal ring slowed to a stop a few seconds later, a different rune glowing over our heads at the spot where it intersected with the third ring. Finally, the inner most ring stopped, and I could see the glow of a rune at the top of the rings. The glow pulsed brighter for a moment, then disappeared completely, revealing an empty platform. Dee gave a squeal of delight as the rings slowly started to return to their original position.

"Can I go with them?" she asked. "I wanna teleport!"

"Not today, sis," I said. "I only bought two tickets. But you and Mom can come up some time."

"There is a Parent's Day every month or so," Dr. C said. "And students can earn off campus passes for weekends."

"Liberty Plaza," the transit operator called out. "Ten minutes to transit to Liberty Plaza. All on the platform for Boston."

"That's us," I said. I squeezed Shade a little closer for a moment, and her arms tightened around my ribs.

"I'm going to miss you," she said for about the thousandth time.

"You know I'm going to be crazy without you," I said as I kissed her.

"Promise to wither away and die?" she asked.

"I'll even write depressing poetry about how much I miss you every day."

"And I'll lock myself in my room for at least a month and mope," Shade giggled.

"Could you two get any more dysfunctional?" Wanda asked, adding an eyeroll for emphasis.

"Still a better love story than-" Dr. C started to say. Wanda's elbow in his ribs cut off the comment.

"Okay, now that the Codepency Channel's off the air, Lucas sent something for you. He said you're not supposed to open it until you've got your room set up." She handed me a black gift bag from Lucas's grandfather's store, Mitternacht's Books. "We're gonna miss having you around to make things interesting. Hopefully, no one tries to destroy the city while you're gone,' she said as she hugged me.

"I'm sure you guys can handle it," I said as I wrapped her in a hug.

"Great," Wanda said with a grin. "Now you've pretty much made sure something is going to happen while you're gone. We'll be stuck trying to make it an episode where you come back right after we beat the Big Bad and we act all cool like nothing happened, instead of one where you have to rescue us at the last minute from our own stupidity."

"I got you something, too," Shade said with a sly smile as she pressed something into my hand. When I looked down, I saw a sleek phone laying on my palm.

"Baby, I can't afford this," I said as I tried to push it back into her hands.

"I can," Shade said, her smile turning a little feral as she closed my hand around the phone. "And it's not for you. It's for me. I want to see your face when we talk. I want to talk to you for hours and not have your minutes run out in the middle. And I want you to have something that's just between us."

"Like I don't already," I whispered. Her hand came up and touched the center of my chest, where the vial with several drops of her blood hung from a leather thong. One with filled withmy blood was nestled between her breasts, both given under a waxing moon, so our love would only grow. I leaned in and kissed her, then stepped back.

"Why is it I keep saying goodbye to you every time I turn around?" Mom asked when I turned to her.

"Because life sucks," I said. Both our voices were a little rougher than we wanted anyone else to hear, but I wasn't about to go all stoic and stiff-upper lipped on Mom. Dee put her arms around my waist and held tight for a few moments, then turned and shrugged the straps of her purple backpack off her shoulders. At least today it almost went with the plain blue t-shirt she had on. Lately, she'd taken to wearing plain shirts, refusing to wear even her Dr. Hooves t-shirt, which I was pretty sure was her favorite shirt ever.

"Take Pyewacket with you," she said as she pulled the black stuffed animal from her pack. "I'd give you Dr. Hooves, but I need him if you're not home."

"I'm sure he'll keep me safe," I said as I took the black cat. It had a little hand-made wizard's hat sewed to its head now, and wore a little pewter pendant with symbols carved into it.

"I don't recognize these symbols," I said as I went to one knee.

"I made them up," Dee said. I almost heard Dr. C's shoulders unknot. "That one's so you don't have bad dreams, that one is for protection, and that one is so you don't have too much homework."

I hugged her tight, and tucked Pyewacket into my backpack next to Lucas's gift bag. "I hope that last one works really well," I told her before I stood up and hugged Mom.

"Everything I can give you, I already have," she said as she took my hand in hers. "The gifts of my bloodline, the love of a mother, and a home to return to when your travels are done. I'm proud of you, Chance." I choked up for a moment, so all I could do was hug her to me.

"I won't let you down," I said when I pulled back. Mom smiled and shook her head.

"You never have," she said.

"The gate's open," Dr. C said. I shrugged my backpack on, then grabbed the dolly that had my book trunk on it and wheeled it toward the opening in the railing. Dr. C wheeled the one with my clothes in it along behind me. Junkyard trotted along behind us, carrying his own luggage in the red harness vest that Mom had made for him. His food and water bowls were on either side, and his blanket was rolled up and tied to the harness across his shoulders, with a few little items in the backpack behind that. His most important possession, a big rawhide bone, he carried in his mouth. And as always, he wore his two bandanas around his thick neck. Once we had my stuff on the platform, I went back to the gate and gave one last round of hugs and kissed Shade.

"Liberty Plaza, transiting in one minute!" the transit operator called out. I backed away from everyone.

"You ready?" Dr. C asked when I reached him. I looked down and saw the paper bag he held in his hand.

"No. Are you?"

"Eh," he said with a casual shrug. Junkyard looked up at us and thumped his tail. At least one of us was happy to be there.

"Transiting to Liberty Plaza," the operator called out. Dr. C nodded and turned so that he was facing away from me. His shoulders pressed against mine, and I felt his weight shift as his right hand went to his side, where a pistol would be if he was armed.

"Old habits?" I asked.

"Bare is the brotherless back," he said as the world outside of the platform turned blue. Reality seemed to spin and lurch at the same time, while my mystic senses were bombarded by a scream of static. Then everything stopped at once, and that was almost as bad as the onslaught of sensation. My ears felt like they were cringing and I blinked like I'd just been flash-blinded. As disorienting as it had been, it was a lot smoother than some of the transits I'd made with Dulka to the various Infernal realms. Behind me, I could hear Dr. C moan and gulp.

"You gonna make it, sir?" I asked.

"Oddly enough…I think I will," he said. "That's a first."

The blue haze faded around us, and I was treated to my first sight of Liberty Plaza. Unlike New Essex's Underground, Liberty Plaza was entirely open to the sky.

The transit rings rotated back into position, and a man in a long coat and white knee breeches opened the gate set in the wrought iron fence that surrounded the platform.

"Arriving, New Essex Underground," he said. We grabbed my two trunks and wheeled them toward the gate as another man spoke up.

"Preparing to depart, Capitol Greens," the man on the opposite side of the platform said. First call, Puget Sound." Junkyard and I followed Dr. C across the open space surrounding the transit platform as a mixed group waited on the other side to enter the transit stage. Most of the buildings were either white-washed wood or red brick. The one Dr. C led us to had a green sign above the door that read "Brannock's Livery, Est. 1706" in gold letters. We muscled my trunks through the door, and almost immediately, a large man in a blue work shirt and jeans hustled out from behind the counter to help us.

"Good afternoon," he said as he gestured at the trunk Dr. C was pushing. "Welcome to Brannock's. Where can we take you today?"

"The Franklin Academy," I said, reaching into my pocket for the pouch full of trade silver I carried. He turned and looked at me for a moment, then nodded and put a smile on his face.

"We don't get many going out to the Academy," he said. His tone was carefully neutral, but I could see Dr. Corwin's shoulders tense when the man stopped and turned to face us. The man nodded and took the trunk to the back, then came back for mine.

"Is the dog going back with you?" he asked Dr. C after both trunks were stowed.

"He's my familiar," I said. I turned to Junkyard and undid his harness. "It's okay, buddy. Let him take the bone. You'll get it back, I promise." Junkyard gave me a long suffering look, then lowered his head and laid the rawhide

11

bone at the man's feet. The guy slowly bent over and picked the bone up then took the harness from me.

"What's so damn funny?" I asked Dr. C while the livery keeper took Junkyard's stuff back. He was grinning like he'd just heard a dirty joke with a pun for a punch line.

"It's just funny when people underestimate you," he said.

"As long as you're enjoying yourself," I muttered.

"Immensely, my young apprentice," he said. "Now, we have a little bit of shopping to do before we go. You still need a couple of books and your school uniforms." I did my best not to groan at that, and if he heard me, he at least acted like he didn't. We left the livery with the time we'd be going to the Academy, and Dr. C led me toward Hobart's Haberdashery. Like most of the shops in the Plaza, the only thing that stood out about it was its sign, and even that wasn't very original. The name was split up in an over and under style on a white oval, with a spool and crossed needles taking center space. Other than that, it could have been any of the three story red brick buildings. My first impression of Boston was a boring one.

A bell rang somewhere in the shop as we came in, and a stooped little man with thin black hair that was combed over the blank acreage on top of his head emerged from the back. Dr. C handed him his card as he walked up, and the man just about simpered at us.

"Ah, Wizard Corwin," the little man said in a breathy voice that sounded like a passable Peter Lorre impression. He offered one limp little hand to Dr. C, who took it just long enough to give a perfunctory handshake. He nodded to me, then lowered his hand for Junkyard to sniff, which of course earned him the dog's approval and a few points in my book. "So good to see you again. Apprentice Fortunato's uniforms are ready. Shall I have them sent ahead to the Academy?"

"We'll take one now," Dr. Corwin said as he wiped his hand on his pant leg. "Have the rest sent ahead, if you please. I'll handle payment via a draft from Bjernings, as agreed."

"Of course, of course," Mr. Hobart wheezed. "So good to see a wizard who still knows the value of tradition. So many apprentices bound for Franklin don't have a proper master to teach them. These past few decades, it's been all tutors and family expense accounts. No one properly overseeing their students." He shook his head as he went to a rack of hanging clothes and started checking tags. About midway through, he stopped and pulled a black suit out, then returned to us with it half draped over his arm. The Franklin Academy crest was on the left breast pocket, and a dark red tie with broad black stripes bordered in white was draped around the hanger. I took the suit, and he offered Dr. C a black box. "You'll find such accessories as needed to turn your young apprentice out in proper style for today inside. And of course, once he is properly settled, you can order accessories to match his house affiliation."

"Of course," Dr. C said with a smile. "We'll notify you as soon as we know."

"Houses?" I asked under my breath as we headed for the dressing room.

"Yes, each dormitory is under the house system. You'll be assigned to one house the entire time you're there."

"Sounds a lot like-"

"Yes, it does. Only without that stupid hat. And there's no cup at the end of the year."

"You didn't like the hat?" I asked as I went into the dressing room.

"I didn't like the idea of lumping all the same kind of people together in the same place. That's never a good idea. Hell, even the characters in the books knew how that worked out and they still put all the potential power hungry maniacs in the same two houses. And then they act surprised when the same thing happens again and again? But, it's fiction. I guess I should expect a little creative license."

"So, she didn't just make up the part about the houses on her own?" I asked after I pulled the pants on.

"No, the house system is pretty common in boarding schools in Britain," he said. "It's also pretty common at boarding schools here, at least the older ones. But the idea is to keep the houses diverse, not homogenous."

The shirt was a soft white linen, and the jacket was a black wool blazer. I tucked the tails of the shirt in and stepped out with the tie in hand.

"Is there a secret knot?" I asked.

Dr. C laughed. "No, just the usual four-in-hand. Remember, some magick uses knots to bind and release spells, so the Academy has to keep the everyday stuff very mundane. Especially around hundreds of young mages with varying levels of control over themselves and their magick." He helped me with the knot, then handed me the cufflinks from the box. Unlike the ones I'd seen my father wear, these were two disks connected by a single link of chain. One bore the school colors in diagonal bands, the other with white dots on a red field. Dr. Corwin ran them through the buttonholes so that the two cuffs came together beside each other instead of having them overlap like all my other cuffed shirts did. He held out a slim, rectangular wristwatch on a narrow black band, and I gave him a distrustful look. "Oh, go on," he teased me. "It's just a time piece, not a manacle." I slipped it on and buckled it into place.

"Lucas would probably say something about being a slave to the clock," I said.

"Most likely," Dr. C said. "Now, the watch case and the cuff links are made of silver. I know it's tempting to use them as charm focuses, but that would be frowned on, so

14

don't do that." His tone had all the sincerity of a used car salesman.

"Of course not, sir," I said. "Because none of the other kids are going to be doing it either, right?"

"Not at all," he said. We went back to the counter where Hobart was waiting. His eyes ran up and down as I approached. He smiled and nodded as Dr. C signed the draft approval, then ushered us to the door.

"A fine fit," he breathed happily. "A fine fit indeed, Apprentice Fortunato. Wear it in good health and don't hesitate to call upon me if you need anything repaired or replaced. The rest of your uniforms will be waiting for you upon your arrival at the Academy."

We found ourselves on the sidewalk with a paper bag that held my street clothes and the accessory box, and Hobart's business card in our hands, with Hobart himself bowing and smiling behind us. Dr. C turned to the left and headed toward another shop, this one with a white wooden sign in the shape of an open books. "Harper and Taylor, Booksellers" was printed across the white paint in the same kind of black letter as every other sign around it.

"It's awfully quiet," I said as we approached the door. I'd seen maybe ten people outside the transit stage, and most of them looked human.

"Boston is home to some of the wealthiest mage families in the US," Dr. C said. "They don't *go* shopping. They tell the help what they want, and it shows up later that day. Most of these merchants make a fortune with customers they rarely see or meet."

"That sounds boring," I said.

"I wouldn't know," he replied.

The smell of Harper and Taylor hit my nose and almost made me feel homesick. It smelled of old paper and leather, a lot like Mitternacht's did. It was missing the aromas of pipe smoke and coffee, though. Rows of books filled the middle of the space, and the walls were lined with bookshelves as well. A blonde woman smiled at us from behind the counter on our right, her hair smoothed back and gathered into a bun so tight I wasn't sure even light could escape it, much less a stray hair. Her eyes flicked to Junkyard and her lips twitched a little, but the smile stayed put.

"Good morning," she said as we approached the counter. "How can we help you?"

"We need these three titles," Dr. Corwin said as he handed her the small page from his notepad. She took it and held it gingerly between her thumb and forefinger, then snapped her fingers. Almost immediately, I heard the flutter of wings, and a blue skinned sprite flew down from the rafters. He wore a simple white tunic with the back cut out to make room for his wings, with a cord belt that had several small pouches and a net dangling from it. His antennae jutted from his forehead and dipped forward, with three small nodules on the end.

"Zip, help these two gentlemen with their purchases," she said. Her smile slipped just a little, and there was an almost imperceptible pause before the word 'gentlemen' as she spoke. I looked at the sprite, and felt my jaw tighten as my teeth clenched. The little fae dropped down and accepted the list from her, then turned in midair and drifted over the bookshelves, his shoulders slumping as he dipped out of sight. A couple of moments later, he reappeared with a book dangling in the net, his wings tinged red from the effort, and his face a darker shade of blue. He set it on the counter and proceeded to unwrap the book, but Dr. C was there in a heartbeat.

"Perhaps you could just show us where the other two are," he said as he lifted the book free of the netting. Zip looked over at the woman, his big eyes darkened with worry.

"If sir insists," he said.

"Sir does," Dr. C said as he handed the textbook to me. "It's a personal preference, pay it no mind." Zip gathered the net up and tucked it back in his belt, then took to the air again, his two antennae quivering as he led us through the stacks. I took a look at the book he'd brought, *History of American Magick: Civil War to 2010.* The next book he led us to was *Transformative Properties: Alchemy In the Modern Age.* It was a thick book, and judging by the orange and red design on the cover, the Modern Age was sometime back in the 70s. Zip led us up a set of narrow stairs and to the back for the third book. Of the three, it was the skinniest, and the smallest. *Counterspells and Wards: Theories of Magickal Defense* was printed in fading gold ink on the cloth cover. I took it from Dr. C with a frown.

"Have I made a mistake?" Zip asked. "Is it the wrong title?"

"No, Zip, you did just fine," Dr. C said with a smile as he fished in his pocket. "It's exactly the right book. You certainly know your shop. Your service was exemplary. Thank you." He laid his hand on one of the shelves, leaving a silver trade bar and a cinnamon candy behind. Zip's eyes went to the shelf, then he nodded and flew off, his wings making a higher pitched hum.

"I thought it would be...I don't know, thicker?" I said as I held up the book.

"It assumes you know a lot about the topic already," he said as he led the way back toward the stairs. "Which you do." He stopped only long enough to sign the draft approval and gave the clerk a perfunctory nod, then headed straight for the door. Once outside, he stopped for a moment and took a deep breath, blowing his breath out through his lips as he seemed to deflate a little.

"Was it the sprite?" I asked as we walked along.

"I can't stand the way people treat them sometimes," he said, his voice tight. I let the subject drop, and we made the rest of the walk in silence.

By the time we made it to the livery office, my feet were beginning to hurt in the new shoes, and I wanted nothing more than to take the damn things off. Preferably to throw them in a fire. I kept them on through force of will, and took a moment to look over the carriage that waited for us. The bottom was a dark red wood polished to a high shine, and the top was black, with a cloth roof that arched forward from the rear. The driver's seat had its own black awning and a black bench with red cushions. My trunks were tied to the back, with a small basket on top. Junkyard pretty much quivered at the prospect of a ride, and his tail was a blur behind his butt. The driver came out and opened the door, ushering us out to the carriage and opening the door to the carriage as well. As we crossed the wooden patio, I saw what was pulling the wagon.

The front looked like a brass horse, complete with a mane of black hair. But where its shoulders should have been was the edge of a large, spoked wheel. The center of the wheel was cut out, and a horizontal copper ring ran through it. A bright blue nimbus of energy floated inside the copper ring, and a pair of thick bars curved forward and down to connect the carriage to the ring. Junkyard jumped into the carriage and looked back at us, his tongue lolling out. I let Dr. C get in first to spite the pain lancing up from my toes, but I wasn't above a sigh of relief as I sank into the leather padded seat.

"Shoes?" Dr. C asked. I nodded. "They take some getting used to. Hobart will likely include some stretchers for them. I suggest you use them."

"I wish I could just wear my sneakers instead," I said.

"You'll have to abide by the manual's instructions," he said as the cart surged forward. We came out onto a side road in a wooded section. The road curved around until it came out onto a path the followed the Charles River. The track we were on ran parallel to the road, but slightly below it. I could see the slight shimmer of the *glamer* that hid us from the cowan drivers, a little deflection spell that barely brushed against the brain's frontal lobe and urged it to ignore what didn't fit with 'normal' perceptions. We rode along, keeping pace with the cars on the road to our left with little more than the sound of the wheels humming on the road and the soft whine of the magickal engine. Most of the time, we were actually hidden from view by the trees, but as the road curved to the right, we emerged near a freeway, and I could see three taller buildings ahead and to our right. We followed the river's bank, crossing the water using a lane no one else seemed to see. Finally, we veered away from the banks near a subdivision called Waltham. Once we slipped under the interchange after Waltham, we started seeing more carriages on the road. A couple passed us like we were standing still, both floating along effortlessly.

Eventually, we turned off the hidden road and found ourselves in front of a set of gates with three carriages and a limo ahead of us. Men and women in dark suits flanked the gate with clipboards and wands in hand. One approached the limo and spoke to its driver, checked his clipboard, then waved them through. The carriage after it got the same treatment, but the next one was waved onto a side road to the right. As we pulled forward, I caught sight of a blue robe and a silver ankh atop a silver staff.

"That's new," Dr. Corwin said as he glanced at the Sentinel. Ahead of us, the man with the clipboard was waving the carriage forward when one of the curtains in the cabin parted near him.

"What is the meaning of that?" I heard as an arm emerged from the window. The man didn't exactly point. He swung his hand in the general direction of what he was talking about, apparently assuming the person he was talking to would get the point. Before the staffer could answer, he continued. "I pay enough to send my sons here;

19

I don't want them to have to look at those people all day long."

"The headmaster will explain why they're here, Mr. Abernathy," the staffer said patiently. "Rest assured, Master Carlton and Master Wilforth won't be seeing them any more than is absolutely necessary for their safety and security."

"They shouldn't have to see them at all, and you can be certain I'll be having a word with the headmaster about your attitude as well. When Master Draeden hears about this, he'll have your job and the headmaster's I'm sure." The hand retreated back into the carriage and it pulled forward, leaving us as the next in line.

"Good afternoon, sir," the staffer said as we pulled up.

"Good afternoon," Dr. C said. "Wizard Corwin and Apprentice Fortunato." Up close, I could see that the man had an ear cuff on his left ear. It glowed blue when Dr. C stopped talking and the man nodded. I guessed it was tuned to tell if someone was lying, and it had just verified that we were who we said we were. The staffer ran his finger down the clipboard, then looked up at us, his eyes hooded as he glanced at me.

"Fortunato," he said slowly. "Scholarship. You'll be checking in at Strathorn Hall."

"Strathorn?" Dr. C said. "I thought check-in for all students was at Chadwicke."

"No, sir," the staffer said with a practiced looking smile. "Scholarship students have a streamlined check-in process now. Much less confusing." He stepped back and gestured at the driver, and the carriage lurched forward.

"That's new, too," he said as he frowned and leaned back in the seat. The road curved along the inside of a stone wall on our right that came up about five feet and sprouted iron fencing above that. Square towers of stone supported the fencing every twenty feet or so. I caught glimpses of the school through the trees, but never more than a stolen glance of red brick or white trim. Ahead of us, the woods ended, and the wall went from half-stone and half fence to all iron fencing except for the intervening stone towers. Outside the forested area, the support columns were topped with painted statues of mystical beasts.

When we cleared the trees, I got my first good look at the Franklin Academy. Like most things in Massachusetts so far, it was mostly red brick with a little white wood for contrast. The doors, shutters and roof trim were bright white. The front of the place looked like one very wide four story building that had sprouted a couple of smaller buildings along its wings. To the left, I could see cars and carriages, and a crowd of students in Franklin black in front of the main building in the middle. The boys were easy to tell from the girls by the flash of pale legs in skirts.

Then we were around the corner, and a much smaller group of people were waiting outside of an older looking building. Cars and carriages were evenly represented here, but none of them looked very expensive. In fact, the newest looking carriage there bore the crest of the livery company we'd rented ours from. As we pulled up, I could see some of the kids lounging near the steps that led into the building. Unlike what I saw at school in the cowan world, this group didn't split off like normal kids did. Some of them were sitting on the lowest step staring at handheld game consoles, while another group was at the corner of the steps and a third was only a few feet away. The corner group was a mixture of different performers. A couple of girls worked with hula hoops, doing impossible twirls and tricks. A trio of guys and two girls spun poi with an intensely casual air, while another kid worked with a set of small rings next to one who was weaving intricate energy designs between his fingers. The group further from the steps was almost all guys, and my summer spent working with Dr. Corwin, Steve Donovan and the Hands of Death, Todd Cross and T-Bone, told me all I needed to know

21

about them. These were the martial artists, or the guys who liked to think they were. Smooth katas were mixed with rapid, jerky sequences of strikes and kicks, each more elaborate than the last.

The carriage stopped, and Dr. C was out the door before I could even sit up straight. When my feet hit the grass beside the road, he was already several steps ahead of me. Even Junkyard seemed to have springs in his feet as he bounded around me. I slung my backpack across one shoulder, then followed Dr. C as fast as I could, and we found ourselves in a large, open room with tall, narrow windows. A large fireplace dominated one end of the hall, and three heavy tables that formed a squared off U shape. Grown-ups sat on the outside of the U, while students filed along the inside of it with papers in hand. Parents and students chatted with each other and the handful of staff in the open area in the middle of the hall. A handful of the parents had a sort of shell shocked look on their faces, mostly those with younger kids in the Academy's uniform beside them.

"Excuse me," a man's voice called out when we were halfway across the hall. "Pets are not allowed." We turned to see a thin faced, blond man in his mid-20s crossing the wooden floor toward us, his leather shoes clomping against the hard surface as he came our way.

"He isn't a pet," Dr. Corwin said, sounding about as irritated as I did when I said it.

"I beg your pardon?" the man asked, pulling up short.

"He's my familiar," I said.

"Where's his control collar?" the man demanded. "All familiars must be under strict control of their owners at all times. You can't control an animal without one. And where are his papers and registration as familiar?"

"I don't own him," I said. By now, heads were starting to turn toward us.

22

"The bond between mage and animal is the entire point of a familiar," Dr. C said with a frown. "You can't just buy one." The man just smiled and shook his head.

"Typical," he said. "I'll take you to Washington Hall and you can make arrangements to send the animal home. Come with me." He turned and strode toward a side door, and we found ourselves in a hallway that connected the building we were in to the rest of the school. The staffer's feet clacked on the marble floor as he set a quick pace down an endless hallway. We went through another building and turned left into a larger marble hall. Another building and another hallway passed before we hit the steps leading into the main building. Even then, we ended up going down a long hall with several old wooden doors on either side before we hit the main hall. Through it all, Junkyard stayed by my side, and Dr. C maintained his glare at the other man's back.

The biggest difference between the two rooms was the number of staff here. And the number of chairs. Row upon row of tables had been set up like individual desks, with one chair on one side, and three on the other. As we entered, a family got up from one of the tables and left the room, and another family was ushered into their place. One half of the room was also given over to a waiting area, with padded chairs and tables covered with bottles of water, soda and juice next to trays of hors d'oeuvres.

"Good morning, Mr. and Mrs. Endicott," the woman on the other side said as they took their seats. "We'll just have you sign a few forms here, and give you Reginald's syllabus and student manual, and he'll be enrolled."

"Excellent," Mr. Endicott said as we passed the table. "I have a meeting at three, I can't be held up with paperwork..." The rest was lost in the low buzz as we headed for a line of kids at the back of the hall. Each of them wore the Franklin school uniform, and all of them had an animal either next to them, on them or in their arms. I

23

slowed down, but the stampede of panicked animals never happened. A few started to act agitated, but at a gesture from their owners, they calmed. I turned and gave Dr. C a confused look, but his glare only seemed to focus down to a laser-like intensity.

"Wait here," the staffer said and then headed toward the front of the line. I looked back over my shoulder toward the table we'd passed. A woman was handing the over a thick file to the man behind the desk, who nodded at her before she went toward the back of the room. I could see several more runners moving between the tables, pulling files from a long table at the back of the room. I turned my attention back to the line of kids and animals. Winthrop Gage had also mentioned a collar when he'd first seen Junkyard, but we'd fought a demon not long after that, and that little detail just sort of faded into the background. And these kids either had very strong bonds with their familiars, or animals that were familiar material just weren't phased by all the demonic crap that had stuck to my aura while I was working for Dulka.

"That is just...*wrong*," Dr. C said through gritted teeth. "Those animals aren't familiars." I looked down the line. One girl held a koala, while another had a spider monkey clinging to her shoulder. Two other boys had huge hawks, and a third had a colorful parrot on his shoulder. There were a few exotic cats, all well bred and groomed, and a couple of owls. All bore some sort of jeweled collar or band around their neck or leg.

"What do you mean, sir?" I asked. "They certainly act like it." He tapped the center of his forehead, then raised his eyebrows at me expectantly. It took a second before I got what he wanted me to do. "Oh, right!" I said, and blinked a couple of times to let my eyes unfocus and my Aura Sight open.

Bright blues and purples covered most of their auras, with curious gaps in places. The animals, on the other hand, had light green aura covering their natural one, with dark red streaks extending from the collar through the overlaid shell. Each of the kids had a small red and green blotch on their aura, centered on a ring or a bracelet. I looked down at Junkyard, with his bright gold aura, and the streaks of black and red around his heart. A similar patch of gold ran through my aura near my heart chakra, the little bits of ourselves that we had shared when we bonded.

I blinked and shook my head. "There's no bond between them," I said.

"The collar suppresses the animal's will, and the master device lets the owner control them like a puppet." He was almost trembling with anger now, and I could understand why. Dr. Corwin might have been a bad ass wizard, and he sure as hell didn't cut me any slack with my lessons, but as strict and sometimes just flat scary as he was, he had a huge soft spot for anything with fur or feathers. As hard as he pushed me, he spoiled Junkyard twice as much. Seeing this must have pissed him off to no end. Dr. C was usually pretty mellow, but right now, he was almost as angry as I'd ever seen him.

"Dr. C," I said softly. "In the words of your generation, be cool, man." One side of his mouth dipped down as he turned toward me and pulled his head back. "What?" I said off his look.

"Hearing you be the voice of reason is a little…odd," he said.

"I'm the one who knows when fighting is a bad idea, and losing your shit right now…kinda at the top of the whole bad idea list."

"This is definitely not the time, or the arena," he said after a moment. By then, the officious little prick who had pulled us from the enrollment line was dragging another, older man toward us. Most of his hair was gone, leaving gray tufts above his ears that matched his faded eyebrows. His face was round and pink, with wrinkles at the corners of his eyes and mouth that looked like he spent most of his time smiling.

"Really, Mr. Preston," he was protesting as the younger man pulled him forward. "I don't see the need for…oh." He stopped as he saw Junkyard.

"Yes, sir," Mr. Preston said with a quick nod. "We can't have this animal wandering loose."

"You look familiar," the older man said as his eyes fell of Dr. C.

"I was a student here back in eighty-one, Professor Abernathy," Dr. C said as he offered a hand to the older gentleman. "I'm Trevor Corwyn."

"Ah, Wizard Corwyn, yes, I recall you," Abernathy said with a smile. "You did a semester to qualify for Sentinel training. Chomsky's last apprentice. I was saddened to hear of his passing last year; terrible loss. The boy is your student, then?"

"Yes, sir, and the animal in question is his familiar. A real familiar, not some…" he stopped for a moment, then waved his hand toward the line of students. "Not like those."

"An old fashioned bond, eh? Haven't seen anything like that in a while," Abernathy said. "Well, the test should be easy enough to see to."

"But, Professor, the animal's registration and paperwork," Preston sputtered. "We can't let just any animal in here. It has to be from a certified breeder and…and…"

"I told you it had been a while," Abernathy said to Dr. C. He turned and ushered us up the steps to the curtained off stage area, with Preston following behind. Behind the curtain, several men and women in longer coats sat behind a single table. An empty seat waited on the right side, and Abernathy wasted no time in taking it. Still he wasn't fast enough to shut Preston up.

"Professor Abernathy, these traditions have been in place for over thirty years," he said.

"Yes, I know," Abernathy said. "And I've been here for sixty-three years. By your logic, *I'm* a tradition, and an older one at that. Young man, what's your name?"

"Chance Fortunato, sir," I said. "And this is Junkyard." Junkyard took a step forward and promptly sat.

"Junkyard?" the woman to Abernathy's left asked, her pen poised over a form.

"Yes, ma'am. That's where we first met."

"And this is where you shared the bond gaze?" Abernathy asked. I nodded. "Very well then, let's put him through his paces."

"How do you propose we do that?" a woman who looked like she was in the early twenties asked. "

"The same way we do all the others. First, we verify the bond."

"How do we do that without documentation?" the younger woman asked. Abernathy sighed and shook his head, adding in an eyeroll to up the difficulty.

"Have none of you been here more than thirty years?" he asked. Heads shook up and down the table. "Look at the boy's aura and then at the dog's. There will be some overlay around the heart. There, do you see it?" Half a dozen pairs of eyes went to me, and I could see the shock and revulsion on their faces as they each got a look at my aura, then glanced over at Junkyard.

"Nadia," the older man said when one woman let out disgusted sound deep in her throat. "Are you capable of conducting yourself impartially at this time, or is your objectivity compromised?" The question had the cadence of a formal request, but his tone made it sound a lot sharper to me, as if the question itself was a reprimand.

"I'm okay," the woman said after a moment.

"Then we're agreed that a bond exists?" Six quiet acknowledgements answered him. "Mr. Fortunato, please direct your familiar from one side of the room to the other, then back to your starting point."

I looked down at Junkyard, and he looked up at me. His tail hit my ankle as it wagged. "Over there, buddy," I said. He trotted to the place I was pointing, then turned and looked back at me. "Other side now," I said, and pointed to the other side of the room. He crossed the room, turned around and sat, giving me a tongue lolling look. "Back over here." Seconds later, he was next to me again, and I found myself facing row of frowning faces.

"The familiar failed to complete the task properly," one of the men said.

"Failed?" Abernathy laughed, "Or exceeded your expectations?"

"There is only pass or fail," the man said. "He did not do what was instructed. The task was to cross the room and return to his owner. The fault lies with the owner, but that changes nothing."

"He did cross the room," Nadia said. "And he did return to his owner. Most students do it as a straight line and back because that's all they can manage, Harris. Is *your* objectivity compromised? No? Then the dog passed." Shrugs and head nods answered.

"Very well then, next test," Abernathy said with a slight smile. "Step forward. Stop. Now, keep the animal in place." Nadia, Harris and two others stood up and came around the table toward me, stopping only a couple of feet away from us. I looked down at Junkyard and gave him a little nod and smiled, and his tail thumped again.

"So far so good," I muttered. As if they'd been waiting for me to relax, all four of them closed in around me, almost but not quite touching us. Junkyard leaned into my leg and went very still. After a few seconds, all four stepped back, then took another quick step to one side so that they ended up moving one place to the right. A moment later, they did it again, then did it all in reverse before backing away.

"He handles crowding well enough," Harris said, each word sounding a little reluctant. "But I still have my concerns about an uncollared animal roaming about."

"Nonsense, Harris," Abernathy said. "Familiars roamed these halls uncollared for centuries without incident. It wasn't until these collars were invented that we even felt the need to test them to make sure they'd be safe. It used to be that you couldn't go a week without seeing a familiar running or flying back and forth to fetch a forgotten wand or homework or some such. Now they're about as useful as those little dogs rich *cowan* women carry around in their purses."

"Then maybe we should make this animal prove it can do that before we let it roam around. At least that way, when it pees in one of the halls, we can justify it!" Harris said, his tone heating as he spoke.

"That is uncalled for!" Abernathy said. As he addressed Harris, I knelt beside Junkyard and whispered in his ear.

"I think it's entirely called for," Harris said. "We have to prove to some of the most influential families in America that they're children are safe from any foreseeable threat while they're getting the finest education on two continents. I'm not going to let some stupid animal walk unsupervised on this campus." He leaned toward Abernathy as he spoke, and didn't see Junkyard raise up on the table and paw his pen toward him. His eyes went wide, though, when he saw Junkyard's big furry head pop up in front of Abernathy with his silver pen in his mouth and drop it onto the desk in front of him.

"What's this?" Abernathy asked as he reached for the pen.

"It's a pen, you use it to write with," I said. "But that's not important right now." Beside me, Dr. C choked on a laugh. "It's his. Junkyard can go get something and take it somewhere, as long as he's seen it before and been to where he's going. He's still working on doorknobs, though." Abernathy covered his mouth as his smile widened. He looked at the pen in his hand, then held it back out to Junkyard.

"Would you return this to its owner?" he said. Junkyard leaned forward and gently took the pen in his teeth, then dropped down and trotted back to Harris. This time Harris watched as he put his front paws on the table and leaned forward, his tongue and jaw working the saliva covered pen out of his mouth.

"He's drooled all over it," Harris said, picking it up with his handkerchief.

"I don't think he liked being called a stupid animal," I said. A couple of giggles made it past tight expressions.

"I believe we are satisfied," Abernathy said. "Any objections?"

"We're satisfied for now," Harris said. The frown on his face convinced me that he wasn't happy about it, though.

"You may return to your enrollment."

We turned and headed back through the curtain to the main enrollment area. By now, it looked like everyone who had been at the tables was gone, and a whole new group of kids were being enrolled. Preston was waiting for us, looking like someone had just asked him to smell something nasty. As soon as we came into view, he turned and headed back across the room.

This time, I could see the stares as we walked through what felt like hostile territory. Some of the looks we got were disdainful, some hostile, and a few were just curious and aloof. None of the eyes on us seemed friendly. The whispers started as we passed.

"That's the demon boy; don't talk to him and make sure you burn all ..."

"Don't look him in the eye, son. That goes for all of them, especially those African girls…"

"…if that little fox boy doesn't try to seduce you, he'll try to steal your soul…"

"… know my Reginald *earned* his place here. I can't believe they expect him to mingle with trash like …"

"I can't believe you dropped an Airplane reference on them," Dr. C said as we made our way to the edge of the crowd.

"It seemed like the thing to do," I said. "You inflicted it on me, I figured I should pay it forward."

"Inflicted? It was only one night."

"Yeah, but you made me watch *both* of them."

"Okay, so the sequel wasn't as good as the original but that's because-"

"It was made in 1980?" I said as we left the hall through a side door. There was a cart with bottles of water and soda next to the door, and I grabbed a soda as we passed by. The trip back felt a little shorter than the first time, probably because Preston was walking as fast as he could without breaking into an actual run. When we came back into Strathorne Hall, another man hustled up to us and pulled our guide a couple of feet away.

"I thought I gave you specific instructions to get rid of that thing," he whispered a little too loudly.

"It's the boy's *familiar*," Preston almost whispered back.

"No scholarship student can afford the collar!"

"Abernathy pushed it through," Preston sighed. "You'll have to take it up with him."

The other man made a disgusted sound. "This complicates things immensely. We'll have to give him a different room, and he'll be…well, you know." Preston nodded. "There's nothing for it. I'll get his paperwork started. Contact someone over at Chadwicke and have them send the proper form over." Preston headed to another door

31

and the other man pasted a smile on his face and walked back toward us.

"So sorry for the inconvenience," he said as he put his hand out. "I'm Fenton Lowell."

"Dr. Trevor Corwin. Is there a problem, Mr. Lowell?"

"A minor disruption, nothing to be concerned about. You see, since scholarship students usually don't bring familiars, we have never needed to request a room equipped to accommodate one. It's just a matter of requesting the proper form and having you fill it out." The words flowed smoothly, but the smile he gave us never seemed to reach his eyes as he ushered us toward the tables. A tired looking young woman greeted us as we approached.

"Tabitha will get you started on the enrollment forms," Lowell said. "Then we can get your housing, meal plan and text book forms filled out."

"These were already filled out for the students over in Chadwicke Hall," Dr. C said as we gathered the forms. The woman looked to Lowell.

"I'm sure you must be mistaken, sir," she said.

"No, I'm pretty sure I saw it clearly."

"Most of the enrollment paperwork is already filled out," Lowell said as his eyes flicked to the left. "Some families simply take the initiative to pre-fill the forms we're taking care of today." There was a faint note of disdain in his voice, but it was hard to pin down. "It is an option offered to the children of previous alumni. Shall we get started?" I shrugged and Dr. C gave him a skeptical glance before he nodded.

For half an hour, we filled out form after form. I only got the point behind a few, like the one that gave the school permission to give medical treatment. Junkyard laid down beside me as I went to work on my share of the forms. Even after handling demonic contracts for Dulka, the maze of forms was baffling. Twice, the girl on the other side of the table handed me something back and pointed to a place I needed to initial.

Finally, my fingers feeling like they were seconds from cramping, I handed the last form to the weary looking man at the final station. He slid it into the folder with my name on it without looking up and handed it over his shoulder to Preston.

"If you'll follow me," he said as he led us out a different door. "You been assigned to Jefferson Hall, and your luggage is being moved there now." We came out on the lawn behind the school buildings, and he pointed us toward one of the halls at the corner opposite and gave Dr. Corwin my folder. Junkyard trotted along beside me, his tongue lolling out and his tail bobbing as he went.

Dr. C led me through the main door and to the reception desk that sat in the middle of the hall. When he laid my folder down in front of her, the corners of her smile wavered a little, and she looked to him, then to me.

"Dr. Corwin," she said with a steady voice. "Welcome to Jefferson Hall. We were just notified that Mr. Fortunato will be joining us."

"Thank you, do you have his room assignment?"

"Not yet," she said, drawing the two words out. "We're having to do some rearranging to work out the best placement for everyone." She glanced to one side, and I followed her gaze to see a tall, blond haired man standing in a semi-circle of people further down the hallway. She brought her hand up when he looked her way and nodded toward Dr. C. He nodded and held up his hands for a moment, then broke free of the group and came our way with a purpose.

"Mr. Emerson, Dr. Corwin is here to-," she said, but Emerson nodded and cut her off.

"Corwin, I'm glad you finally made it," he said as he pulled Dr. C. away.

33

"Just have a seat over there," the girl said as I started to follow, pointing to a carpeted area with a fireplace. Dark brown furniture contrasted with a pale green carpet with a pattern of small brown squares running through it. The chairs were smooth leather that offered just enough friction to keep me from sliding off if I held very still. I could hear the murmur of voices further down the hall, but the chairs weren't in line of sight, which eliminated most eavesdropping spells. I set my backpack down on one side of the chair; Junkyard laid down on the other side and put his head on his front paws.

"I'll take this up with the headmaster if needs be, or would you prefer I contact the Council?" I heard a baritone voice from behind me.

"I share your concerns, Dr. Endicotte," another voice said, this one higher and speaking faster. "But I'm afraid there's nothing to be done about it. The boy is here at the order of Master Draeden himself."

"I don't care who ordered it, I will not allow some demon worshipping little warlock anywhere near my sons without adequate protection. You obviously don't care that you're putting my sons in the company of a boy whose reputation includes a body count! It's bad enough he's even at the same school, but in the same *building*? That's beyond the pale." I heard steps on the carpet as the staffer and Endicott moved to stand right behind the chair I was sitting in. I felt Junkyard move beside the chair, and I put a hand out to touch his shoulder. He looked over at me, and I shook my head.

"And of course, you know private security is not allowed on the campus for various reasons, Dr. Endicotte. But, I feel I can share this with you in the strictest confidence, in light of your family's patronage over the years. The headmaster has arranged to have a contingent of Sentinels assigned to the Academy for the duration of Fortunato's enrollment, though I doubt he'll last long here.

Your children will have the best security available as long as he's here."

"Don't insult my intelligence, young man. Sentinels are soldiers, police officers at best. They don't know the first thing about security or protecting people. Where is the housemaster? I demand to speak with him." The sound of footsteps started moving away, and I risked a glance over my shoulder to see a man in a gray suit heading for the reception desk with a staffer in tow. I sat back in the seat, suddenly not caring if I fell on my ass or if anyone saw me. I was a bogey man to most of these people. All they knew or cared about was my past. It was like nothing I'd done over the past year mattered.

"Come on," Dr. C said from beside me. I turned and looked up at him. I hadn't heard him come up, but it was going to take more than that to make me jump.

"If I punched a parent, do you think that would be enough to get me expelled?" I asked as I got to my feet.

"Probably just in time for our jail sentence to start," he said. "Look, Chance, I know this is all strange, but it's nowhere near as bad as some of the things you've faced. No one here is actively trying to kill you." He led me to a stair case and started up the first flight.

"I can punch vampires and demons," I said as we climbed the steps. "I don't know how to fight this kind of battle."

"You'll learn," he said. "Just… learn to fight it the right way."

"What's the right way?"

"Most of these kids are going to try to bring you down, somehow. Don't try to do that to them."

"Right," I said, not getting it at all. We kept going up until we ran out of stairs, and came out at the end of a hall. To our left was a big common room, with several couches set around a TV over a fireplace on either side of the room. A set of tables with hard backed chairs sat between the two groups of couches. We turned right and headed down the hallway. Red doors loomed on either side, each one buzzing with faint traces of magic. We reached the end, and Dr. C closed his eyes, put his hand up and held his palm toward the door on the left. After a moment, faint wards traced themselves out in golden light on the wood. Some were elegantly traced in spidery thin lines, while others were precise but blocky. Varying levels of skill had gone into creating each one, and each had been infused with different amounts of power. None of them pulsed with active power, though.

"You could learn a lot from this door," Dr. C said right before he rapped it with his knuckles. The door opened a few seconds later, and we were faced with a young man a little taller than Dr. C. His black hair swept down across his forehead, accenting a narrow face. He studied Dr. C, his hooded eyes scanning down then up before he moved his attention to me. His eyes widened for a moment, then his gaze dropped to Junkyard, and his expression darkened a little. He had a skintone almost the same as mine, with the distinctive eyelids of Asian ancestry. Just this side of masculine, his looks bordered on pretty.

"I'm Dr. Corwin, and this is Chance," Dr. C said. "Chance has been assigned as your roommate for the semester. May we come in?" The kid nodded and stepped back.

"Sure," he said. "I'm Hoshi Nakamura." His voice was a smooth contralto, hard to tell if it was a guy's or a girl's unless you already knew.

"This is Junkyard," I said as a hundred pounds of fur and slobber trotted in past me and sat down in front of Hoshi.

"Uh, yeah," he said. "I'm not really… exactly good with dogs."

"Of course," Dr. C said. He rattled something off in Japanese, and Hoshi nodded before he responded in

Japanese as well. I caught the word for mother in the sentence, but the rest was lost to me, even though, through the memories I shared with Dr. C, I had some access to the language.

Hoshi turned to me and gave me a smile that didn't quite reach his eyes. "I am *kitsune*, on my mother's side. Her people don't get on well with dogs." Junkyard made a plaintive little noise in his throat that sounded like he was either expressing his dismay at being lumped in with all other dogs, or apologizing for the bad behavior of his species.

"Junkyard's pretty cool," I said. "Hell, he's the only animal that'll hang out with me."

"Excuse me for a moment, boys," Dr. C said and headed out the door.

"So, you must be the second least popular dude here," Hoshi said.

"I was gonna say the same about you. So, what's your story?"

"Mom's a Japanese trickster spirit. What about you?"

"Used to work for a demon."

"So you're the demon guy," Hoshi said as the smile finally reached his eyes. He went over to the bed on the left side of the room and sat down. "Way some people are telling it, you sold him your soul for power, then shafted him on the deal somehow and got your soul back."

"That's a new one. Mostly people just think I apprenticed myself to him. Someone thinks you're going to try to seduce their son."

Hoshi's laugh was a series of musical little sounds, almost like barks, and he rolled his eyes. "I get that one a lot. They think I can turn into a girl."

"Can you shapeshift? I know *kitsune* are supposed to have at least two forms."

37

"So, far, I can only turn into a fox at night. Other than that, what you see is what you get. What about you? Anything I need to look out for?"

"Just bad dreams," I said. "And sometimes I blow shit up. But I'm doing better about that. It's been about six months since I did any serious property damage."

"That's reassuring," Hoshi said.

Chapter 2

~ Many are the fond farewells that started with awkward greetings. ~ Myrddin Emris, mage, adviser and friend to Artur Pendragon

"Remember," Dr. Corwin said. "You're never truly alone. Any time you need me, day or night, you call me. Or your Mom, or anyone. Just remember there are people you can reach out to." He stood in the doorway and shuffled his feet, suddenly quiet. After fifteen minutes of non-stop talking, it should have been a relief.

"I will," I said. "Probably more than you like."

"Well," he said. I cracked a smile.

"Yeah." We stood there for a moment, then he reached out and gave me a quick hug. When he pulled away, he put his arms on my shoulders and gave me a quick nod, then turned and headed down the hallway.

"Awkward much?" Hoshi asked. He was curled up on the bed, looking a lot like a fox as he looked over his class schedule.

"All the damn time," I said.

"Must be nice," he said. He stretched and rolled onto his stomach. "My folks took off as soon as they could. Barely a goodbye or a handshake."

"Yeah, it is pretty cool," I said as I picked up my class schedule from the desk. "Considering the last time I said goodbye, there was a firefight. Time before that, I blew up a school."

"You blew up a school?" Hoshi rolled off the bed and came to his feet. "That's so freaking cool!"

"Yeah, demons don't like it when you tell them to piss off." I tried for casual, like I was that much of a bad ass. Hoshi grabbed his desk chair and pulled it up, but an insistent knock at the doorframe interrupted us. A tall, red-haired guy stood there, his brow furrowed and his lips pinched together. He wore the same uniform we did, but he had a pair of gold cords draped across his neck and

39

dangling down over each shoulder. Junkyard stood and put himself in the middle of the room, conveniently between the possible intruder and us.

"Come on, you two," he said. "The housemaster wants to speak to the plebes before first assembly." We followed him down the hallway, amid a group of whispering kids. Hoshi and I stood taller than most of them, and it looked like we were among the oldest. Another student with gold cords on her uniform was ushering a group of girls from the opposite hall. Two more groups joined us from the other side, and we were led down the stairs to the dining room on the first floor. At the far end, a man and a woman in uniforms similar to ours, but with a longer cut jacketsand brass buttons on the coat. Both held a staff with an inch-thick brass band at the top and a narrower band about six inches below it. The man looked like he'd just stepped from an action film, with perfectly coiffed blond hair, a classic chiseled, square jaw and cheekbones high enough to give you a nosebleed, and a smile that made me wonder if we shouldn't be in a hidden lair instead of a school lunchroom. I recognized him from earlier, the man who had grabbed Dr. C to talk about getting my room. The woman beside him was equally blonde and just as much a walking fashion doll as he was. Standing to their right were two older students with white cords draped down the front of their coats. The boy was dark haired to the girl's blonde, and both had the same Stepford smiles and good looks as the two adults. The four with gold cords joined them after they got everyone in a chair. Once the last of the older students joined them, the man tapped his staff against the floor, and the soft buzz that had started to fill the room died.

"Welcome to Jefferson House," the man said. His smile got wider and he lifted his left hand. "The best house at the Franklin Academy. This will be your home while you are students at the Franklin Academy. Everything you do here reflects on your house. Your behavior, your academic performance, even your extra-curricular activities will be seen as an extension of this house's honor and reputation. And make no mistake, Jefferson House has never failed to have one hundred percent enrollment in extracurriculars, nor have we failed to hold at least three cups for excellence every semester. You are now part of that tradition, and every member of your house is depending on you to carry on our legacy of excellence into the future." He paused for a moment, and the woman next to him started clapping, which seemed to be a prompt for the rest of the hall. After a few seconds of clapping, the man held his hand up, and the hall quieted again.

"Now, for introductions. I am Mr. Emerson, your housemaster, and this is Mrs. Emerson. To our right are Rebecca Saunderson and Stewart Hampton, the Head Girl and Head Boy for Jefferson House. The boys and girls on either side of us are your Hall Captains. Hall Captains, would you please introduce yourselves?" Each of the students in gold cords stepped forward and said their name.

"Ethan Stanwicke," ours said.

"Your Hall Captains and the Head Boy and Girl speak with our authority, and are authorized to take disciplinary action including house merit and demerit points, house detention and other administrative or academic measures as they see fit. You will treat cord bearers from other houses with the same respect and deference as you would your own. They've earned their cords through academic excellence and moral integrity. Finally, your own grades and participation will dictate your standing within Jefferson House. House rankings will be updated weekly. Now, First Assembly starts in half an hour. If you have any questions, ask your Hall Captains. Dismissed." There was a mass scraping of chair legs on linoleum as everyone got to their feet. Fortunately, Junkyard seemed to grant us a little more leeway, with the younger kids automatically moving to one side as we approached. Hoshi and I made it back to our room with time to spare.

"Man, no pressure or anything," Hoshi said as he fell back on his bed. "You're just competing with everyone else at the school, all the time, every day for everything!"

I sank to the floor and sat tailor-style. Junkyard came over and gave me a look that reflected what I felt, like he wanted nothing more than to go back to Boston and transit back home. I put my arm around his shoulders and pulled him close while I rubbed the fur along his side.

"No kidding," I said. "Still, could be worse."

"Not sure how it could get much worse than constant competition. This is like the Roman Colosseum only without all the bloodshed."

"The night my father sold me to a demon, it broke both my legs to make a point. Believe me, it could be worse."

"I stand…well, sit corrected," Hoshi said as he sat up on the bed. "I guess it could be a lot worse. Dude, that must have sucked."

"More than a little. Demerits kind of lose their sting after that."

"You must be hella hard to scare."

"Not a good idea to find out," I said. "I tend to punch first and apologize later."

"Gotcha. Important safety tip. So, awkward subject change, do we have any classes together?" I had to reach for the folder on my desk to get my schedule. I looked at the schedule for a moment and saw eight classes listed, way more than I took at home, but only four classes per day. There was no way that worked out right during a five-day week. Then at the bottom, I noticed two more, but they were redundant, and they only happened on Wednesday. When I looked back at the other two lists, I realized that the days were Monday and Thursday for the first one, and Tuesday and Friday for the second list.

"So," I said slowly, "I think I have American Mage History first period, Alchemy III second, lunch, then English and Conjuring III."

"So, we have History and English together in first block. What about second?"

"Evocation II, Enchantment III, Magickal Defense AP and Botany and Herbalism II."

"Only Botany and Herbalism second block, but we have Botany lab together on Wednesday, I think. But dude, how did you rate advanced placement in Magickal Defense. I'm in a remedial class for that." Hoshi planted his butt on his desk and crossed his legs, then folded himself over so that his elbows rested on the wood.

"The hard way," I said with a slow smile. "Lots and lots of practice."

"First Assembly is in fifteen minutes!" Ethan yelled down the hallway. I got to my feet and put my left hand on my pants pocket. The place where I expected to feel my TK rod was disappointingly flat. Across the room, Hoshi had unfolded himself and was pulling a wand from a duffel bag at the end of his bed. I pulled my new wand from the pocket on the side of my backpack and went to tuck it into the big pocket on the right side of my coat, only to find a second, slimmer pocket next to it that fit the wand like a glove, and still left the handle free to grab. We hit the hallway and followed the stream of other students down the stairs and across the commons toward Chadwicke Hall. Once we got inside, the older students led the way to the big hall on the ground floor, where five long tables had been set up running the length of the room. Another table ran perpendicular to the others, and it took up the entire width of the room. The other Jefferson House students took the table second from the left, with the boys on one side and the girls on the other. Each seat had a name card, and Hoshi and I found our names a few seats from the middle of the room, with one name between us. It didn't take long for S. Lodge III to find that spot. Tall, dark haired and possessed of a jaw strong enough to break bricks, he assumed his place with all the dignity of an aircraft carrier. The two flunkies on either side of him, however, pulled up short, evidently not used to finding the spots beside the USS Lodge filled. They ended up on Hoshi's right, further from the front of the table. To my left, the Head Boy and Head Girl took their place at the head of the table, then the Hall Captains, then several older students, followed by a couple my age.

"How did you end up there?" Lodge demanded as he towered over me. I looked over my shoulder at him.

"Same way you ended up there," I said. "I read the little card that had my name on it." His eyes went to the card, and the furrow between his brows deepened. He put his hands on the table and leaned down until his face was close to mine.

"There's no way trash like you rates a better seat at the main table than I do," his voice bordered on a growl. "You don't even deserve to set foot on this campus."

"Card says different," I said. "You got a problem with how they set the table, talk to the guy who wrote the guest list." That started a round of whispers, as everyone looked to Lodge, then to me. His hand fell on my shoulder and started to squeeze.

"How about I talk to you someplace dark and quiet?" he hissed as his hand tightened like a vise.

"Last guy who put a hand on me," I said through clenched teeth, "ended up in a cast. Or maybe they didn't tell you about the body count."

His hand came away from my shoulder like he'd grabbed a live wire, and I fought to keep from sighing in relief. "Body count?" he said. I just smiled and gave him a quick nod. His frown softened for a moment, then he jumped and looked down. I followed his look to see Junkyard nudging his ankle. He pulled back, looked up at

Lodge, then bared his teeth silently for a split second. Before anyone could react, he was back to his friendly looking canine self, leaving Lodge to wonder how close he'd come to losing a leg.

A loud boom echoed through the room, and everyone's head turned to the front table. A silver haired man with a close trimmed white beard stood at the center place, with a silver staff topped with three prongs holding a pale blue crystal.

"Everyone, take your seats please," the man said, his voice carrying through the hall. Seats scraped across the floor as the last holdouts sat down, including Lodge. "For those of you who are new to us, I am Mr. Caldecott, the headmaster. I want to wish all of our new students a warm welcome, and express my joy at seeing our returning students. Ours is a tradition of excellence that reaches back over two hundred years, and you are the next to carry that tradition forward, into the future." He paused and let his hand drop from his staff, which did that cool wizard trick of staying upright like it had been nailed to the floor. For a moment, he stood there with his head bowed and his hands clasped in front of him, looking like he was about to do something unpleasant. "You may have noticed the presence of Sentinels today as you arrived. There has been no shortage of rumors and speculation regarding their presence. The truth, however, is not as exciting as the conjectures. Indeed, it is far more tragic. It pains me to inform you all that Leonard Cargill was killed over the summer, and that Josie Hart disappeared at the end of term." A collective gasp went up at that, and I saw several of the girls put their hands to their faces. The girl across from me sat blank faced, tears running down her smooth brown cheeks.

"Len?" one of Lodge's buddies said. "Len died? How? What happened?" He wasn't the only one with questions, because the room started to buzz with conversations.

45

Caldecott held his hands up, and the room went quiet after a few seconds.

"A memorial service will be held on Sunday in the chapel for those who wish to attend. For those of you who knew Mr. Cargill and Miss Hart, grief counselors will be available for you to speak with should you need to. Master Polter has asked us to keep the details of these cases confidential until the investigation has been concluded. If any of you have information regarding your lost classmates that might be of use, we encourage you to speak to your housemaster right away. In the meantime, if you see a Sentinel during the course of your day, do not approach them or impede them in their work. If you are approached by a Sentinel, cooperate with them fully."

"They should just arrest you and be done with it," Lodge leaned over and whispered to me as Caldecott continued talking. Teachers were being introduced, each one standing as he said their name.

"I wasn't even here last term," I said between the short bursts of applause.

"Doesn't mean you shouldn't be arrested for being a warlock."

"Been there, done that. Got the fancy sword." I could feel the disturbance in the Force as Lodge's face screwed itself into a confused look.

"I know we can expect your best this year as we continue our tradition of academic excellence and leadership through the new term," Caldecott concluded. Chair legs scraped on the floor as hundreds of chairs slid back at the same time. Junkyard got up and yawned as I got to my feet. Lodge stopped in front of him and looked down at him.

"Get that fucking mutt out of my way before I step on him," he said with his upper lip curled.

"That's a good way to end up with a permanent limp," I said.

46

"Are you threatening me, plebe?" Lodge asked.

"Just stating the obvious," I said. "You're the one who made a threat."

"No one's going to believe a warlock," Lodge sneered. He turned and walked off with his two escorts in tow. Hoshi waited for me with a grin on his face.

"Well, that was fun," he said as we turned and headed for the door along with the rest of the students. "And informative."

"Kind of a downer," I said.

"Maybe for you," Hoshi said with a laugh as he pulled two slips of paper from his pockets. "I got a couple of numbers." I shook my head. We crossed the commons to Jefferson Hall and eventually found ourselves back in our room. My trunks were next to my bed, and a trio of soft sided suitcases sat next to a large cardboard box on the other side of the room.

"Well, nothing got lost," Hoshi said as he went to the suitcases and started unpacking clothes. I pushed the trunk holding my books against the wall, and turned it on its side before I unbuckled the leather strap holding it closed. The sides opened out, then I flipped the catches on the middle and flipped it up to rest on the top of the trunk so that the top was right at eye level for me. Once the top was secured, I pulled the cover holding the books in place out, then doubled it over to make a compact writing desk. The middle was filled with books, older leather bound tomes sharing space with my newer text books, as was the right side. The left side held ten leather scroll cases in leather loops, with an old fashioned dip pen, ten small ink bottles and a box containing different nibs for the pen.

When I turned to the clothes trunk, I found a receipt for the rest of my school uniforms from Hobarts. A quick glance in the closet by the door showed them hanging up, with another pair of shoes on the floor and several pairs of socks in a box on the dresser. With my school clothes good

47

to go, I opened the clothes trunk and started putting my normal clothes away. It didn't take very long.

Finally, I was down to the important stuff. I sat on the bed and unzipped my backpack. First out was Pyewacket, who got the place of honor on the desk. Then I pulled out my laptop and got it set up. My meager magickal gear was next, which at this point was only my hawthorn wand in its case. My new TK rod, my retrieval ring and my amethyst scrying stone were locked up somewhere in the dorm, along with my athame and other working tools. All of my other charms had been left in New Essex. I tried to shake the naked feeling that had been pushed to the back of my head all day, and mostly succeeded again. I was at a school, protected by Sentinels and some of the best educated practitioners of magick in the US. I wasn't supposed to *need* the stuff I usually carried around in my backpack. My paintball gun and its specialized alchemical rounds were still in Missouri. *I'm safe here,* I told myself. *I don't need it. I'm safe.* Except I didn't believe me. I was a good liar, but I'd never been able to fool myself for long. Even if I was safe, I hated having to depend on someone else to keep me that way, even the Sentinels. They might have been total badasses in the magick department, but they weren't always around. My hands itched as I opened the case and pulled the long leather pouch out the held my wand. The thirteen inch wand was still in perfect shape, with the copper and silver wire that was wound tight through its core wrapped around the seven sided channeling quartz tip and the garnet sphere at the base. The wood was smooth and warm, still holding the slight sheen of oil that I'd applied right before I left. It was good work, even if I said so myself. With it, I could cast pretty much any spell I knew, though a specialized rod would have made it twice as potent. Still, it was better than nothing.

I slipped the wand into the little pocket for it in my jacket and went back to the backpack. The package from

Mitternacht's was next, and as much as I wanted to open it and see what Lucas had sent me, there was still one last thing to do. I closed my eyes and reached into the pack, letting my fingers run along the bottom of the pack. My hand brushed the cool metal of the little tin I was searching for, and I whispered the command word for my chameleon charm before I pulled the tin it was wrapped around into sight. The charm came off with a gentle tug at the knot, and I ran my thumb up the side to push the top open. Inside was a layer of cotton that held several semi-precious gemstones in place so they didn't slide around. A miniature stylus was held in place along two small bottles. The first was filled with a mix of sage, ginger root, holly leaf and St. John's wort, the second with dragons blood ink. In the top, I'd replaced the pages that represented the sum total of my knowledge with blank rice paper for scrolls on the fly. And finally, below the padding that kept the stones in place, I'd laid a broken bit from a CD, a narrow silver ring, a silver skull pendant and a razor blade.

"What's that?" Hoshi asked as he perched his butt on the corner of my desk.

"My best friend calls it my prison kit," I said. One corner of my mouth lifted in a half smile. "It's all the stuff I'd need for spell casting and making a couple of charms or scrolls in a pinch." The contents clicked softly as I put them back into place and closed the lid.

"Ever have to use it?" Hoshi asked.

"Once, when I escaped," I said. "I hid the blades I used to cut my pentagram into the floor in it." I wrapped the cord for the chameleon charm around the box as I spoke, and it shimmered from view when I whispered the command word.

"Seriously?" Hoshi asked. "That's so legit, man." It looked like Hoshi had his stuff pretty much set up. He'd put his text books in the shelves next to the closet, along with some other, more colorful books and CD cases. On the wall, he'd put a bright poster of a manga character. Dressed in a trench coat, the character held a katana with tassels dangling from the pommel in his right hand, and an oversized revolver in his left.

"So, who's the manga dude?" I asked with a nod toward the poster.

"That's Chikao Nishimara, from Five Tail Fox Detective," he said. "It's my favorite manga. He's a kitsune who fights crime in New Tokyo as a PI, trying to stop the Veiled Mistress and her crime syndicate from taking over the whole city. But she's also his older sister, and she's a seven tailed kitsune, so she's more powerful than he is. The last series ended with the Mistress getting Chikao's *hoshi no tama*, the pearl that holds his soul. I can't wait for the next series to start."

"I might have to start reading it so I can keep up," I said while I opened the bag from Lucas. Inside was a white cardboard box with a note taped to the front. *Get your computer and wi-fi set up before you open,* it read. Grumbling, I grabbed the orientation packet we'd been given while we were enrolling and turned to the section on how to connect to the school's Wi-Fi. I shook my head as the connection completed. Somehow, a magick academy with Wi-Fi seemed … wrong.

The school's website came up in my browser, and I spent a couple of minutes checking out the bells and whistles. Mission statements, history, and a gushing blonde named Tiffany offering a virtual tour of the campus. I followed Tiffany's virtual self as she showed the features of the familiar friendly dorms, like the little lever on the bottom of the door that opened it from both inside and out, and the folding roosts on the windows. The beds had foldout places for most small animals to sleep literally at their masters' feet. She ended her tour of the dorms by reminding me to check my school mail drop daily as she turned to open what looked like a small cabinet door set into the wall. Hoshi and I traded surprised looks and scrambled to the two drop boxes set in the outside wall. Sure enough, both of us had several thick envelopes waiting for us. I sat mine on the desk and closed the school's intranet browser. The rest could wait for later. I'd waited long enough to see what Lucas had for me.

I opened the box to find a small white square with a lens in it and a thumb drive. Below those was a mount and a USB cord to connect the external camera to my laptop. The camera had a sticky note attached to it that read "*Plug in first.*" It only took a couple of moments to get it into the mount and the USB cord connecting both ends. Then I plugged the thumb drive in and waited. The little boxes with the slowly filling bars popped up, and were eventually replaced with one box that read "*Hit this button.*"

"What to do next?" Hoshi asked from over my shoulder. "You'd think he'd leave clearer instructions." When I did move the cursor over the button and clicked it, a larger screem popped up and I heard a tone over the speakers. It repeated two more times, then Lucas' face appeared in the video chat.

"Hey, Lucas," I said. "Working hard?" The background was dominated by old wooden bookcases and tall, plate glass windows. Over his shoulder, I could see the sign for his grandfather's bookstore backwards against the glass.

"I got off a couple of hours ago," he said. "I just didn't feel like moping around upstairs all afternoon. I see you made it to wizard school okay. Who's your shoulder surfer?"

"This is Hoshi, he came with the room," I said. "Hoshi, this is my best friend Lucas." In the smaller picture, I could see Hoshi raise his hand and wave behind me. On the larger screen, the background moved, and Lucas' face started bobbing around.

"Hey, Hoshi," Lucas said. "So, now we can talk and if I need to consult with you on things, it's as easy as hitting a button on your computer screen."

"Are you on your phone?" I asked.

"Yeah, it's an app that's compatible with the service the camera uses, only this one can be made more secure. All you need to do is open the file marked 'Blooming Onion' on the thumb drive I included and follow the directions. I'd walk you through it, but it's better if you learn how to do it on your own." His face took on an amused expression that I took to mean there was another reason I should learn it for myself, a look that I'd long since learned meant he was keeping a secret.

"Cool, I'll check it out later," I said. "By the way, we missed you this morning, man." His expression clouded and he nodded quickly.

"Yeah, I'm sorry about that," he said with a tight voice. "I've said goodbye a few too many times lately, if you know what I mean."

"Yeah, I get it," I said, trying hard not to think about his parents' funeral back in June. The scars were still pretty raw from that. "Man, I wish you were up here. You should come out on one of the family weekends or something."

"That'd be cool. And you'll be back during the holidays and over the summer, too. Of course, it's probably going to be pretty boring here without you around to get us into trouble."

"You'd think you'd be happy about that part."

"You would," Lucas said with a half-hearted smile. "But, I do a lot of cool things when you're around. Anyway, I'm glad you got the camera working. Now it'll be easier to keep in touch. Look, Grandpa wants to go to lunch here in a few, so I have to run. But this comes to my phone and my computer, so you can use it to contact me any time."

"Uh, okay, cool. So, I'll talk to you later?"

"Yeah, dude. Catch you later." The screen went blank, and Hoshi let out a low whistle.

"That went to awkward fast," he said.

"His parents were…they died a couple of months ago. He's still trying to deal with it."

"Sure, okay," Hoshi said as he stood up, leaned against his desk and pointed at his face. "This is me, not judging." I narrowed one eye at him, and he shrugged. "Okay, not judging out *loud*."

"It'll do. I don't know about you, but I'm hungry. I'm going to find the cafeteria and eat like a bear."

"And I'll silently judge everyone else's table manners and diet while they look down their noses at my fashionably poor wardrobe."

Chapter 3

~ Second chances are rare. Do everything on your power to keep it that way. ~ Common saying in the Abyss.

My first class was American Mage History, and I was almost late to it. Hoshi and I did our best to run quietly though the almost deserted halls, but the sheer emptiness worked against us. Every footstep was amplified by the walls, and we nearly passed the room we were looking for. When we got into the room, the only two desks that were still open we right in front of the teacher's desk. The room was a sea of smirking faces, all of them younger than Hoshi and me. I slid into my seat with a smile as Junkyard laid down beside my desk No sooner than I had my butt in the chair, the teacher walked in. He was tall, pudgy and had already lost most of the hair above his ears, leaving the slightly pointed top of his head exposed.

"Good morning class," he said as he walked in and laid his leather attaché on the desk. "I am Mr. Goodwin. Welcome to American Mage History. Now, before we settle on our seating arrangement, I thought I'd share some statistics for class. Students who sit on the front rows tend toward A grades about eighty-five percent of the time, which means that those of you already on the front row stand an excellent chance of making the Dean's List, and becoming Hall Captains after your first year. So I guess I can see who my natural acheivers are. It's good to see some scholarship students up front." There was a nervous buzz behind me as the freshmen reevaluated their choices to sit at the back of the class. "Now, let's get started."

An hour and a half later, the first five pages of my notebook were crammed full of notes. Far from being the snooze fest that Mr. Strickland's American History classes were back at Kennedy, Mr. Goodwin managed to make history kind of interesting. Every once in a while, he'd stop and ask someone what they thought of something he'd just described. After the first couple of freshmen got caught stammering, more pens came out and a lot more notes seemed to be taken.

"Read Chapters two and four, specifically the socio-economic causes behind the Kentucky Rift," he told us as the bell chimed the end of class. Hoshi and I went our separate ways from there.

I ended up in the last building on the end of the left hand prong of the U of the main campus. It looked older than the rest of the buildings, built on thick stone slabs with black, natural rock for the walls. It was almost as tall as the main building, stretching four stories above ground. The stone arch above the main door read "Denham Building" in simple black letters. Inside, it was even more hushed than the other building I'd just left. My footsteps and the click of Junkyard's claws on the floor seemed too loud for the somber quiet that laid over the hall. My class was on the fourth floor, so I hit the stairwell, careful not to slip on the smooth stone steps.

Once we got to our floor, I noticed one thing that was different already: a row of cushions and perches was arranged outside of each classroom, and several animals were already lounging on them.

"Looks like you're gonna be waiting this class out in comfort," I said as we walked down the hallway. Junkyard responded with a messy sounding sneeze. "So it's like that, huh?" He sneezed again. Then we were in front of the room I was looking for, and he turned to an empty cushion and laid down, giving me puppy eyes as he laid his head on his paws. The moment I opened the heavy wooden door, I understood why familiars stayed outside.

Alchemy isn't what most wizards would call a *neat* discipline. Part chemistry, part magick and part culinary art, it combined all of the messiest aspects of all three to create some of the most spectacular effects I'd ever seen. The rare healing draught that my former master Dulka had kept on hand were still some of the most disturbing concoctions I'd ever experienced; feeling bones shift and body parts move in the healing process were the only thing worse than the horrendous taste of the damn things. All of that should have prepared me for the smell that hit my nose the moment I opened the door. The pungent odor made my nose wrinkle up, even as weak as it was. I could only imagine what Junkyard's nose would have made of it.

I had done enough alchemy that they'd stuck me in a third level class, which put me in with a bunch of students who were my age or the next year older. I looked for an empty seat at one of the lab tables, and saw Stewart the Head Boy gesturing for me to join his table. I shrugged and headed that way. It never hurt to get in good with people in power, even if that power was limited to one residence hall. What was important was that it was *my* residence hall.

"It'll be fine," Stewart was saying as I sat down on the tall wooden stool. My back was to the door, which I hated, but it was the only seat left at the table. "Chance is a good fellow. Don't you mind the rumors. I know better. Our man Chance here is the guardian of the Maxilla Asini itself. Isn't that right, Chance?"

"If I was," I said carefully, "I wouldn't be allowed to say anything about it." That got a belly laugh from Stewart and the other guy at the table, while the girl across from me giggled without seeming too dedicated to it.

"But," Stewart leaned forward and glanced both ways, "You also wouldn't be able to lie about it."

"Where are you getting all of this?" I asked. "Like you said, it isn't something I could just talk about."

"My father has friends on the High Council," Stewart said. "The Hampton name carries a lot of weight with some of the Council members."

"So you're Fortunato," the guy across the table said. "Lance Huntington. This is my girlfriend, Ginger." He put his hand out and I took it. We played a microsecond game of Who-has-the-better-grip, then he sat down and leaned back. The usual tingle of power that I felt whenever I touched someone with magick ability lingered on my skin. I also nodded to Ginger and put my hand out. She looked at it for a moment, then took it briefly and let go, her expression neutral the whole time. I looked down at my hand, hardly believing what I had just experienced. Where Lance had registered about like most mages I'd met, Ginger's touch had felt like grabbing live wire by comparison. She was the stronger of the two by far. I felt the subtle shift as the door opened and the teacher came into the room.

"Good morning, class. I'm Professor Talbot," the man said. He was tall, cadaverously thin and tanned. He reached into his coat and pulled out a pair of thin glasses, opening them with a flick of his wrist. Slowly, he slid them on, his dark eyes scanning left and right until the glasses came to rest on the narrow beak of his nose. Thin, dark eyebrows furrowed together as he pulled out a black notebook and opened it.

"We'll skip the formalities of roll call, as I can see that we have twenty seats filled, and twenty students in the class, so I believe it's safe to conclude that everyone is here. Now, class, is this inductive or deductive reasoning?" Dead silence spread through the room, and I could see people at other tables glancing at each other.

"Mister Fortunato, deductive or inductive?"

"Uh, inductive, I think," I said.

"You think?" Talbot said, his tone getting sharp. "In alchemy, there is no room for 'I think.' No room for uncertainty when you are mixing chemicals and reactants. You had better *know. What. You. Are. Doing!*" Soft laughter filled the air, and Talbot's eyes narrowed.

"You're amused. That's nice. So, let's assume Mister Fortunato's guess was correct. Now tell me why. Mister

Hines." Hines, a soft featured guy with aristocratic looks, looked over at me then back at the instructor.

"Should we assume he's correct, sir?" Hines said with a casual smile. "Or should we be certain he's right?"

"Nice try. Try that kind of evasive nonsense in political science. Any volunteers?" One girl raised her hand, but Talbot pointed to another guy. "Mister Howerton? No? Very well. I shall explain. Inductive reasoning takes two things and assumes they are connected. There are twenty people in the classroom, therefore everyone who is enrolled is present. The assumption is that all twenty people in the classroom are also enrolled. Deductive reasoning would use statements that connected two sets. For instance, there are twenty juniors at Franklin Academy. There are twenty juniors in the class room. Therefore, all of the juniors are in the classroom. However, if any of you had done the assigned reading from your syllabuses last night, you would also have known that my previous statement could also have been abductive reasoning. So, let's see if you can disappoint me for a third time, and complete the shame you're all bringing on your houses. Try to tell me why it would be abductive reasoning." When no one raised their hand right away, I slowly raised mine.

"Seeking redemption Mister Fortunato? Very well, are you certain?"

"Yes, sir. With abductive reasoning, the conclusion is the most likely one, because it's the simplest."

"Please, do tell me what makes *that* true," Talbot said with a sneer.

"Requires the fewest assumptions or actions to be true," I said, remembering Detective Collins' explanation. "If your conclusion wasn't true, that would mean someone would have to either be in the wrong class and too embarrassed to admit it, or someone is here impersonating someone else. Or something like that. Simplest explanation is that everyone is here who is supposed to be here. Basically, it's a guess that could be wrong, but it's the most likely conclusion because it's the simplest."

"Hmm, not the most scientific of answers," Talbot said, "but sufficient to avoid a demerit. If you haven't figured it out by now, at this level of alchemy, we'll be concentrating more on the finer points of the exact science that is alchemy, and less on basic brewing and mixing. By the end of the semester, you'll be able to create a formula of your own. Perhaps one of you will go on to create something worthwhile someday. Now, since none of you did the reading last night, let's catch up. Turn to page seventeen in your texts for the section on alchemical theory." Stewart leaned in close to me as I pulled my textbook out of my backpack and laid it on the table.

"Okay, how did you know that stuff?" he asked. I turned and looked at him.

"It's how cops think."

"Spend a lot of time behind bars, Fortunato?" Lance asked.

"That's beneath a Franklin man, Lance," Stewart said. "We're not petty."

"Maybe you're right," Lance said. "Sorry, Fortunato."

"It's okay," I said. "I get that a lot. My master is an occult crimes consultant for the New Essex Police Department." Lance's face turned a little red and he muttered something before he buried his nose in his book. I followed suit, not wanting to end up on Talbot's radar again. That lasted until the bell chimed to signal the end of class.

"Fortunato," he said as I headed for the door along with everyone else. I stopped and went to his desk. Without a word to me, he kept working in his gradebook while the classroom emptied. Finally, the room was empty and quiet, but he still kept working.

"You wanted to see me, sir?" I finally asked.

60

"Are you aware of a little thing called classroom etiquette, Fortunato?" Talbot asked.

"Not specifically, sir," I said.

"When an instructor calls on you, you are to acknowledge them *immediately* by name. So in this instance, you would have correctly answered 'Yes, Professor Talbot.' And then waited for me to speak. Is that clear, young man?"

"Yes, Professor Talbot," I said.

"Good. Now, I was disappointed in your academic performance today. Of all people, you should have read the syllabus ahead of time and known there was assigned reading before class. You are among students who have always been held to a higher standard. As a scholarship student, I have higher expectations of performance for you than of the rest of the class, so I expect to see your performance improve dramatically." I felt my face heating as he finished, and wondered why he wasn't delivering this same lecture to the rest of the class. Hell, I'd done better than the rest of the class, and I was the one being told I was a disappointment.

"I understand, sir," I said, instead of protesting.

"Good. You may go." He turned back to his papers, and I couldn't get out of the room fast enough. Junkyard fell in beside me as I headed for the stairs. When I hit the bottom landing, I found myself facing the connecting hall between Denham and the next building in the U. Going back in really didn't appeal to me, so I headed down the walkway. There was a door in the middle of each connecting walkway, so I could just take it and go back to Jefferson Hall for lunch.

As we got closer to the door, the sound of voices, pitched low but fast, reached our ears. Junkyard's floppy ears perked up a little, and he looked at me with a little sound in the back of his throat.

"Yeah, I'm curious too," I said softly. I slowed as we approached the door. The voices were coming from the right, outside of the U. As we got closer, I could see that the door was slightly open. Through the glass, several people were visible. The first person I recognized was Lodge. Then I saw one of his cronies at the door, probably the lookout but too engrossed in what was going on to notice me.

"Come on, fox boy," Lodge said. "Cough it up."

"Cough what up?" Hoshi's voice came from somewhere out of sight. Lodge moved, and there was an unpleasant sound of flesh on flesh.

"Don't play dumb with me, you slant-eyed little shit. Your pearl. Give it up or I'll beat it out of you."

"Man, you got me all wrong," Hoshi said with a laugh. "I don't wear pearls. Not that it wouldn't be a good look for you, with all that pale skin, but nothing but gold graces my extremities."

"Bullshit!" Lodge barked, and several more thumps followed. "All you little fox fuckers have a pearl. It protects whoever has it from your magick. Now cough it up before I make you puke it up!"

I'd heard enough. Without another thought, I put my right shoulder to the door and pushed hard. Caught off guard, the guy on the other side went stumbling, and I gave him a little bit of an extra push as I went by. The other guy from the table last night moved toward me, but found himself facing a snarling Junkyard as I made it to Lodge. With a yell, I shoved him away from Hoshi. As he stumbled away from me, I realized that even with Junkyard and Hoshi, I was still outnumbered. I looked around to see several other kids closing in on us. Hoshi was kneeling by the trunk of a big tree that shaded us, and also gave us a little bit of coverage to our rear. I counted four more closing ranks in front of us.

"Back off, Fortunato," Lodge said as he got to his feet. "This is between me and Hoshi."

"You brought six friends," I said as he came closer. "Seems like it isn't as private as you say."

"Private enough that you're not welcome," Lodge said. "You don't want to be on my bad side, plebe. Get the hell out of my way, and I'll forget all about this."

"And if I don't?"

"Then every secret you have is gonna be mine."

"Trust me," I said with a slow smile. "You don't want to know my secrets."

"Oh, yeah? Why not?" Lodge asked.

"My secrets will get ya killed," I said. I heard Hoshi yell a warning, and then I was being tackled from behind. I twisted just enough to keep from doing a faceplant into the grass, but before I could recover, there were more hands on my arms, and my wand was being pulled out of my jacket. Upright and kneeling, I found myself face to face with Lodge.

"Why don't I hold onto that for you…for safe keeping," he said as one of his cohorts handed him my wand. "Now, let's see what's inside that head of yours. You've heard of the Horus Gaze, right?"

"Yeah," I said. "I've done it a couple of times. Didn't work out so well for the other guy. Besides a Horus Gaze goes both ways." Lodge shook his head and his grin grew wider as he pulled a purple cloth pouch from his jacket pocket. He pulled a small circle of glass out of it, and I could see the glimmer of enchantment sigils around the outer edge. A gold frame ran around the edge, with raised wires attached to it, and a thin gold chain linked to the outer frame. After a few seconds, I realized he was holding a monocle.

"Not with one of these," he said as he held the monocle to his eye and pushed it into place. "My great grandfather had it made. The mind of a Lodge is sacrosanct. I won't have rabble like you in it." He closed the other eye and leaned in, his gaze intent, compelling…and ineffective. I felt the pressure of his mind against my mental defenses, almost like when Dr. Corwin had first tried it, just not as strong.

"What the hell?" he blurted out when the Horus Gaze didn't start.

"My brain is a scary place," I said. "And I don't like letting random assholes into it."

"But…you can't stop a Horus Gaze," Lodge said.

"Surprise! Yes, I can."

"You're no match for me," he sneered. "I've got centuries of magick in my blood." He leaned closer and glared at me even harder, but the assault on my defenses didn't get any stronger.

"I kept a Count of Hell out of my head," I said. "You're only human." Lodge's eyes narrowed, but before he could say anything, someone called out, and suddenly, my arms were free, and people were scattering. Lodge's head came up, then he looked around for a moment. I got to my feet to see Ginger pointing toward us from the door, with Stewart pushing it open and coming our way. Lodge reached for the monocle and turned away, but Stewart's voice cut through the air like lightning.

"Sterling Lodge, stay right there!" Lodge's shoulder's hunched up, and he turned to glare at me. "What's going on here?"

"Fortunato was just showing off his new wand," Lodge said as he pulled my wand from his pocket and held it out to me. I grabbed it and tucked it back in my jacket.

"Oh, is that what was going on here?" Stewart asked with a lopsided smile. "Because it looked to me like you were trying Horus Gaze him. We've had that talk before."

"Backoff, Stu," Lodge said. "Fortunato here will tell you I didn't do a Horus Gaze. Besides, who cares what happens to trash like these two?"

"I do, Sterling," Stewart said. "They're in my house. Now, you can give me the monocle, or I can take this to my House Master."

"I'm not giving this up to anyone," Lodge said, holding up the pouch for emphasis. "It's been in my family for generations."

"We'll mail it back to your parents, and we'll say it got packed by mistake. It won't go any further than that. Otherwise, I *have* to report it. I really don't want to, but I will if I have to."

Lodge didn't say anything for a moment, and I could see the thoughtful look on his face. I could imagine the gears turning in his head as he weighed his options, but even a goon like him could see the end result. Forcing a Horus Gaze was considered a violation of the First Law, a breach of free will. My own use of it against Dominic King had been overlooked because he wasn't human, and he'd been doing his best to kill me at the time. Even so, it was still high on a long list of sins I'd committed, even if it might have fallen under the broad caveat of "for the greater good." For Lodge, being reported for it would mean facing the High Council, and probably a lenient, but still humiliating, slap on the wrist as punishment. He held the pouch out.

"Here," he said.

"You made the right decision," Stewart said as he took the proffered bag. "Now, get the hell out of here." He didn't have to tell him twice.

"What the hell?" Hoshi said as Lodge walked away. "You can't let him just walk! He really did try to Horus Gaze Chance, He was trying to make me give him my *hoshi no tama* until Chance jumped in."

"Your what?" Stewart asked.

"It's a piece of my soul," Hoshi said. "If he had it, he could control me, even kill me. You can't just let him walk!"

"He won't be doing it again," Stewart said as he hefted the pouch. "Sterling is usually a pretty good guy, but he's under a lot of pressure. So he makes bad decisions. All he needs is some guidance, and he'll come around."

"He tried to beat me until I gave him part of my damn *soul*! And he tried to mind-fuck Chance!"

"But he didn't," Stewart said calmly. "And if I pushed it, it would come down to your word against his, and that's not enough to destroy his life over. So, this never happened, and I'll make sure Lodge never bothers you again, okay?"

"Man, this sucks," Hoshi said.

"Yeah," I said. "He gets a pass this time. But if he crosses me again, Hell is gonna seem like a vacation."

"Chance, you can't take these kinds of matters into your own hands. If he gives you any more trouble, you come find me and I'll deal with it. Now, go get lunch." With that said, he turned and headed back toward the door. Ginger waited until after he went past her, then looked back at us, her gaze intent and searching for a moment before she followed Stewart.

"Dude, what was that?" Hoshi said as he got in front of me. "He practically tried to mind-rape you, and you're ready to let him walk? What the hell?"

"Remember who I am," I said. "I might not like my reputation, but I can't say I didn't earn it. But I got my shot at redemption. So when it comes to giving someone like Lodge a little room to turn himself around, I can't turn him down." I walked past him, but he followed.

"So, what are you gonna do when he tries to gaze you again? Turn the other cheek again?"

"You only get one pass," I said. "Next time he wants to do a Horus Gaze...I'll let him."

"Yeah, that'll show him," Hoshi said as we reached the door. When I smiled, he frowned. "You weren't kidding when you said it went bad for the other guy, were you?"

66

"No."

"Ummm, how bad was it?"

"Bad."

"Like on a scale of bruised ego to dead, how bad?" he asked as he stopped me with a hand on my arm.

"Curled up on the floor in a little ball bad." I kept my face blank, and Hoshi reached inside his jacket. His hand came out holding a pair of sunglasses, and he slid them on slowly.

"You have issues, man," he said before he turned and headed for our Hall.

Chapter 4

~ We are never so strong...or vulnerable...as when in the company of boon companions. ~ Benjamin Franklin, "Wizard Of the New World"

Lunch at a normal high school had taken some getting used to. Even normal people give off a pretty fair amount of mystic energy. Cram enough of them in one place, and it's like being inside a nuclear reactor. At first, my control over my mystic senses was so sketchy that being in a crowd was almost overwhelming. But, Dr. C had taught me how to shield myself from it so that every nerve didn't feel like it was on fire.

Walking into the cafeteria reminded me just how much I had to learn. More than a hundred young mages sitting in a room without a single focus generated so much energy that it felt like I had just stepped into a smelting furnace. Reflexively, I sent a tendril down to tap into ambient Earth energies, and found a ley line nearby. The slow, ancient pulse of energy flooded my tap line, and I created a simple shielding bubble, whispering *"Tutus loco,"* as I curled my ring and middle finger of my left hand to my palm and set my thumb parallel to my index finger. The push of unfocused energy abated, and my nerves stopped telling me it was four hundred degrees in the room.

As my skin stopped tingling, I could look around. When we'd been in here yesterday, it had been only minimally staffed, and parts of the place had been closed up. And I'd slept late this morning, so I'd skipped breakfast. Now, though, everything was open. There was a deli section, a grill and a salad bar along one wall, and the back wall was dedicated to beverages. Coffee, exotic teas, smoothies and even different flavors of water were all on offer behind a counter manned by staff in crisp white uniforms with perfect little green hats. Even their soda selection was unique, since this was the only place where

I'd seen both major brands in the same place, alongside a variety of bottles I'd never seen before, some obviously in other languages.

I got a burger with bacon, mushrooms and cheese, while Hoshi got some kind of lettuce and meat filled wrap. When we sat down, I looked at the pile of fries on my plate, then over at the stack of multi-colored crispy things next to his wrap. He had some kind of pale blue water in his glass. My only concession to good nutrition was the glass of ice water next to my soda.

"Man, you're going to have your first heart attack before you're old enough to buy liquor," he said as I gulped down most of the water. Defiant, I grabbed the burger and took a bite.

"At least I'll die happy," I said around a mouthful of meaty, cheese drenched bliss. "What the hell are those?" I pointed to the multicolored sticks.

"Vegi-fries," he said. "Although they're actually oven baked, so there's no oil in them."

"Vegi-*whats*? Hoshi, that's not food. That's not even what food *eats*." I washed down the burger with a deep swig of water, then tried the seasoned fries. My eyes rolled back at the combo of spice and crisp outer layer, and I took a moment to savor the whole thing before I finished the water off and took another bite of my burger.

"At least you'll die well hydrated," he laughed.

"More than likely," I said with a grim smile. Odds were, I wouldn't die in my sleep or of old age. Part of my training regimen with T-Bone and Cross, the aptly named Hands of Death was that I drink at least one full glass of water with each meal to stay hydrated while they drilled me in the hybrid martial art that Dr. Corwin had dubbed "mage-fu." I wasn't anywhere near as lethal as they were, but since I'd escaped from Dulka, I'd had my ass kicked more times than I cared to count, and I'd nearly died twice. Any advantage I could get was a welcome one.

70

More people came to sit at our table, usually at Hoshi's invitation. Unlike most of the other students, all of these kids seemed determined not to blend in with the crowd. No two hairstyles were alike. For that matter, there weren't that many hair *colors* that were the same, and most had at least one facial piercing. The seat next to me was taken up by a larger girl with long black hair that she'd done in Betty Page bangs. Long black gloves covered her from fingertips to above her elbow. She undid a set of buttons at her wrist, then pulled the gloves far enough forward to take her hand out. With her hands uncovered, I could see the black nails on her hands, similar to Synreah's black talons. When she had the gloves tucked into the wrist, she turned to me and gave me a smile.

"Hi," she breathed. "I'm Desiree."

"Chance," I said, offering my hand.

She held up her left hand and shook her head. "I eat my emotions so I don't chomp on yours," she said with a smile. I curled my fingers in and gave her a thumbs up.

"I don't think I'd taste very good," I said.

"You must be the demon guy. I'm a quarter cambion. Or an eighth succubus, however you want to put it."

"Good to meet you," I said.

Her smile widened and she tilted her head to one side. "Most people don't mean it when they say that," she said. "Especially when they know I've got demon blood in me. But you do."

"You're an empath?" I asked. It made sense; Synreah was an empath, and if they both fed on emotions, it figured they'd be able to sense them.

"Yeah," she said. "That's part of the reason I'm here, so I can learn to control it and shield myself...and everyone else." Her gaze went down, and I could see something in her seem to withdraw. I wondered if I looked like that when I walked up to the edge of something painful in my own head.

"Dangerous," I said after a few seconds. "But useful."

"What?" she said, the withdrawal now a spark of anger.

"That's why I'm here. Someone thinks I have 'potential,' I just need guidance. Which basically means, dangerous, but useful. Welcome to the club." Desiree's smile came back.

"Thanks, I think," she said. "By the way, you'd probably be delicious. Your emotions, I mean!" Her face turned a dark shade of red, probably part of her demonic ancestry.

"I thought the part about feeding on negative emotions was bullshit," I said.

"It is. It's the primal stuff that really does it. Anger, fear, lust, joy. The really strong ones, the feelings people have the hardest time controlling, those are like crack. Going to a rock concert used to give me a buzz for days. You," she looked at me with narrowed eyes before she went on. "You're like a buffet, a lot of strong emotions."

"What about love?" Hoshi asked. I took a sharp breath, remembering how sensitive Synreah had always been about that particular emotion.

"We can't feed on love," Desiree said with a smile. "My grandmother always said it was the one thing demons can't feel, so that part of us can't feed on it."

"Makes sense," Hoshi said.

Moments later, a tall girl with long black hair done in cornrow braids sat down across from Desiree. Large, dark eyes fell on me for a moment, then she smiled when Desiree greeted her, and her face lit up.

"Kiya, this is Hoshi, and that's Chance," Desiree introduced us.

"The two baddest boys in school," Kiya said as she put her hand out to me. When our hands touched, I got the same kind of warm feeling I got when I touched Wanda any more, except I got the sensation of plunging my hand into a warm river current.

"What?" Hoshi said with raised hands. "I'm as pure as they come. Whatever it is they're saying I did, I have an alibi."

"I'm sure you do," Kiya said. "Des, hook a girl up. Conjuring was a total bitch." Desiree pulled a handful of miniature chocolate bars from her purse and plucked three out to give Kiya.

"Swiss chocolate with honey," she said seriously. "That should take the edge off your nerves for a while." Kiya took one, unwrapped it and popped it in her mouth. After a few seconds, she closed her eyes and smiled, letting out a sigh as her shoulders drooped a little.

"That's so what I needed," she said after a few seconds. "You are the bomb, girl."

"What did you mean about the two baddest boys in school?" I asked.

"You didn't know?" Kiya asked, her eyes wide. "Hell, nobody wanted to room with either of you. They were afraid Foxy here was gonna bite their precious boys in their sleep, or turn 'em all pansy ass. And they figured you were gonna be cursing their little snookums or start turning 'em to the dark side or some bullshit."

"What is it with the gay thing?" Hoshi asked. "It's not like I go around flirting with guys or anything!"

"It's because you're so pretty," I said, only half joking.

"I am pretty damn easy on the eyes," Hoshi admitted. He excused himself and headed for the soda fountain.

"Damn, he's gorgeous," Desiree said as she licked her lips.

"No shit, girl," Kiya said. "That's saying something, coming from you. And look at that ass! Damn! So, Chance, quick, before he comes back, what's he into? Music, TV, whatever."

"Um, he's into manga and anime, but I haven't looked at his MP4 player or anything," I said. "No wonder no one wanted to room with him."

"Aw, don't be like that," Kiya said with a smile. "We all know you already got a girlfriend. And nobody wants to piss off a werewolf."

"How do you know this stuff?" I asked. "I live ten states away. And I don't know any of this shit about you."

"Well, the werewolves out here certainly know about your girlfriend," Desiree said. "And they don't like her. Which makes me like her even more."

"Wait, you're from Boston?"

"Yeah, my mother has a place down on Talismonger Way in Squattertown. The Clans held a meeting a couple of weeks ago to discuss what to do if she comes out."

"What did they decide?"

"They don't talk about that part in public," Desiree said. "If you're not Clan, you pretty much don't exist to them."

"Great," I said. "One more thing to worry about."

"I don't think they'll do anything drastic," she said. "Probably rough her up a little to make a point and get her to grovel on her belly a little in front of the Clan Heads, and that'll be it."

"You don't know my girlfriend," I said, determined to call her as soon as I could. Hoshi made it back, and the rest of lunch was mostly spent discussing anime and manga, which was an education all its own for me. When the warning bell finally chimed, Hoshi and I headed for Hawthorne Hall.

"Okay, so everyone knows everything about everyone else," I said as we walked along. "Except me."

"Who do you want to know about?" Hoshi asked.

"I don't know. Anyone?"

"Well, you know Desiree's part succubus, right? And Kiya's got some spirit that no one's ever heard of attached

74

to her. They think she's a summoner, but they can't get a bead on the spirit's name. All they do know is that it helps her do some random ass magick."

"How do they not know what spirit's attached to her?" I asked. "Can't they scry it or something?"

"They've tried, but they can't find its name, so it's immune to everything they've done. Me, I think they just don't want to admit there's a spirit they don't know." By then, we'd crossed the quad and were almost to class.

Mr. Leopold started us off right away on Chaucer's unabridged Canterbury Tales, which included the Alchemist's Tale, the Wizard's Tale and the Apprentice's Tale. My brain ached after an hour and a half of breaking down each line from Old English to modern English.

By the time the bell for the end of class tolled, I was more than ready for Conjuring II, even if it meant a little extra walking. The Grotto was outside of the main campus area, out past Denham Hall and down a short path through the woods that came out near a small lake. The building was a round, stone structure that was enclosed halfway around, with six thick stone columns that supported the roof on the open side. A round tower jutted another story from the dome of the roof on the far side from me, with a black iron railing around the edge.

Inside, the marble floor was inset with rings of different metals and different sizes, as well as rings that were carved into the stone itself and left open. While none of the rings crossed each other, they weren't concentric. By habit, I skirted the edge of the outermost circle, even as I saw other students stroll through them. As I went, I visualized where each circle would appear, imagining each in different colors, starting from red inside and moving through to violet and then white for the outside circle. In doing that, I realized that while none of the circles shared the same center-point, all of them included the center of the room and thus the outer circle.

75

The actual classroom was set inside the hill, next to the smaller cave that looked like it was the original feature. I stepped into the room to find the teacher marking his roll book in front of the class. He was the youngest teacher I'd seen so far, and if he hadn't been wearing an instructor's longer coat, I would have pegged him as a senior. A chalkboard was mounted on the wall behind him, with a series of complex circles drawn on it in different colors of chalk. At the top of the board, he'd written "Professor Kenneson, Conjuring II"

"Ah, Mister Fortunato, do take your time to find a seat. Perhaps you'd like to circle the room *widdershins* before you do?" he said.

"*Deosil* is fine," I said as I looked for a seat. Unlike the rest of the classes I'd been in, there were no individual desks. Instead, long tables were set up in rows. The only seat I could find was in the back of the class. I headed up the shallow steps to the table and sat down. Junkyard took a spot just behind me and plopped down.

"So, are there any more obsolete superstitions you need to observe before you're ready to begin?" the teacher asked.

"Excuse me, sir?" I asked. He gave a long sigh, then turned to the rest of the class.

"Who else found it necessary to go *around* the edge of the circles on their way to class?" he asked, making a walking motion with his fingers as he moved his hand in a broad circle. A few snickers answered him, then he turned his attention back to me with a smug smile on his face.

"I was taught to treat a circle with respect," I said. "Especially a permanent one."

"Which of your recent masters taught you that bit of antiquated nonsense? The demon or the fossil?" All eyes in the class turned to me, and I narrowed my eyes at the insult to Dr. C.

"Both of them," I said. "For different reasons."

"Well, it's a good thing you're here, then. We'll disabuse you of those outdated ideas, and bring you into the twenty-first century. Now, let's get started with a little real education, shall we?" He turned and pointed to one of the circles on the board, with a main circle in yellow and a smaller circle in red that just barely touched the larger one. "So, who can tell me what is wrong with this circle?"

"What kind of circle is it, Professor Kenneson?" one of the blond guys near the front of the class asked.

"Excellent question, Mister Davenport. Excellent question! That's the kind of inquisitive approach that will serve you well! This is a summoning circle."

"What is it summoning?" I asked.

"If you can't tell, Mister Fortunato, then let me explain. By the colors it should be obvious that it is for the summoning of an elemental, yellow for air, red for fire. Please try to at least act like you know enough to even waste my time in this class." More laughter rose at that, and I leaned against the back of the chair. My face felt hot as I realized that Mr. Kenneson probably had it in for me. Even if I laid low, he'd probably find some way to make that a bad thing. He had us open our books to the second chapter, and we read about elemental summoning.

"So, Mr. Fortunato, now that I've practically spoonfed you the answer, what is wrong with this circle?" Kenneson asked.

"The summoner's circle," I said, drawing a raised eyebrow from Kenneson. "Air is moist and warm, with the first being the dominant trait. So the summoner's circle should be water, instead of fire if you're trying to summon and control an air elemental."

"Well, you can regurgitate facts," he said. "Well done. Perhaps you'd care to recite it verbatim? No. Well, then, let's see what more refined minds can do. Mister Winthrop, why is this relevant?" Winthrop basically recited the book. There was no way this class was going to end well for me

77

this semester. As I left the classroom, I saw Lodge standing a little too casually in the hallway between me and the door to the common area. I tensed, expecting him to step out and try to stop me, but he just watched me pass, his eyes on me like he thought he'd bore a hole in my head if he just looked hard enough.

Stewart caught up to me outside Jefferson Hall as I waited for Junkyard to finish baptizing an obscure and undeserving bush. Overhead, the air was buzzing with sprites going back and forth between buildings.

"So that's how our mail gets delivered," I said as he stopped beside me.

"Oh, yeah," he said, as if I had just mentioned that the sun came up in the east. "I saw Lodge waiting outside class for you today."

"Yeah. He didn't actually do anything, he just stood there."

"That's what he usually does. He'll show up in different places, and just watch, at first. Then, he'll do something, beat a kid up, cast a hex on them or something. Then he goes back to watching for a few weeks. Before long, his victims either transfer to a different school, or go to great lengths to avoid him. I've seen him do it every year after his first."

"Why do they let him keep getting away with it?"

"Because he's a Lodge," Stewart said. "No one dares accuse him of anything. He'll be a Hall Captain next semester, and Head Boy his senior year, just because of who his father is."

"And you're telling me this because?"

"Because he thinks you're his next victim, Fortunato. He's decided you don't belong here, no matter what the Board of Scholars or even Master Draeden and the Council says. He's taken it on himself to *correct* their error. I think it's high time he learned what disappointment and failure taste like."

"Are you sure you're not violating some Boston Brahmin Code of Honor or something by doing this?" I asked. "I mean, you're pretty much breaking ranks just talking to me, right?"

"There's bit of doggerel about the Boston Brahmins that the cowan use, about the Lowells only speaking to the Cabots, and the Cabots only speaking to God. You think there are equals here? There's a pecking order among the older families, and an expectation of how things are supposed to be. The Lodges are at the top of the heap, and everyone else kisses their ass in a very specific order. I'm a much better mage than Sterling, but he'll be the one with the seat on the Board of Mages someday, or sitting on the International Council. So talking to you might be breaking ranks, but it's better that an outsider deals with him than one of his 'peers' tries to do it."

"Because that's just not the way things are supposed to be for you," I said. "And you people call poor folks 'entitled.'"

"Look, I'm trying to help you out here, Chance."

"Then help me. Just telling me that he's going to do shit he's going to get away with isn't as useful as you might think."

"Okay, okay," he said, holding up his hands. "Look, when he's going to do something, he'll bring friends. He'll use magic, but most importantly, he'll try not to leave any physical marks, especially not where they can be seen. So aim for the face. Go for black eyes, broken noses, busted lips. Make it hard for them to cover up what they're doing."

"What's to stop him from accusing me of attacking him or his buddies?"

"That's the beauty of it," Stewart chuckled. "He doesn't dare accuse you of attacking him. It would make him look weak to the rest of his peers, and he can't afford that. If some of the other guys smelled blood in the water,

79

they'd go after him in a heartbeat. One black eye, he can explain as a lucky shot, but not two or three."

"Five is right out," I said.

"What?" Stewart asked.

"Nothing, just a movie quote. I got it. Aim for the face. I can do that." So that was what that felt like. After almost a year of being the one on the ignorant side of pretty much every pop culture reference, I was finally the one making the obscure reference no one else got.

"Good. Now, we can't be seen talking too much, or it will look like I'm...you know..."

"Doing exactly what you're doing?" I said. "I get it; you're not hanging out with the unwashed masses. But thanks for the heads up and the advice." I turned and headed into the dorm. Day one was almost done, and I had an enemy and an ally of almost equal standing. On the plus side, I had some new friends, too. Hell and high school weren't all that different. You had rigid factions vying for power, and everyone smiled to each other's faces while they sharpened their knives behind their backs. At least in high school, I'd found a few people I could trust.

Hoshi was already in the room, lounging on his bed with Canterbury Tales open in front of him. "Hey," he said without looking up. I looked around, and immediately went stiff. Something felt off.

"Someone's been in here," I said.

"Yeah," Hoshi said. "One of the sprites left your dog some food." About that time, I heard the crunching of Junkyard's kibble.

"Junkyard, stop," I said. To the big guy's credit, he did, but the look he gave me was calculated for maximum guilt. I knelt and plucked one of the hard chunks of food from the bowl. It looked like the small bag I'd brought with me, but sprites were still fae, even if most fae considered them lower caste. Accepting food or gifts from them

brought certain obligations. Services, on the other hand...
that was a little fuzzy.

"Did he ask for anything?" I demanded.

"Only if he could feed the dog. Put the flag on the
campus mail box up, he'll probably be here in a few
seconds."

"He better be," I said as I crossed the room to the foot-
wide wooden door in our wall. When I opened it, I found
myself staring at an oval face with large, almond shaped,
lavender colored eyes.

"Hi," the sprite said. His hair was a pale green, like
spring grass, and he stuck one slender hand out. I grabbed it
and pulled him into the room. His dragonfly like wings
snapped back out straight and his two antennae sloped
backward over his head, the two lobes at the end of each
bobbing up and down. He dangled from my hand, wings
very still, with a nervous smile on his face.

"What's your name?" I asked.

"I'm Ren, Jefferson Hall messenger cadre, messenger
third class. Can I...can I play with your dog?"

"What?"

"Your dog. He seems so nice, and he's not a dumb
drone like all the other critters here."

"Is that why you fed him?" I asked.

"Yes!" Ren chirped. "I used your food, so there wasn't
any kind of obligation, even if it was to a sprite, who serves
in your house, so technically, there really couldn't be any
kind of enforceable debt. I just wanted to pet him and throw
the ball for him sometimes." The words tumbled out of his
mouth almost too fast for me to understand. I set his feet
down on the desk and let go of his hand. On the desk, he
was about two feet tall. His feet were bare, and his tunic
was a simple affair, not much more complicated than a
poncho, or maybe a pillowcase with holes cut out for his
head, wings and arms, and a belt to hold it on.

81

"That's really up to Junkyard," I said. Behind me, Junkyard let out a low whine. "Oh, yeah, sorry. It's cool, you can eat it." Crunching resumed.

"You leave it up to him to decide?" Ren asked.

"He's a good judge of character. I trust him," I said as I set my backpack down and opened it. I tossed my books on my bed, then opened the compartment on the back and pulled out the peanut butter, honey and cracker packets that I'd taken from the cafeteria at lunch.

"Is that…peanut butter?" Ren asked as I opened the drawer.

"Yeah," I tossed a packet of the peanut butter to him. "You're my guest, the obligation is mine." He smiled and tucked it into the pouch on his belt. Junkyard had emptied his bowl, and was sitting by the bed eying Ren. "Don't eat him, he wants to get to know you." He tilted his head to one side, then opened his mouth and let his tongue loll out, what I'd learned was his version of a smile. I gestured to Ren. He fluttered his wings enough to get himself a little lift and drifted to the floor in front of Junkyard.

Slowly, the sprite lifted his hand and presented his knuckles to be sniffed. Junkyard took a few whiffs, then ducked his head under Ren's palm so that he was petting him. For a few moments, Ren simply ran his hand down Junkyard's coat, then he scratched him behind the ears and earned my dog's undying loyalty for the next few minutes.

"Can we go downstairs?" Ren asked.

"Sure," I said. "It's nice enough, I can do some of my homework down there. I'll be right behind you." Junkyard went to the lever at the bottom of the door and pawed at it, then went out into the hallway and headed for the stairwell, while Ren went back out through the box.

"What's his deal?" Hoshi asked.

"I'm not sure," I said as I grabbed my Alchemy book. "I know sprites are very domestic. They tend to live on farms and ranches or near gardens, and they love plants and animals. I didn't see any cats or dogs when they were testing Junkyard, so maybe he just hasn't seen a dog in a long time."

"What, he can't get all cuddly with a koala?" Hoshi asked.

"Doubt it," I said. "You ought to come on down, too." He shrugged, and I made my way to the stairs.

Outside, I saw Ren flying low and just ahead of Junkyard, who was at a full out run. They headed into a stand of trees and I watched as they wove in and out between the trunks. Junkyard's barks and Ren's laughter were musical sounds as I sat down on the broad steps facing the outside of the U.

No sooner than I had planted my butt on the stone, another sprite, this one dressed a little better in an actual shirt and pants, floated down in front of me. His wings were a crimson blur behind him, and his face was set in a neutral looking mask. Apple red hair fluttered in the wind of his wings as he crossed his arms and looked out at Ren and Junkyard playing.

"I'm so sorry, sir," the sprite said, his words short and sharp. "I'll make sure this miscreant stops harassing your dog." Something about this sprite rubbed me wrong, and I found my blood racing at the thought of him disturbing Ren and Junkyard while they were having fun.

"He's not harassing him," I said. "He's exercising him for me." The new sprite's head turned, and his antennae shook as they dangled in front of him.

"You mean he's doing this…"

"At my request. So I'd appreciate it if you didn't interfere in my dog's run."

"I…I…I'm so sorry, sir," the new sprite said. "I didn't realize."

"I'm sure you didn't. Think nothing of it." I gave him my best imitation of a dismissive wave, and he flew off. Once I was sure he was gone, I allowed myself a smile.

After a few minutes, my pocket buzzed, and I fished out the phone Shade had given me. There was a text waiting for me, a picture of her in her car, blowing me a kiss. Under the picture, it read:

>Shade: Hey, hottie. Whatcha doing?

Chance: Wishing I was kissing you.<

>Shade: I miss you so much. I've been thinking about you all day.

Chance: Miss you, too. Thought about texting you, but I really don't want anyone to take this phone.<

>Shade: Can I call?

Chance: Please!<

A few seconds later, my phone was playing the opening bars of Love N' Chains' "Full Moon", and when I swiped the answer bar, I was treated to Shade's face smiling at me.

"I needed to see your face," she said with a smile.

"And I needed to hear your voice. I miss you so bad."

"Miss you too, baby. How was your first day of wizard school?"

"Rough. Already pissed some people off, made a couple of friends. Give me a couple of weeks, I'll probably be in the headmaster's office. How was your day?"

"Boring," she said with a little pout. "Depressing. I realized today you're not going to be here for Homecoming."

"Maybe I can skip a day and come home for it."

"That would be ironically apropos," she said with a wicked little grin. "Or maybe I could come up there for yours. I'll wear something sexy, maybe get that dress I wanted with the leather bodice. We could scandalize all the blue bloods."

"That's why I love you," I laughed. "You think like I do. I have it on good authority that you'd make all the old clans of werewolves out here pretty much pee all over themselves if you showed up."

"I hadn't thought about that." Her grin got wider.

"Maybe you should talk to Sinbad about it."

"Oh, yeah," she purred. "I'm sure they sent someone to talk to him. I bet he's just waiting for me to show up on his doorstep. Ugh, enough of that crap, though. Tell me about your classes, your dorm room, tell me everything!"

I was in the middle of telling her about alchemy when I heard another ring tone.

"Crap, it's my mom," she said. "Hang on." She put the other phone up to her ear, and for a few moments, she was the dutiful daughter. When she finally put her other phone down, her face was creased in a frown.

"What's up?" I asked.

"Mom's on this kick again where she thinks I should be 'over' you by now and getting back with Brad or finding myself a respectable boyfriend that she can show off at the faculty get-togethers. I've got to go. She wants me home in ten minutes. But I'll call you later tonight."

"Okay," I said. "Stay under her radar. I'll talk to you later. Love you, babe."

"Love you, hot stuff," she said before the screen went dark. I went back to poring over alchemical equations.

As the light faded to the point that I was starting to have trouble reading, Ren flew back with a panting Junkyard following behind him. His wings glowed in a light purple blur behind him as he set foot on the rail beside me.

"I saw Egle talking to you," Ren said as I rubbed Junkyard's head.

"Yeah, I told him you were exercising Junkyard for me."

"Really?" Ren said, his lavender eyes getting wide. "So, is it okay if I do it again sometime?"

"Let me check. Did you have fun, Junkyard?" I got an enthusiastic bark in response. "You want to do it again sometime?" Another bark, and he turned around in a quick circle, his tail going so hard his bony little hips were wiggling. "Looks like you're hired," I said. "As long as it doesn't interfere with your other obligation to the school."

"Oh, no, I promise, it won't! We're usually free between three and eight. Egle likes to deliver the evening dispatches late. He likes making students scramble."

"What a dick," I said. "So, I have a question, if it's not too sensitive. Most sprites' antennae bend forward. Why are yours backward?"

"Because I'm fast! Before the school bought my contract, I used to work with the Sentinels' advance teams. We used to scout out places for them and tell them where the bad guys were. Then that jerk Polter took over, and made the Sentinels human only. Now I just deliver mail. Which is important stuff, don't get me wrong. But man, it sure doesn't compare to being a scout."

"Sounds kind of dangerous," I said. I closed my book and looked at him with new intensity.

"Nah, most people take us for granted, and we're so fast, most people miss us anyway. So, can I do this again Wednesday?"

"You can do it every day if you want," I said.

"I wish I could, but I have to go into the Commons tomorrow evening to deliver some orders. And Wednesdays are half days for labs and extracurriculars."

"Can you deliver one for me? I'm going to need food for Junkyard pretty regularly."

"Sure," Ren said, his wings glowing pink as they fanned the air behind him. "I know of some places with good prices."

"Good. Then I'll see you Wednesday." I stood up to go back inside, and Ren flew off, leaving a pink glow in his wake.

86

Chapter 5

~ You've never seen it all. Keep learning and
exploring. It will keep you sane over the centuries. ~
Mordecai Straj, ancient wizard

Tuesday dawned gray and rainy, and I woke up to the rumble of thunder in the hour before dawn. Junkyard stirred as I got up and grabbed my blanket. Oddly enough, I didn't remember any bad dreams, which I chalked up to being too tired to dream at all. For me, there were no other kind of dreams than bad dreams. Not even Junkyard could stop those entirely, though they weren't as bad as they used to be.

My first class of the day was Evocation II, which was across the quad from Jefferson House. I grabbed my cloak and swung it over my shoulders, then headed out the door. Very few students seemed willing to brave the rain, which was fine by me. I let my memory walk through the conversation I'd had with Shade late last night. Her mother was serious about breaking us up, and Shade had called me with puffy eyes and a long face. We'd only talked for a few minutes, and most of that had been us trying to reassure each other that we'd be okay, and trying to say 'I love you' as many times as we could. Even now, I still didn't know what we were going to do.

The rain tapped against the oiled leather of the cloak, and I let the deep hood hide the frown on my face as I walked through the wet grass. Junkyard trotted along beside me, acting like he wasn't getting wet. I'd told him to stay in the room today but he didn't listen. I just hoped he didn't show up to class all wet and smelling of dog. My class was on the top floor of the main hall, and it took up the front half of the building. Mr. Hamilton was a round, balding little man who paced in front of the board the whole class as he went over the basics of manipulating magic as pure energy in the form of light, heat and kinetic force.

"By the end of this semester," he said while he practically bounced from one side of the room to the other, "you will all have an appreciation of and proficiency in the geometry of energy forms. The higher Art of Evocation is not about fire and lightning. It is the mastery of form and the ability to mold energy with precision. It is the mastery of Magick in its purest form. We will start with the most basic form in geometry, the line." As he finished, he put his index fingers together, then muttered a word. When he pulled his fingers apart, a glowing line of green light appeared between his fingertips. "Turn to page twenty-two." The classroom exploded into motion as we started turning pages.

My next class was Enchantment III, and it was just a floor down. A blonde woman in glasses stood almost motionless as we filed in and took our seats. The board behind her read "Professor Kincaid." Most of the students in the class were older than I was, and there were several hall captains and one Best Girl in the mix. Once again, I was pretty much the youngest person in the room.

Once the final bell chimed, the teacher stepped to the podium beside her desk and cleared her throat. "Mr. Fortunato," she started clearly, and I give up any hope of making it through class unnoticed.

"Yes, Professor Kincaid?"

"I understand you not only have a great deal of knowledge regarding enchanting foci, but also, several years of experience in making and using them." Her voice was high and bordered on musical, with a tone that sounded very prim and proper.

"Yes, ma'am. It was how I learned magick."

"Forgive my prying, and know that there is a point to this. To what end was your education limited to enchantment?"

"To control me," I said, my face burning. "So I couldn't cast spells on my own. I needed to prepare my spells ahead of time using a focus, usually something just for that one spell and one person."

"And did your…were there advantages to this?"

"Yes, ma'am. Using a single use focus made it next to impossible to track the spells back to me, or to my boss."

"And the…disadvantages?"

"I was limited in the spells I could cast to what I could prepare ahead of time. I also had a harder time learning to cast a spell without a focus."

"Thank you for your candor, Mr. Fortunato. I bring up this case as cautionary example. Enchantment, while it has many advantages, can lead to a dependency upon those same advantages to the detriment of other vital skills. Also, the dependency upon, shall we say, prepared or refined components for charms and tools can leave you rather ill-prepared should you need to enchant an item under less than ideal circumstances. This semester, we will learn to formulate the sigils, runes and glyphs required to enchant a single subject item, and to enchant a working tool. As our class project, we will also use common materials to create working tools, similar to Mr. Fortunato's Telekinesis Rod."

"Professor, why would we need to know how to make tools from junk?" one of my classmates asked, a guy with Hall Captain braids draped down from his collar.

"An excellent question, Mr. Camdenton. But tell me, are you not in a three level class?" Kincaid asked. "One where each of you are presumed to have mastered the basics?"

"Of course."

"Improvisation is the hallmark of mastery, Mr. Camdenton. The objective of this class is to teach more advanced techniques of enchantment. This includes methods which would seem otherwise unconventional. We will also learn how to enchant otherwise ordinary objects to hold specific spells for discreet use among the *cowan*. Now, in your texts, you will find on page three-seventy-five a table of basic sigils." I let a little bit of a smile through. This was a class I was likely to do well in.

After lunch, my next class was Magickal Defense. This one was an Advanced class, not even required for graduation. The rain had gotten worse, so I was stuck with all the rest of the students taking the breezeways between buildings. Fortunately, it was on the top floor, so the crowd thinned considerably by the time I found myself in the right hallway. As I got closer to the door, though, my mystic senses started to tingle, and Junkyard stopped a few steps from it and let out a low *hruff*. I looked down at him, and his eyes were fixed on the doorway. I blinked and opened my Third Eye a little, and saw a faint shimmer in the open doorway. After a moment, the illusion faded, and I could see that the door was actually closed. And behind the illusion was something else. A suggestion, not much more than a slight compulsion. Technically, it should have been illegal, but I nodded as I realized that the only way to actually defend against most things was to actually face them. And for an advanced placement class, it made a certain amount of sense to start with an object lesson.

Challenge accepted, I thought as I brought up my full set of mental defenses. First came the interlocking shields, each one helping to power and bolster the next, standard fare in Dulka's arsenal. Any spell or defense worked best when powered with emotion, so I had linked my defenses to anger. The more someone tried to attack me, the more pissed off I got. Also standard demon fare. Finally, I brought up my own little bit of clever, a sort of buffer zone that ran a remembered thought pattern like a computer subroutine. It was designed to do two things. One, give Dulka something to "hear" when he tried to read my mind, and give a compulsion spell something to latch onto instead of my real thoughts. It would do its whammy inside the shell version of me, and I would be okay. I hadn't brought my full set of defenses up for almost a year, even when I ran into the occasional mental assault. Up to now, just clamping my Third Eye shut had been enough to stop almost everything I'd run into, and my basic defenses had done the trick with almost everything else. Pure willpower and contrariness had handled the rest.

With my defenses firmly in place, I reached out and turned the doorknob. The illusion shimmered and faded, and I felt the second ward go off but it splintered against my defenses like a paintball against glass, which wasn't far off from the actual intent of the spell. If I hadn't had my defenses up, it would have "painted" my aura. Dulka had used the exact same spell to designate marks in a crowd for scrying spells later. A third ward flared as I stepped through the door, and it was sucked into the buffer shell. It registered as a compulsion, something to do with color. Even as it hit my defenses, I felt the delay as it shifted between Junkyard and me a few times before it aimed for the shell.

Inside, the classroom walls were covered in sheets of paper. Each one had an inert warding symbol on it, and a different message written in red.

Don't look here.
Eyes front.
Smile.
Listen.
Call your parents tonight.
Put your right hand on your desk.
If you can see the color red, shake my hand.

Standing at the front of the room was an older man with curly, steel gray hair. He had his hands on his hips, and as I stepped inside, his seamed face broke into a smile. The second thing that stood out about him was that he didn't wear the standard slacks. Instead, he wore black cargo pants, and I saw the silver ankh of a *paramiir*

91

dangling from his belt. I stepped forward and offered him my hand, not bothering to hide the frown on my face.

He chuckled as he took my hand, and I felt a strong buzz across my palm. "Most kids miss that one. What's your name, son?" he asked, his voice pitched low enough that it barely reached my ears.

"Chance Fortunato, sir."

"Figures," he said with another chuckle as he put a hand out to Junkyard. "Jacob Buchanan. Take a seat." I turned to see the room about half full. In the middle of the front row, there was an empty desk with a sign on it in red ink: *Don't sit here!* Of course, I sat right there. A couple of minutes later, there was the heavy sound of someone running into a door they didn't think was there. Two more people caught the first two wards, but fell for the third, which I could see from the inside was set on the wall opposite the door and triggered when someone walked more than a foot into the room. The fourth person through the door after me was Stewart, who opened the door, splattered the marking charm, then promptly went and shook Mr. Buchanan's hand, before he took the seat right behind me.

"Did you shake hands with him, too?" he asked softly.

"Yup," I said.

"Kinda figured."

"Well, Mr. Hampton makes it a full class," Buchanan said. He reached behind him and held up a square of red cardboard. "Mr. Fortunato and Mr. Hampton, please sit this question out. What color is the card I'm holding up?"

"You're not holding anything in your hand, sir," someone behind us said. I could hear the smug smile in his voice, and a split second later, a girl on my left echoed the sentiment.

"We're not fooled," she added.

"Very well, who sees a card?" I heard the rustle of cloth as hands went up behind me. Two people snickered, and I wondered how well they were going to handle the truth. "What color is it?" The closest anyone got was orange.

"Is this like that dress thing on the internet?" someone asked.

"No, Mr. Hogkins, it isn't," Buchanan said. "It's because most of you can't see the color red right now. Also, about half of you ran into the door because you thought it was open, and a third of you have aura marks. There is a cowan saying that I've heard many of you repeat, 'What he doesn't know won't hurt him.' Well, this is an object lesson in how that isn't true. Those of you who didn't fall down an elevator shaft when they thought they were stepping into an empty elevator would be marked for later scrying or targeted for remote killing spells. And those of you who didn't accidentally run a red light while driving home would have been open to a myriad of suggestions. Observe!" With a gesture, I felt the slight pressure against my defenses fade, and the whole room gasped as they saw the messages written in red.

"You can't do that!"

"That's illegal!"

"My father will be hearing about this!" Of course, someone had to threaten to tell Mummy and Daddy what the big mean teacher was doing.

"Quiet, people!" Buchanan barked. "Your parents already know about this, they signed a release permitting me to subject you to these kinds of spells. Advanced Level classes are strictly voluntary, but I will remind you, you *did* sign up for this, and if you don't *like* what goes on in this class, you can always opt to drop it and take the failing grade. The spells you faced today are the same kind of spells and wards that you could face in the real world, and out there, you won't have the option to run home to Mommy to tell her what the bad man did to you. You'll be too busy trying to please your new master to worry about anything else."

"How are we supposed to trust you, then?" the girl on my right asked.

"You can trust what I teach you, Miss Kingston," he replied. "And you can trust that no spell or compulsion you encounter will last beyond the confines of this class. Now, back to actual learning. Look around. Each of these signs has a message on it, written in a color most of you couldn't register. Mr. Hampton, why would I find that useful?"

"It would let you plant suggestions without having to leave a compulsion spell in place," Stewart said after a moment. At a gesture from Mr. Buchanan, he went on. "Just because you can't see a color consciously, your eyes still see it, and your subconscious processes the message. And you still act on it."

"That's all pseudoscientific crap," someone behind me said.

"Mr. Fortunato, please hold up the sign that was on your seat. If it didn't work Mr. Fortunato would be sitting where you are, instead. Remember, bad guys can be subtle. And, like those who still pretend that the Earth is flat, just because you believe a thing doesn't make it true. Suggestion works. Cowan businesses use it very effectively every day. Now, Mr. Fortunato, how did you know to have your defenses ready when you entered the classroom today?"

"Junkyard alerted to something, and I felt the magick," I said.

Buchanan nodded. "Your familiar...excellent attention to your environment."

"Why did his familiar catch it and mine didn't?" a girl behind me asked. I turned to see her holding a long, brown creature that looked like a ferret, but with a patch of white fur on its upper lip. Like most familiars I'd seen here, it had an ornate collar around its neck.

94

"I don't use a control collar on Junkyard," I said.

"All familiars need a control collar," someone else said with almost as much disdain in their voice as I had in mine.

"Only when you buy one and enslave it instead of bonding with it," I said.

"It's just a dumb animal," the girl with the ferret said.

"No, *he* isn't," I said. "Junkyard is my friend, we're...to him, I'm his pack, his family. And I will be for as long as he lives. He always has my back, and he can see and smell things I never could. I trust this 'dumb animal' more than I trust most people, and if any of those spells had been real threats, this dumb animal would have saved my ass three times over just today. You can't say the same thing about your ferret."

"That's because it's a mink," the girl said with a sniff.

"Great, another white knight tree hugger," another boy sneered.

"Enough," Buchanan snapped. "Miss Kilcannon, Mr. Hartness, you've both earned your house a demerit. And Mr. Fortunato, another outburst like that will earn a demerit for your house. Am I clear?"

"Why do we get demerits and this charity case gets a pass?" Hartness demanded.

"Two demerits, for you, Mr. Hartness," Buchanan corrected him. "First, Fortunato's remarks were aimed at an exhibited behavior, as opposed to being personal attacks. Secondly, he was right, and a Franklin student should have the presence of mind and self-awareness to recognize that."

"How was he right?" Kilcannon asked.

"Did your mink alert you to the spells waiting for you? No, by your own admission, it didn't. Also, I've seen familiars like Junkyard here, without control collars. I've seen them give their own lives to protect their partners. One of them...was my familiar. Your casual disrespect for the person, Mr. Hartness, is what earned you both demerits. Which brings us to the root cause of the very *need* for this

95

class, ladies and gentlemen. The warlocks casting every spell, hex and curse I will be teaching you to defend yourself against have, at the core of their being, a total disregard for the victim. If you can't grasp that basic concept, you will fail this class. And if you adopt that same disregard, make no mistake, someday, someone like me will show up on your doorstep to hold you accountable for it." There was a moment of silence that stretched out to the point where it was getting uncomfortable before Buchanan said anything else.

"Now that you have a feel for the stakes, we can get started. Get your textbooks out and turn to page thirty-four. We'll start with mental defenses."

As we read, I started to realize just how clunky and crude my mental constructs actually were. Like most things I had figured out or learned under Dulka, my defenses relied on brute strength to keep unwanted influences out of my head. The defense structure in the book was more of an overlapping lattice of separate, supporting defenses. Rearranging the bulked up, overpowered mental wards I used in the more intricate pattern from the book took some work, and my head was pounding by the end of class.

Fortunately, my last class on Tuesday was Herbalism and Botany with Mr. Whitcomb. Whipcord thin with curly red hair that went everywhere, he lectured in a warbling voice that he pitched just low enough to make sure you had to listen closely. Still, it was partly dirt therapy, though there was also a little bit of mixing and preparation to make the most effective use of the plants.

After H and B, all I wanted was to change into t-shirt and jeans and chill for a while, but Housemaster Emerson had other ideas. Less than ten minutes after I got back to Jefferson House, I found myself in the common room for my hall, poring over the list of extracurricular activities and listening to the members of the hurligan team extol the virtues of the game. Hurligan was a lot like lacrosse, only with specialized wands instead of sticks. The object was to get the hurligan through the other team's goal, which was a hoop set sideways about twelve feet high on an angled stone wall. One of the hurligan players was decked out in the heavily padded uniform, which featured an open faced, padded helmet and solid pieces of plastic covering every joint. That was enough to make me decide I didn't want to play the wizard version of lacrosse and football. I had a bad habit of putting life and limb in danger on a regular basis. The last thing I needed was to go looking to get hurt playing a game that required almost as much padding as football. I turned my attention back to the longer list of clubs that didn't require so much armor.

"Narrowed it down any?" Stewart asked from over my shoulder a few minutes later.

"Well, it's a toss-up between the fencing and pistol clubs, but I'm pretty sure I want to do cross country," I told him.

"Have you considered the equestrian club?"

"Not on your life. Most animals freak out if I get too close. Junkyard is the first and pretty much only animal that will get close to me short of using a control collar."

"It was a thought. I'm a member of the fencing and pistol club. I'll introduce you around at the gym tomorrow afternoon. The pistol club meets on Saturdays, and, you're in luck, the cross country club meets on Wednesday morning before first lab period." I tried not to be too enthused, but all I managed was to seem unimpressed. Three extracurriculars. What utter joy. How would I ever contain myself? I shook my head and got up. Mr. Emerson immediately showed up to block my escape.

"Now, Mr. Fortunato, you'll need to choose at least two clubs to maintain the Jefferson tradition of well rounded interests."

"I figured three was rounded enough, Mr. Emerson," I said. Emerson looked over my shoulder, and I caught Stewart's head nod.

"Well done then," he said, and stepped aside, zeroing in on Hoshi as I left. As I headed down the hallway, I wondered if the Draeden had finally found a way to do what a werewolf, a demonic vampire and even the Sentinels themselves had failed to. Instead of trying to kill me with magick or violence, he was going to let the Franklin Academy kill me through sheer exhaustion.

On the up side, there would be fewer nightmares that way.

Chapter 6
~ Eternal and infinite, the soul can only be given by its own consent. ~ Faust

I woke up in the dark, covered in sweat and scrambling to get away from…something. Something pressed against my back, and all I knew for certain was that I was awake, and not beside my own bed. My arms were covering my face, my feet were cold and I could feel the cool trails of tears on my cheeks. My arms came down by fractions of an inch, and I scanned the room for whatever I was afraid of. In the dim light from my clock, I could see my side of the room. A quick glance to my left revealed Hoshi's desk, easy to tell from mine, even in the dark, because of the clutter. Somehow, I had crossed the room on my hands, ass and feet and ended up against his bed. Movement on my bed registered, and I saw Junkyard raise his head.

"I'm okay, buddy," I said. Junkyard gave me a quizzical head tilt, probably not believing a word I said. Assuming he understood anything I was saying, which I did. The continued silence nagged at me until I realized I hadn't heard anything out of my roommate.

"Hoshi?" I whispered. I reached behind me with my right arm and patted the bed, but only found rumpled sheets. I turned around to see the expanse of white linen, unmarred by my roommate's presence. Focusing on the moment seemed to calm the static in my head, and I found myself able to think a little more clearly as my pulse slowed to a steady pounding in my head. The sheets came free of my legs with a couple of kicks, and I gathered them up before I went back to my side of the room. Some part of me couldn't shake the feeling that something bad had just happened, and my roommate was missing. I slipped out of my sweat pants and grabbed my jeans, all the while wishing I could listen to the part of my brain that was trying to convince itself that it I was reacting to the dream, and that there was a perfectly reasonable explanation for why my roommate wasn't in his bed in the middle of the night. After I'd had a case of night terrors. My braing paused to do a little math. The first time in the three weeks I'd been at the Franklin Academy.

I heard the click of the door opening as a memory. By the time I knew what I was reacting to, my body was already moving, and I had my hawthorn wand up and pointed, ready to go all Han Solo in Cloud City on whatever came through the door. When nothing immediately presented itself for summary blasting, I lowered the wand. With my hand out of the way, I saw the large, silver fox standing in the doorway, looking at me with wary eyes. Irrational fear, meet reasonable explanation.

"Sorry," I said to Hoshi. "I'm a little jumpy." He padded to his bed and hopped up on it, then turned around a couple of times before he curled up and looked at me over his paws. Taking comfort that, for once, there actually was a reasonable explanation for everything that didn't seem to include danger to life and limb, I grabbed my sheets and laid back down on the floor to get a couple more hours of sleep before my alarm went off. Junkyard jumped down and curled up beside me, ready to keep the worst of the dreams at bay. I reached for my cellphone and hoped Shade answered.

"Hey, baby," she murmured, her face lit up by the screen. "Bad dream?" She peered at me with puffy eyes, and smiled gently. Even in the middle of the night, with no make up or anything, she was beautiful.

"Yeah," I said. "But seeing your face chases it all away."

"I wish you were here, in my arms," she said. "You'd never have bad dreams again."

"We'd never sleep."

"I know," she said with a wicked grin. From his bed, Hoshi fox let out a low groan.

"That's enough out of you, fuzzball," I said before I turned my attention back to the call.

A group of instructors and two Sentinels were waiting at the front of Jefferson House when the cross country club finished our first timed run. Stanwicke and a senior named Rothwin were the only two ahead of me, which meant I had a good chance of running with the A team at the first meet next month. It was a little unsettling how much I liked that idea. Maybe that was why I didn't get the screaming heebie-jeebies when I saw the wall of adults waiting on the steps of the dorm hall.

"Chance Fortunato," one of the Sentinels said in a booming voice as he leveled his *paramiir* staff at me. "Step clear of the group and face the yard. You are bound by order of the Council to stand down." The rest of the club scattered like I'd dropped a live grenade. Being on the wrong end of a *paramiir* staff was a lot like that, so I couldn't really blame them. I turned around and backed toward the Sentinels with my arms straight out and my hands splayed, palms facing away from them.

Minutes later, I was standing in the Headmaster's office in a pair of spellbinder cuffs, surrounded by Sentinels and teachers. The Sentinels all looked pretty much the same, but the faculty was looking pretty ragged. Professor Kenneson was missing his tie and vest, and one of his cuffs was undone, and Professor Talbot was in his shirtsleeves and vest, with his tie hanging loose and his top button undone. Only Buchanan looked like he hadn't dressed in a hurry, and even he hadn't bothered with his tie. Caldecott, on the other hand, hadn't missed a thing, in spite of the dark circles under his eyes.

"So what did I do?" I asked.

"Do you always assume you're going to be accused of a crime when you speak to someone in authority, Mr. Fortunato?" Professor Kenneson asked.

I held up my hands and rattled the cuffs. "Unless these are normal attire for visiting the headmaster's office, there's only one reason I'm wearing these. Something bad happened and no one else has confessed." That brought a round of gasps and a couple of laughs.

Kenneson glared at me. "This is no laughing matter, Mr. Fortunato."

"The kid's right, Tom," Mr. Buchanan said. "Spellbinders pretty much mean an accusation's already been made."

"Mr. Fortunato," Caldecott said as he leaned forward in is chair. "Can you account for your whereabouts between lunch yesterday and the time you were taken into custody this morning?"

"That's a pretty long stretch," I said. "And you know where I was from yesterday morning until about three yesterday afternoon. It isn't like there aren't dozens of witnesses. But no one has told me *why* I'm standing here in cuffs."

"A student has been attacked, Mr. Fortunato," Kenneson said. "Something I think you are very much aware of, since of all the people here at the academy, only you have the knowledge and background to have ripped the soul from a person's body. And of all the students here, only you have the motive to have attacked Sterling Lodge."

"I've danced to this tune before," I said. "Broad time frame to fill in, getting rousted at oh-dark-thirty, being the only possible suspect. You've got nothin' on me or anyone else. You're fishing. Because as much as you'd *like* to think I can just take a soul by force, that just ain't happening."

Caldecott shook his head and gestured to the Sentinels. "Keep him under guard in the detention room."

It was noon before I saw anyone but a stone faced Sentinel, and even they got to change shifts in the middle. The detention room was a plain brown brick place with no decorations, no windows and unadorned lighting. One desk faced two plain wood tables, and that was pretty much it. Not even a cheesy motivational poster. Probably the single most boring room in six states, and I was stuck in it for half the day. I meditated for hours. And if meditation looked a lot like napping, my technique was obviously very advanced, and I was very relaxed.

When the door finally opened, Caldecott himself stepped inside.

"Mr. Fortunato," he said. "While we haven't eliminated you completely as the person who attacked Mr. Lodge, it is beginning to look as if your protestations of innocence are sincere. There are a few questions we would like to ask you, informally. Would you consent to being questioned?"

"Sure," I said. "The other option probably means I end up getting knocked out cold and brought before the Council, and I've had enough of that shit."

He drew up and looked down his nose at me for a moment. "Well, then. Follow me, if you would." I got up and followed him out of the room. We ended up in an empty classroom with two Sentinels, Mr, Buchanan, Professor Kenneson and Professor Talbot. Somewhere along the way, Talbot had found his jacket but lost his tie, and Kenneson had secured the wayward cuff. My backpack was on a table in the middle of the room, its contents neatly arranged beside it. Another table was set up beside it, and Caldecott led me to the chair on the near side to the door, and pointed to it. I took a seat to face Caldecott and Buchanan.

"You were the last person to see Mr. Lodge before he was attacked," Buchanan said. "And you have no witnesses who can verify your whereabouts between the end of your

Alchemy class and when you arrived at Jefferson House cafeteria. Tell us what happened."

"He was waiting for me outside the classroom, like he had been for the past week. There were a few people still in the hall, so I figured I'd get a shot in on him. So I went up to him and told him that if he was going to stalk me, at least overdo it with the gifts or something. Write me some bad poetry, tell me how we're meant to be together or something so I can play my part right. He got a little huffy about that, and he said I'd never graduate from Franklin. That was when Professor Talbot came out of his classroom and called him over. He told me to get going, so I did."

Buchanan looked over at Talbot, who was nodding. "Yes, that's right. I addressed Mr. Lodge's disappointing behavior. Our conversation was brief, and it was witnessed by two other students. No, three, though Huntington was so absorbed in something on his phone that he seemed hardly cognizant of what was going on. After that, Sterling left in something of a hurry. At the time, I presumed he was eager to catch up to Mr. Fortunato."

"And what about last night, between three and five A.M.?"

"My roommate came back from his own night time rambling, and I called my girlfriend. But you probably already know that, if you talked to him and checked my phone records." *That* got a round of wide eyed looks, and one of the Sentinels left the room in a hurry. "Which thing was a surprise to you guys?"

"The phone," Buchanan said. "Divination is usually all we need to determine the truth of a matter, but the usual methods are bearing little fruit at the moment."

"I know how that goes," I said, recalling my attempt to find the Maxilla.

"I'm sure you don't," Kenneson said, adding an eye roll for extra snark.

"I had to find a sword that didn't want just anyone finding it," I said. I leaned forward and pointed at him. "When divination didn't work, I had to use the evidence we found on my dead mentor's boots and clothes to figure out where he'd been so I could find out where he hid the sword. Turns out, it wasn't exactly on Earth, but in this little dimensional pocket. So, yeah, I know how to find shit when it doesn't *want* to be found!"

"Of course!" Talbot said. "Forensic evidence! If Mr. Fortunato was at the site where the spell had been cast, there will be certain energies still attached to him. For that matter, there may still be particulate matter from the casting of the circle itself attached to clothing or skin."

"Are you determined to make excuses for this warlock?" Kenneson demanded. "He's guilty, I know it and you know it. All that remains is to prove it."

"If you know the boy is guilty," Buchanan said slowly, "then perhaps you should recuse yourself from this panel."

"I'll do no such thing! I'm here to see justice done, even if the two of you are not. All you have to do is look at his aura to see the evil that flows in his veins. Perhaps it's you who needs to recuse himself."

"I sat on the committee that approved this boy's familiar," Buchanan said. "And I was at his trial. I've seen his aura, Wayne. It has healed considerably since then. If he was responsible for tonight's attack, I'm sure it would have left its mark on him, but I see no deeper taint upon him."

"Which could be avoided if he had a proxy do the actual casting of the spell," Talbot said calmly as he leaned back in his chair. "However, he has raised a valid option, one I think we would be well served to explore. Mere heartfelt certainty of someone's guilt, Wayne, is not enough to convict. If you're right, then one would think that the opportunity to *prove* it would be more than welcome. Headmaster Caldecott, I hereby suggest that we subject the

105

boy to alchemical testing for components and energies from the circle's casting."

Caldecott looked down at the table for a moment, then up at me. "Very well. Mr. Fortunato, will you willingly submit to these tests?"

"Sure," I said.

"Will this also satisfy the Sentinels to the boy's innocence or guilt?" he asked the Sentinel at the door.

"Yes, sir," the Sentinel said.

"Headmaster," Kenneson said, his voice rising almost to a whine, "the conflict of interest here is obvious. We can't use the very test the perpetrator himself suggested-"

"Fortunato didn't suggest it," the Sentinel said. "Talbot did. And even if the kid did suggest it, it would still be a valid test because it's potentially self-incriminating."

"And I suppose *you* want to administer the test yourself," Kenneson said to Talbot.

"None of us three can," Talbot said, barely moving from his slightly reclined position. He scribbled something on his notepad, then tore it off and held it out to Caldecott. "We would contaminate the test because we've all been to the circle. There are other teachers who can administer it. Please give this to Mr. Whitcomb."

Caldecott glanced down at the note, then handed it to the Sentinel, who turned and left the room. "Understand, Mr. Fortunato, that this test only determines whether or not you were at the circle tonight. It does not prove your innocence. There are still gaps in your alibi, which leaves enough uncertainty that you are still a suspect."

I shrugged. Even if I had an airtight alibi, Talbot had also mentioned the idea of using a proxy, introducing plenty of doubt no matter what I did. A few minutes later, the other Sentinel came in with my phone in hand. His face was red as he set the phone down in front of the headmaster.

"The call log matches Fortunato's claim, sir," the Sentinel said. "I verified that the number was to a live phone, and even spoke to the young lady to confirm that she talked to Fortunato."

"Did you get any details to verify with Fortunato?"

"I did, sir," the Sentinel said, his face getting a deeper shade of crimson. "The young lady was very...forthcoming."

"I see," Caldecott said. "Would *you* care to elaborate, Mr. Fortunato?"

"We're two horny teenagers who haven't seen each other for a week and a half," I said. "What do you think we talked about? Baseball? No, we talked about sex. A lot." Now Caldecott was turning a little darker. "You want more? Because we're both pretty frustrated. There was a really good description of her-"

"I'm sure that will be plenty," he cut me off. I raised an eyebrow at him and flashed a smile.

Whitcomb came in a few minutes later with a spray bottle in one long hand, and Talbot's list crumpled in the other. "Who needs to be tested?" he asked. I raised my hand but that just got me a dubious look until Caldecott and Kenneson gestured my direction. "If you'll stand over here, please."

"This isn't going to ruin my sweats, is it?" I asked as I got up.

"It's just silver nitrate suspended in a solution with a simple divination cast into it. It shouldn't stain." With that, he started spritzing me from shoulders to feet.

"What's supposed to happen?" I asked. "Aside from nothing."

"If you had been exposed to any of the elements of the circle, they would be glowing," Talbot said as he got to his feet.

"Assuming this mixture even works," Kenneson said. Talbot came to stand beside me and gave Whitcomb a nod as he gestured toward himself. Whitcomb sprayed him like he had me, and almost immediately, small spots began to glow below the knees of his pants and around his hands and up to the elbows of his jacket sleeves. Kenneson came over and grabbed the bottle to spray himself down, and began to glow from the knees down, as well as his hands and cuffs of his jacket sleeves.

"All right," Caldecott said. "So we can rule out Mr., Fortunato for being at the circle tonight."

"This does not exonerate him," Kenneson added quickly.

"But it goes a long way toward it," Buchanan said.

"You're excused young man," Caldecott said. "Classes have been called off for today and tomorrow. Return to your hall." I went to the table and started putting things back in my backpack.

"I'll escort the boy back to his hall," Buchanan said, and the other three left the room. After a moment, he went to the door and locked it, then came back to the table and laid the tin with my emergency gear in it down.

"Why didn't you mention it?" I asked as I picked it up and slid it back into the hiding place under the titanium plates.

"Because I have one, too," he said as he reached behind his back and pulled a round metal box into view. The top of his was engraved with a complex ward, unactivated but ready. He uttered a command word, and it shimmered from sight, then he tucked it back away. "It was the food that made me think to look for it." I looked over at the packages of peanut butter, crackers and honey lying next to the plastic spoon and condiment packet I'd snagged.

"You have an MRE tucked in there somewhere?" I asked, pointing to his cargo pockets.

"Usually just a granola bar and jerky," he said with a laugh as he patted his left pocket. "I keep the MREs in my car. But that's the point, Chance. I started doing this kind of thing because I never knew when I'd end up following someone across six states or staking out a coven for twelve hours before relief could get to me. Twenty six years of being a Sentinel made me think about being prepared all the time. You're only sixteen. You shouldn't be worried about that. Is this Corwin's teaching?"

"No," I said, grabbing the packets and stuffing them into the bag. "I was doing this before I met him. I never knew when Dulka would remember to feed me. Or when he would decide I needed to go hungry for a few days to remind me who was in charge. I never knew when or if one of Dulka's rivals would try to nab me and either hold me for ransom or try to pry my master's secrets out of me…or just want to have some fun before he let me go. So, yeah, I'm always prepped. And armed with my TK rod, if I can swing it."

"I see," he said. "I'm sorry, Chance."

"For what?"

"That you never got to be a kid, I guess," he said. "For what it's worth, you'd make a good Sentinel."

"No I wouldn't," I said. "I don't take orders very well."

"Not all of us do."

Hoshi, Junkyard and Ren were waiting for me when I got back to the room, along with a huge mess. Hoshi and Ren looked worried, but Junkyard just looked sleepy. He'd curled up on my clothes on the bed, with Ren perched behind him, his tiny hand stroking his fur. Hoshi came up out of his desk chair as soon as I opened the door.

"Dude, what's going on?" he asked. "They said you got arrested, and that you killed another student and summoned a demon or some shit like that!"

"Slow down," I said as I looked at the aftermath of having my room searched. Junkyard got up, stretched and hopped off the bed, then came over to me and reared up so he could put his paws on my chest. Once I'd rubbed his head a little, he dropped down and went to his food bowl, then looked back at me. "Yeah, I can see why you missed me today." I poured some food into his bowl and went to my desk to sort through the books and papers that had been dumped out onto it.

"So? What happened?"

"I don't know exactly, but I'm going to find out. Whatever it is, they were pretty sure I did it at first. Hell, I'm still a suspect. Now what?" My cheap phone chirped in my pocket. I pulled it out and flipped it open to see Dr. C's name in the little ID box.

"Chance!" he said as soon as I hit the little green answer button. "I just now heard. Are you okay? What did they do?"

"I'm fine, sir," I said. "They just asked me some questions and sprayed magic water on me to make sure I wasn't there. My room might never recover, though."

"Let me guess, you were their first and only suspect."

"Pretty much. It's like you know me or something."

"That's it," he said. "Draeden can do whatever he wants to me, but you're coming home. I'm not going to let them railroad you-"

"No, sir," I cut him off. "I'm staying."

"You're just asking them to pin this on you."

"They already *want* to pin it on me! If I go now, I'm as good as confessing to this. Even if they found out who was doing this for real, they'd still figure I was a part of it somehow. But that's not why I have to stay."

There was a short pause before he said anything. "You think you can stop them."

"I *have* to stop them," I corrected him. "I can't just run from this. I made a promise. I have to make this right."

"Chance, you don't have to-" I hung up on him.

"Okay, that was dramatic," Hoshi said. "So, why the white knight routine?"

"What do you mean, white knight?" I said with a glare for emphasis. I'd heard or rather read the term directed at Lucas online, and it wasn't meant as a compliment.

"I have to stop them," he shot back, making his voice deeper and rougher.

"That whole conversation, and that's the only part you heard? That's the *only* thing you decided was important?" I asked as I crossed the few feet between us.

"Dude, you don't have to do anything you don't want to," Hoshi said, stepping back. "I mean, it's not like you're gonna get laid or anything for doing this."

I gave him a level stare for a moment. "I don't think with my dick, Hoshi. Not about things like this." I turned away from him and started back toward my side of the room. The bed looked like a good place to start, so I grabbed one of my shirts and a hanger.

"Whatever, man. You take this shit way too seriously."

I closed my eyes and tried to keep my mouth shut, but that didn't work worth a damn. My feet pivoted so that I turned in place and I looked across my shoulder at him.

"Fifty-seven," I said after a moment.

"What?"

"I helped send fifty-seven people to Hell. And I made a promise to make that shit right. So, yeah, I take this very seriously."

"Oh." He sat down on his bed and looked across the room at me with blank eyes.

"Ren, I'm going to need your help," I said after I took a moment to hang up the shirt I'd grabbed and calmed down a little

The little sprite launched himself into the air with a buzz of wings and landed on the only unoccupied corner of my desk. "What can I do?"

"I need to know where they found Sterling Lodge, to start with, so I can go take a look at the scene. I also need to find out where they're keeping him so I can try to get a look at his aura."

"I can do that," Ren said, his face alight. "Can I come? I can scout for you, and be a lookout if you need one." He floated off the desk until he was at eye level.

"Ren, I don't want you to get in any trouble."

His smile got bigger as he floated closer. "If you don't get caught, I won't get in trouble."

So help me, the little shit sounded like me. "Okay. You can come along."

The sound the little sprite made barely registered in my hearing, but Junkyard whined for a few seconds after he was gone. I sat down and felt my shoulders slump, finally able to relax. I looked out the window, but my mind and my gaze always came back to the school and the forest around it. The hunt was on.

Chapter 7

~ Action, even fruitless striving, is better than passive acceptance of the status quo. ~ Caleb Renault, protagonist in the Blood and Honor series by Nick Vincente

"It was pure luck that one of my clan even found this place," Ren whispered from his perch on my backpack. "She'd just chased a bogill off the grounds, and she ran across this place coming back. It's probably what attracted the damn thing in the first place." The clearing in front of us was about fifty feet wide, with a dark ring in the middle. The grass was stomped pretty much flat both inside and outside the ring, which meant there was no way I was going to be able to follow anyone who been here while it was in use. Too many tracks, too many energy patterns. I was beginning to understand Detective Collins' frustration with having a bunch of civilians on a crime scene before he could take a look at it. Junkyard pressed against my leg, his own senses probably showing him things I was glad I couldn't see.

"It's like a herd of elephants went through here," I said as I stepped into the clearing. The only two places that didn't look like the flood of feet hadn't touched were the central section of the circle, and the ring itself. The ring got my attention first, simply because it was closer, and I'd have to cross it to get to the center. I walked a slow circuit around it with the cellphone Shade had given me out and recording video. Looking at it through the screen, I didn't recognize the pattern, though the runes were familiar. The grass was dead along the circle's perimeter and in a foot wide swath on either side of the runes. As I went, Ren flitted off my back and flew along inside the circle with me. He dipped low as I completed the circuit, then came back up to eye level with me.

"The grass was just starting to grow back," he said, pointing to the dead vegetation in between us.

"Grow back?" I asked. "Then…this wasn't the first time they used this circle," I said. I glanced up at the moon and moved to the east side of the circle, then stepped across it. There was a slight tingle of energy across my aura as I breached the threshold, then it was past, and I was practically on top of the central point of the whole set-up. Now came the hard part.

I took a deep breath and opened my Third Eye. The cold gray of necromancy lingered in a vaguely human shaped form on the ground in front of me, large enough to show more than one set of limbs. They had used this place more than once, and if I was right, they'd claimed three victims here. It was time to test that theory.

"Ren, I need some of the grass at the edge of the circle." As he flittered to do that, I pulled my backpack off and took the tea candle out of the emergency tin. The withered grass was fed to the candle's flame, and acrid smoke filled the clearing. A quick poke with my pocket knife got me three drops of blood to anoint the candle and added a little life essence to the whole thing.

"Pnévma tou prósfata anachórise , sas kaló na to méros tou thanátou sas," I intoned softly in Greek. Roughly translated, it meant 'Spirit of the recently departed, I call you to the place of your death." In this case, the true meaning of the words was important, since I was making a specific call to an entity, so I used a language I spoke occasionally. After I'd repeated the phrase five or six times, the flame from the candle went pale green as it hit the blood, and the energy in the clearing changed. With that change came visitors.

Junkyard growled and turned his head to the right as another shape shimmered into existence right in front of me. I brought the cellphone up and snapped a quick shot, then turned and tried to see what Junkyard was growling at. Another figure had appeared outside the circle. I hit the shutter in the split second before the figure disappeared. I

114

turned back to the first figure to see it still shimmering in place. I got the phone up and snapped another picture as it reached out a hand before it too faded.

"Time to go," I said as I reached out and pinched out the flame on the candle. In seconds, I had everything stowed and we were headed out of the clearing. Ren flew ahead of me and Junkyard ran beside me as I made my way through the dimly lit woods. The thin crescent of the moon barely gave me enough light to see by, but between that and Junkyard, I managed to keep a decent pace. Once we reached the edge of the woods, I dropped into a crouch, and Ren lowered himself onto my backpack again. Junkyard laid down beside me, his tongue lolling out. Ahead of me, I could see the silvery sheen of dew on the grass, and the lights by the doors of the Academy.

"Are we still on mission?" Ren asked softly. I had to smile at the eagerness in his voice, especially since I was fighting the urge to grin ear to ear myself.

"Yeah," I said. "I still need to get a look at Lodge. If I can, I also want to take a look at the records of the two kids who disappeared last year."

"Oh, I can get you the records for a little while," Ren said. "But I'd need to take them back, and I couldn't get them for you until tomorrow."

"Tomorrow's good. Let's focus on Lodge, then."

"Right! Okay, follow me." Ren launched himself into the air and headed off to the right. I followed him for several hundred yards, until we came to a place where the ground dipped. Ren stopped in a small stand of trees, and I crouched beside his vantage point. About fifty yards ahead I could see two sprites lounging on a pair of boulders that sat on either side of a wooden door.

"Okay, that complicates things a little," I said softly.

"Don't worry," Ren said. "I've got this. I'll need Junkyard's help, though."

I looked down at Junkyard, who had come to his feet. "You got this big guy?" I asked him, certain he understood me on some level. He took a step toward Ren, then looked back over his shoulder at me. "Yeah, you got this," I said, and he turned in place and looked to Ren.

"I'll draw them away from the door. Once you're in, go to the first junction, then turn left and go three openings down, that'll bring you out in the basement for the infirmary. The entrances inside the school aren't guarded. We'll meet you there." He flew over to Junkyard and dropped down onto his back, then grabbed the fur on his neck and made a clicking sound with his tongue. Junkyard bounded out of the trees, carrying Ren toward the door. The two sprites flitted into the air, drawing out bows as big as they were from behind the rocks. When they saw it was Ren, they laughed and called out to him in Fae. I'd heard it spoken plenty of times, but I'd never been able to pick up even the most basic terms, because more than half of it was beyond the human range of hearing. The sprite dialects were also inflected by antenna movements, so no human or other race could speak fluent sprite, either. After a few comments, they laughed along with him, then he flew up and gestured to Junkyard. One of them set his bow down, and his companion followed suit, dropping hers behind the rock she'd originally pulled it from. The first one settled on Junkyard's back, and he took off toward the woods. Ren laughed and took off after him, and the other sprite followed. Seeing my opening, I darted from the trees and headed for the door, careful to stay low and as quiet as I could manage. The Dutch style door was a dark wood with heavy iron hinges and lower latch. The upper latch was a shiny brass lever. Wards flared briefly but didn't go off as I grabbed the iron latch and let myself inside. Once in, I waited for a few seconds after the door clicked shut to make sure no one was going to follow, then turned around and pulled the small angle head flashlight out of my pack.

It was a military surplus model that still had the colored lenses with it. I'd put the red lens in, and down here, I figured I could risk the extra light.

The tunnel was lined with rough, brown stone, with a dirt floor. There were lightbulbs every few yards, connected by metal conduit pipes. There was a switch by the door, but I left it alone. I didn't want to go and advertise that I was down here any more than I had to. My footsteps were muffled by the dirt so I let my pace pick up a little as I went along. Once I hit the first juncture, I found myself in a much larger, much warmer concrete tunnel. Pipes lines one wall, and the caged lights were actually on in here. I clipped the flashlight to my belt as I took the left turn and headed down, counting junctions until I got to the third one. The door opened smoothly, and I found myself in a dark basement as the two latches clicked shut behind me. The red beam of the flashlight revealed that I was in a store room for errant tables and broken chairs. True to his word, Ren showed up a few minutes later, coming in through the upper door. He gestured for me to follow him, and led me through the hallways until I found myself crouched at the edge of a doorway, staring down at the ward hall. A pair of Sentinels stood guard over Lodge's bed, and a nurse sat at a station at the end of the hall, her attention on her computer.

An up close look at Lodge was out of the question. All I really needed was a quick look at his aura, though. I slowly stuck my head around the corner again and took a peek, opening my mystic senses again as I did.

After a few seconds, I pulled back, fighting the urge to gasp. Slowly, I took a deep, ragged breath and let it out. The Sentinel's auras had been bright and clear, both bright blue with duty, mixed with various muted red blotches of anger and streaks of purple that spoke of mild grief or sadness to me. Where Lodge's aura should have been was what I could only describe as a sucking wound. It was literally an empty maw of gray that felt like it would pull

117

me in if I looked at it for too long. He was still alive, but everything that was Sterling Lodge was gone. I turned and headed for the basement.

"I've never seen anything like that," I said once I was safe in the tunnel.

"He just feels like a blank spot to me," Ren said.

"People without a soul still have an aura, it's just...faded, or washed out. This...this was something else completely. Okay, I need to get back to my room. Do these tunnels connect all the buildings?"

Ren nodded. "Yeah, we're not very far from your hall. I'll take you."

Twenty minutes later, I was safe in my room. Well, as safe as I was going to get where someone was going around ripping people's souls out. Ren had gone to bring Junkyard back, and Hoshi was sitting on his bed practicing his frown.

"Did you find what you were looking for?" he asked.

"No," I said. I sat down and booted up my computer, then sent Lucas a text warning him I was about to call. "If I had, whoever did this to Lodge would be in custody. Or in the morgue."

"Do you kill everything you go up against?"

"Not everything." The computer screen changed, and the program Lucas had given me came up with an incoming call. I hit the green button with the cursor, and Lucas's face appeared on the screen.

"Good...morning," he said, rubbing sleep from his eyes. "What's up?"

"I need you to get some files to Dr. C. so he can check them against the special collection. Tell him there are two confirmed deaths linked to this thing. I got pictures of two ghosts, one for sure is a full body apparition, the other is at least upper torso. Once you get them, I need you to play it and make sure nothing is corrupted. Once I know you have it, I'm going to have to delete the files from my phone." I

118

pulled up the video and the pictures, then texted the files to him.

"Okay, I'm transferring them to my laptop now. So, while they're playing, what is going on?"

"It's hard to describe. Someone is ripping people's souls out. They're not even leaving an aura behind."

"What about the one thing you told me about? Some kind of mark on their aura? Or was it on their skin?"

"Yeah, demon's like branding their humans, kinda like cattle. They always leave a demon mark. It takes time to show up in the aura, unless they have your soul, then it's pretty much automatic. I don't know if the victims are marked or not. If they are…"

"Then we use the Big Book O' Demons you and Dr. C were working on."

"Liber de Magna Daemonia," I said, translating the title to Latin. "Dr. C wants to go with Codex Abyssus. Anyway, I'm going to get a peek at the victims' files tomorrow, and I'll look to see if they had any marks on them."

"Okay. Got the files, so you can delete the originals. I'll get these to Dr. C in the morning."

"Good. Just make sure he knows not to go to the Council or anyone with this. I'm not exactly legit here."

Lucas let out a snort. "When are you *ever* legit when you go all Sherlock? I don't think I need to tell him, but I will."

"He does this kind of thing a lot?" Hoshi said, leaning in over my shoulder.

"He's like a damn anime hero, only with normal colored hair," Lucas said. "Ninja Detective Mage Fortunato. He'd be lost if he didn't have to sneak around to solve a case." Hoshi let out a short laugh of his own at my expense. "Look, bro, I gotta bolt. It's almost midnight here, and I have a Calculus quiz tomorrow. I'll give this to Dr. C tomorrow, and I'll tell him to keep it off the books." He killed the connection, leaving me with a smirking Hoshi.

"What?" I asked as he let out a snicker.

"Ninja Detective Mage Fortunato," he said as he turned the lights out and went to his bed. "I'm so gonna draw that."

"And I'm so gonna kick your ass if you do." I laid down on my blankets. Junkyard wandered over and pawed at the thick cloth for a moment before he plopped down beside me.

"Maybe you can get Metallo-Baby to do a catchy opening theme for you."

"Maybe you'll get a bad case of amnesia."

In the darkness, he hummed a few notes, then went silent for a few seconds. "Ninja Detective Mage Fortunato…go!" he sang softly.

"So, this is what madness is like," I muttered. Hoshi snickered, and for a few minutes, it was quiet. Just when I thought I was going to get to sleep, he broke the silence with another chuckle.

"You need a signature fighting move," he said. "And a pose." It was going to be a long night.

Chapter 8
~ If what you're doing isn't working, try something else. You only eliminate one more thing if it doesn't work. ~
Lao Chi, detective.

"Isn't that your dad?" a girl asked as a tabloid fell in the middle of the table. I looked up amid a chorus of snickers and malevolent giggles. My father's face was plastered across a copy of the Boston Ledger. It was a particularly clear shot of him holding his coat up in front of him and his face turned to one side, like he was trying to avoid a camera pointed at him from another angle. Unfortunately for him, it presented the particular scowl he was wearing right at the photographer who had taken this shot.

SPARTAN INDICTED!
Empire toppled by inside informant.

"Why? Looking for a date?" I asked her retreating back. She stopped cold for a second, then glared at me over her shoulder for a moment before walking on. I shook my head and looked down at my plate. Somewhere between my fifth and sixth bites, I'd dozed off and my fork had fallen into my oatmeal still bearing a chunk of scrambled eggs. With a sigh, I pushed my plate and bowl away, then reached for the mug of coffee. Even lukewarm, the black elixir was decent tasting.

"Help me, Sunrise Roast. You're my only hope," I muttered before I took a second sip.

"I'm never gonna make it to the weekend," Kiya moaned. "Wait, what day is it?" I looked over at the paper.

"Wednesday, I think," I said. "September something."

"It's Thursday," Desiree said. "Grapefruit on the fruit bar. Gracie Solomon and Sarah Ellincot are eating breakfast together, because they have the same first hour class."

"So it could be Monday," Hoshi said.

"Too tired for Monday," I said, my legs reminding me that I'd done my qualifying runs for the next cross country meet yesterday. A chorus of weary agreement followed that.

"Thursday," Kiya said. "I'm calling it for Thursday."

"When is your source going to get back to us?" Hoshi asked as the focus shifted back to the table. "It's been three weeks."

"When did you join the Ninja Detective Mage agency?" I whispered back.

"Since the Franklin Honor Code. I get the same punishment you do if I don't report you. So, since I'm not reporting you, I might as well join up."

"Dr. C has a lot on his plate already," I said. "Poring over a crappy cell phone video isn't going to help that much. Bugging him about it sure as all Nine Hells won't speed things up." The morning bell chimed, and I grabbed my bagel as I got to my feet. "He's also got classes to teach," I said.

By that afternoon, even if Dr. C had given me the names and pictures of whoever had ripped Lodge's soul away, I wouldn't have had the time or energy to go after them. I set my stack of books down on the table in the common area and tried to decide which one to start first. Conjuring won, and I pulled the sketch book from my pack. The page flipped to the most recent set of elemental summoning circles, various shades of pastel reds, greens, blues and yellows, all marred by the bright red marks pointing out errors I still couldn't see. No matter what I did, I never seemed to get the conjuring circles right according to Professor Kenneson. For a guy who had managed to summon lesser demons and spirits, that stuck my ego hard.

Today's homework was to do a summoning circle for a weather elemental, a very specific type of air elemental. I read the question from the book, having to go through it three times before I was halfway certain I understood it.

You need to know the weather for three days from the current date. Draw the proper summoning circle for the proper elemental.

My first step was to make sure I used the same color pencil as the chalk I would be using when I drew the actual practice circle. With less than steady hands, I put the colored pencil to the page and started on the central sigil, which would resonate with the elemental and draw it to the circle.

"Temperamental little bastards, aren't they?" Stewart said from over my shoulder. My pencil shifted, and the line went to one side.

"Sorry about that," he said as he plucked the half-used eraser from beside the sketch book. "I just hated Conjure Three with a passion. It's hard to tell who's harder to deal with, Kenneson or a pissed off elemental."

"If I could make a circle to summon and control him, I could retire before I graduated," I said as I leaned back. Stewart bent forward and rubbed at the errant mark.

"Just remember with this one, the point is information, not control. You just want to talk to it, but you want accuracy, so a truth...a truth sigil...right about..." he said, his words slurring as he swayed in place for a moment.

"Are you okay, man?"

"Yeah, fine. Better never..." His eyes rolled back and he slumped over on top of me.

"Ethan!" I bellowed. "Get Mr. Emerson!" The hall captain barely took the time to register what was going on before he bolted from the room. People gathered around before I even had Stewart on the floor. Where his skin touched mine, I felt enough power flowing through him to make my hair stand on end, and it didn't give me the same tingle as regular magick. No, this was the burn of Infernal power.

"Stand back, what's going on here?" Mr. Emerson demanded as he entered the room. With a blink, I opened my Third Eye, and saw the dark purple stain slowly spreading on Stewart's aura.

"I think it's the same people who attacked Lodge," I said. "It feels Infernal." Suddenly, there was a lot more open space around us.

"Mr. Stanwicke, activate the house wards. I'll shield Mr. Hampton myself. Now step back Mr. Fortunato." I moved away and felt the hum of the house wards against my senses. Moments later, Mr. Emerson's circle shimmered into existence, a beautiful golden column in my Third Eye's Sight, and Stewart moaned. After a few heartbeats, a thick, undulating strand of purple energy became visible. I traced it back to the wall, where I could see the fading remains of the house wards. If it had torn through the house wards…my attention went back to Mr. Emerson's shield. His circle was still intact, but the energy strand was punching through it like it was barely even there.

I lunged for the table and grabbed a stick of chalk, then shoved Mr. Emerson out of the way. He tried to protest, but I was already drawing a rough circle around Stewart on the floor. Once I had it done, I did a hasty circle outside it, then started filling the space between the two circles in with symbols I had memorized months ago. Just drawing them felt like having flaming snakes crawl through my brain, but I could also feel the resistance from the attack as it hit the incomplete circle. I drew in the last symbol, then grabbed Stewarts hand and pulled my pocket knife. Too late, Mr. Emerson figured out what I had in mind, but even as he rushed forward, I thumbed the blade open and ran the razor sharp edge across the outside of Stewart's pinky. Blood flowed, and I flicked the knife at the edge of the circle as I pushed myself away from it.

The effect was spectacular. The instant his blood hit the edge of the circle, it sprang to hideous life, a translucent purple and black column that was visible to the naked eye. So was the energy thread that was attacking him, as the sudden appearance of the shield created a resonance feedback. I could see a pulse of energy flow down the thread and hit the shield. It flared, but, having nowhere else to go, flowed back down the energy thread. Instinctively, I laid my hand against the thread, and felt the power pulse brush my aura. Instantly, I got an indistinct image of a girl's face with her lips pulled back in a rictus of fury.

I pumped raw magick down my arm as my palm closed around the thread. Suddenly, the tingling energy strand felt solid under my hand, and it changed from dark purple to pale blue. Whoever it was must have tried to break off the attack. I shoved more raw energy into it, and suddenly the energy strand was all me. I got the impression of surprise and fear as I let go of it, leaving a glowing blow line in the air. Whoever was on the other end would be certain of one thing: I was coming for them.

I vaguely heard my name as I dashed to the stairs, then I was down the flights and bursting out the door at a sprint. My eyes tracked the slowly fading blue arc as I ran for the woods, my hand groping for my wand. A ravine loomed ahead, and I leaped for the far side, my feet sinking into the soft loam just shy of the top. Stumbling, I got my feet back under me and took off again, accompanied by the sounds of people moving through the brush on either side of me.

I burst into the clearing before I realized I was even close. The first clue I had was the tingle when I crossed the circle's edge, and caught the residual barrier with my shoulder and my face. I saw at least two figures running into the woods, and I leveled my wand at them.

"*Ictus!*" I intoned, and a half-focused bolt of telekinetic energy went crashing through the brush. "Damn it!" I yelled when I didn't even get a yelp of pain back for the effort.

"Fortunato, stand down!" I heard from behind me and to my right.

"You guys know this wasn't me, right?" I asked.

"Don't move, kid," I heard a familiar voice say from my left. I looked down, suddenly realizing exactly where I was: right in the middle of the circle.

"Great," I muttered. "Now I'm *that* guy." I felt six wands focus on me in a heartbeat.

"Explain yourself," another Sentinel said. "Who are you?" Understanding dawned in my head a few seconds later.

"I'm still me, guys, still Chance Fortunato, your favorite pain in the ass. I meant that I'm the idiot who stomps around in a crime scene and makes a mess of things."

"You are that," the woman I recognized said. Average height, round, forgettable face and brown hair pulled back into a ponytail, there was only one Sentinel who fit that bill.

"Sentinel Dearborn, good to see you again." I gave her a smile, but it didn't seem to be thawing her attitude out any. Like most Sentinels, she carried two pistols, one a specialized paintball gun that fired alchemical rounds, and the other a regular semiautomatic that I would bet any amount of money carried silver rounds.

"Wish I could say the same, kid," Jane Dearborn said. The last time we'd met, I'd inadvertently broken through her concealment spell while she was following me during my Ordeal. "I need you to try to back out of there in your own footsteps. You know the drill." I nodded and took a careful step backward, stretching as far as I could to match my running stride. Another step, and I was outside the circle.

126

"Sorry about that guys," I said, though I noticed I hadn't been the only person who'd broken the circle. Another Sentinel was standing at the edge looking sheepish, and I knew he'd been closer to where I was a few seconds ago. "I don't think I stepped on the circle itself, though."

"That's nice, but you've still done more than enough damage. Report back to your house. I'll deal with you later." Dearborn moved to my side, her face a blank mask. "If you're lucky, all I'll mention is interfering with Sentinels. Who knows, they might even let you finish out the semester."

"Yeah, that's awful nice of you," I said. I looked down at the symbols scorched into the ground in front of me, a series that actually came close to making sense to me. "You're welcome, by the way."

"What do we have to thank you for? You blunder into the middle of a circle, disrupting any chance we have of tracing it back to the person who cast it, scaring them off in the process. Why should I be grateful for that?"

"Because I led you to that circle and saved the guy they were targeting in the process. I also know that there were at least two people involved, and I know that this circle is different. I know what they were up to." I studied Dearborn's face for a reaction, and was rewarded with an unpleasant look that promised nothing good.

"Start talking, kid," she said. "What were they up to?" In the distance, I heard Junkyard's bark, and I could see half a dozen lights headed our way.

"Okay, this sequence here, it's a nullifier. See those gaps in the runes? They're for whatever spell you want to attach to it. I used almost this exact same thing when I escaped from my old boss to get past his wards. This is basically an armor piercing bullet of a spell. All this circle was designed to do was break through the school's wards, which I'm guessing you beefed up on the sly after Lodge got a soulectomy."

"That's need to know only," Dearborn said. "How did you save the target?"

"Different kind of shield, one they weren't expecting."

"Okay, we need to make you scarce," she said as we heard the crash of brush and someone cursed nearby. "Fortunato, don't let a word of what you just told me slip. Lie if you have to. Drummond. Get him out of sight, take him back to the dorm and check on whoever it was they were attacking," she said to the Sentinel who'd stumbled into the circle with me. He came to my side and grabbed his cloak by the edge, then swept it up over my shoulder with a muttered word.

The moment the cloth touched me, the world went sort of hazy and out of focus, like a watercolor painting. Inside a small area, everything was still in sharp detail, but even the sounds around us were muted.

"Stay still for a few seconds," Drummond said. "Let their senses adjust."

"Is that a chameleon spell on the cloak?" I asked

"New and improved, since you blew past Jane's spells last March," he said, then put a finger to his lips as someone stumbled into the circle.

"Did he see them?" I heard Talbot's voice ask. More people came right behind him, the tips of wands and other items glowing.

"Okay, let's move," Drummond said. He led me way from the circle, not heading straight toward the school at first, then slowly angling us toward Jefferson House. Once we were at the main doors, he flipped the cloak away from me, and the world shimmered back into focus around me. He stopped me at the door with a hand on my arm.

"Officially, you didn't see the circle for right now," he said. "You found me and brought me back to look at your friend. Not a word about anything else. You got it?"

"Yeah, I know how it works," I said. "Leave crucial details out, let the real perp trip themselves up by revealing too much. And leave the detective work to you guys."

"Keep that up, and you might actually survive to adulthood."

"Boy, wouldn't that disappoint a lot of people." Junkyard caught up to us as we got to the stairs, giving me a look full of reproach for leaving him behind. In the common room, we found Stewart sitting in the chair I'd abandoned, with Mr. Emerson hovering near him.

"There you are, Mr. Fortunato," Emerson said with a frown. "And being brought back by a Sentinel, no less."

"Actually, Mr. Fortunato was leading me back here to check on your head boy," Drummond said with a gesture toward Stewart. "Seems as though you saved the young man's life."

"I beg to differ," Emerson said. "I had the situa- excuse me, did you say I saved Mr. Hampton?"

"Yes, I did. Why don't we discuss this in your office, shall we?" Drummond said. Stewart got to his feet and followed slowly. He caught my eye and mouthed a silent "Thank you" as we left the common area and went to the office in the middle ground between the boys and girls sides of the house. The head girl, Rebecca and Mrs. Emerson came in behind us, and Mrs. Emerson insisted Stewart lay down on the couch along the wall. Emerson took his place in the tall, leather chair behind the broad desk, but he didn't offer us a seat. Drummond took a chair anyway and gestured for me to sit down. As I sat, Rebecca left the room.

"Now, as I was saying, I was handling the attack quite nicely on my own when Fortunato here shoved me to the ground and scrawled that gibberish circle around him. If I hadn't..." Emerson said, but Stewart cut him off.

129

"With all due respect to your skills, Mr. Emerson," Stewart said, "it *was* Chance's circle that stopped that attack cold. Yours barely slowed it down."

"Excuse me, Mr. Hampton?" Emerson asked, his face going from stern to shocked.

"It wasn't until I was inside Chance's circle that I could think straight."

"We're going to go with the story that it was Mr. Emerson's circle that protected you, though," Drummond said, which got a smile from Emerson. "At least until we catch the warlock who did this. We don't want to endanger Chance by advertising his ability to defend against their magick now, do we?" The look on Emerson's face told me that was exactly what he wanted to do, but it looked like his vanity won out.

"Of course not," Emerson said. "Our students' safety is our top priority. For the moment, I will continue to claim that it was my efforts that protected Mr. Hampton. However, several people saw what he did with the energy filament, and they saw him run from the common room."

"And he was severely reprimanded for that," Drummond said, which wasn't exactly fiction. "His actions interfered with our attempts to apprehend whoever cast this spell."

"We'll make sure word gets out, unofficially," Emerson said. "Mr. Fortunato, why don't you assist Mr. Hampton back to his room?" I got up and went to the couch. Stewart got to his feet without much help from me.

"I owe you my life, Chance," he said when we were alone in the hallway. "I mean, I literally could have died back there. I can't even start to repay you for that."

"Don't try," I said. "A good man doesn't keep score like that."

"Well, I still feel like I owe you. I'll tell you what, meet me at the Grotto tomorrow evening, eight o'clock."

"What do you have in mind?"

"Let's just say that some folks here know a good person when they find one. I'll see you there." He stumbled into his room, and moments later, Rebecca went in, leaving the door open. Having a girl on the boy's side was strictly forbidden, much less in your room. Rank evidently had its privileges.

The common room was empty by the time I made it back to collect my homework, but almost every room had its door open and people were congregating. Only my door was closed, and I heard Hoshi's voice through it.

"No, he's fine," he was saying as I walked in. "He just walked in, as a matter of fact. Yeah, he did. Big dude, had guns under each arm. No, didn't see a staff, either. Yeah, we'll meet you down there." He rolled off his bed and perched his hip on the corner of his desk as I set my books down.

"What I can tell you is not much," I said, cutting him off before he could ask.

"Did you see the circle?" he asked. "Was there a sacrifice or something?"

"I saw it, but…Hoshi, I can't tell you what I saw. The Sentinels told me not to."

"Dude, you go out and risk getting expelled so you can look at another circle, but suddenly you're all law and order about this shit?"

"On this, yeah," I told him. "The Sentinels are looking for people who might know something they shouldn't, so they're keeping the details under wraps. If I told you something, and you said something to the wrong person, they lose their edge, and someone dies or some shit like that. Or they think you're the perp."

"Okay, chill, dude," Hoshi said. "I know what you're like when you're all serious like this. Come on, Kiya and Desiree and a bunch of other guys are hanging out in the common room downstairs. You gotta at least give 'em something."

I got up and held up my hands. "Fine, I'll go, but I have to get back up here soon so I can call Lucas." We headed downstairs, and ended up in the biggest common room. About eight other people were down there, including Desiree and Kiya. Hoshi sidled up to Kiya and put his arm around her waist.

"Okay, official word is he didn't see much," he started, which brought a moan. "But can you tell me about the Sentinel you came back with?"

"I guess, what do you want to know?"

"Did he have one of those swords?" Kiya asked

"A *paramiir*? Yeah, they all do."

"I didn't see it. Where was it?"

"It was on his belt. The blade was retracted."

"They can make the blade disappear? That's so *dope*!" Hoshi said.

"Yeah, or they can turn it into a staff."

"I thought the staff was for the higher ranks, and the sword was for like the next rank down," Desiree said. Coming from her, I was surprised at the level of misinformation she had.

"No, the staff, the sword and the ankh are all one thing. I thought everyone knew that." All around me, heads were shaking.

"Dude, tonight was maybe the second time I've ever even seen a Sentinel up close," one of the guys sitting next Desiree said.

"And I've never seen one even use his staff or his sword," Desiree said.

"Well, they are bad. Ass," I said. "Last spring, I got to see a whole bunch of them in action." With that one sentence, that room was mine as I recounted the fight at Inferno. It was almost an hour later before I could sneak out.

Lucas answered almost as soon as I hit the call button. "Dude, you've given Dr. C gray hair, I think."

132

"Well, I'm not done," I told him. "There's been another attack. But, good news, I was able to protect the potential victim and disrupt the spell before they did any serious damage. Thing is, this one was different from the last one. The spell was just a straight-up assault. I think they were trying to make sure they could get through the school's wards."

Lucas nodded and pointed at the camera. "Okay, that makes sense, or at least it fits something Dr. C was saying. That circle you sent him wasn't making sense because it was like the symbols were all wrong. He said it was like they were combining sigils, which wouldn't have worked. Let me get him on the call."

"You can do that?"

"Yeah, Chance," Lucas said as he worked. "These newfangled devices can make what modern people call 'conference calls!' They're amazing. Okay...there he is. Hey, Dr. Corwyn. I have Chance on the line. Let me patch him in." Suddenly, my screen split in two, and I was looking at Dr. C's face next to Lucas's.

"Good to see you, sir," I said.

"You, too, Chance," he replied. "Though I wish the circumstances were better. Lucas's text said you'd found something new."

"Yeah, you could say that." I went over what had happened.

"Okay, now some things are making more sense," Dr. C said. "The first kid who died showed signs of severe magickal trauma that targeted his energy centers. Since you saw his spirit, and probably the girl who went missing, we can assume they didn't get their souls, but they got Lodge's. If they used the same place but made two different circles, things make more sense. Now they're trying to get past wards. Each time, the effects are different. I can't believe I didn't see this before, but with this attack, it makes perfect sense! I know what they're doing!"

133

"Clue me in, guys," Lucas said.

"They're experimenting," Dr. C and I said at the same time.

Chapter 9

~ That no Man shall be prevented from traveling freely upon the roads or through the wilderness… ~ Founding charter of the Shadow Regiment

The down side to being ahead of the authorities when you're sneaking around is that you can't tell them what you know without putting your own ass in a sling. But, if the Sentinels didn't know me well enough by now to assume I was investigating this on my own, I figured I wasn't going to screw myself over until I had to. Besides, it was Friday, and this was also the first weekend Mom and Dee were coming up. It was also the first weekend juniors and seniors were allowed to leave the campus.

After dinner, I made my way down to the Grotto. I lit my way with a glowing sphere that hovered behind and above me, one of the things I'd recently learned in Evocation class. Stewart was waiting for me near the door, and gestured without a word for me to follow him. He turned and followed the curve of the building to the edge of the lake, creating a sphere of his own as we followed the bank around to a small clearing that was out of sight of the rest of the school. A rowboat was pulled up on the bank, and Stewart stepped into it, taking a position near the prow.

"Dude, what the hell?" I asked. He responded by putting a finger to his lips, then winking before he pointed to the seat in the middle of the boat. I hesitated for a moment, then decided to play along. My hand went to the wand at my left hip. In my front pocket, I also had a chamelon charm made from the bit of broken CD, a shield cast on the skull and crossbones amulet and the little ring I'd charmed for a TK blast or two. If this was an ass kicking, someone was going to be going back to their dorm with a limp. I stepped into the boat and sat down. No sooner than my butt hit wood, Stewart turned around and held his hand out, and the boat slid into the water. It slid across the surface of the lake almost without a sound until it hit the rocky shore of a small island. Black tree trunks and boughs stood out against the clouded sky, and for a moment, Stewart stood in silhouette against it as well. He stepped off the boat and picked up a bundle from somewhere, then turned to me and put a finger to his lips again, then gestured for me to follow him. I stumbled along after him as he donned a hat, then buckled something around his hips and finally swung a long coat over his shoulders.

After a few moments, we came to a clearing, and he stopped me once we were well inside it.

"Dusk has fallen, the road is dark," Stewart said solemnly.

"The way is safe," another voice spoke from the darkness.

"Who protects the way?" Stewart asked.

"The Shadow Regiment protects all who travel," several voices answered.

"The way is safe," Stewart said in unison with the other voice. Around us, a circle of lights sprang up, showing several people in long coats, hats and domino masks. All of them wore a broad leather belt, each holding a pistol across their stomach and a sword at their left hip.

"I see my brother," one of them said as he stepped forward. "And I see a face unknown to me. Who do you bring among this congregation of your brothers?"

"I bring a worthy man, one who walks the shadows, a man who loves freedom and one I would call brother, for I owe him my very life. I vouch for his character by pistol, sword and wand." For a moment, there was a soft murmur around the circle, and I got the feeling Stewart might have done something he wasn't supposed to. I snuck a look his way, but he seemed confident.

"In that you have vouched for him, having sworn by pistol sword and wand, we would call him brother as well.

Brother to one…" the guy in front of us said, leaving the sentence hanging.

"Brother to all," everyone else finished.

"Then there is only the matter of formalities," the leader said. "Brother, how are you known, by what name and titles are you called?"

"Chance Fortunato," I said. Stewart nudged me and made a circular motion with his hand, so I decided to run with it. "I am the Demon's Apprentice, the Seeker and the Page of Swords, *gothi* to the Diamond Lake pack and apprentice to Trevor Corwin. I am the Wolf Slayer and Demon's Bane." No one said anything for a moment, then the leader nodded and handed me a belt like the one he wore.

"Then it is a given that you have a sword. Do you have a pistol?"

"Not with me, but yeah, I do."

"It is known that you have a wand," he said, then handed me a cloth domino mask "Within this circle, we are the Shadow Regiment. Outside of it, we were once called the Devil's Highwaymen. To outsiders, you may say you are a Highwayman, a group you were inducted into because you are a member of the fencing and pistol clubs. The Regiment is the enemy of tyranny and the defender of those in need. With this mask, you accept the mantle of the Regiment, to safeguard the ideals of freedom and brotherhood among Men. We fight not for glory but for liberty. Brother to one," he said as he offered the mask. I took the mask and the belt, knowing he expected me to finish the phrase. In the dim light, I could see the smile on his face. This was an empty ceremony to him, something fun to do on a weekend. The words were pretty but meaningless. But to me…freedom meant something. I'd been a prisoner, been the oppressed. When I said the words, they were going to mean something.

"Brother to all," I said. I felt the strange brush of magick on my skin and through my hair.

Then the rest of them said it.

It felt like a gust of wind blew into the clearing, then held itself, a bubble of overpressure waiting to expand. The guy in front of me went wide eyed, and I heard several gasps.

"Brother to one," he repeated, as though he was just now understanding the words.

"Brother to all," we all said. For a moment, it felt as if I really was going to uphold some ancient code. Like somehow, all mankind would benefit from what we were doing right here, right now. And I liked being a part of that.

The warm, tingly rush of magick blew through the clearing, tugging at coats and hair, even the strap of the domino mask in my hand. I could hear voices all around me, mostly some variation on "That's never happened before."

"Let us welcome our new brother," the leader said. The solemn tone was gone, and suddenly, the circle of people closed in around us. I shook a dozen hands before a cold can was pressed against my palm. In the dark, I couldn't see a label, but I smelled the fermented hops before I got the can to my lips. I'd never really liked the taste of beer, and I especially didn't like losing control. The hiss and pop of more cans being opened filled the night, and the guy in front of me pulled his mask off to reveal Lance Huntington standing in front of me.

"Welcome to the Regiment, Fortunato," he said as he held a beer up in front of him. I tapped the edge of my can against his, then mimed taking a drink. The lights came up around us, and more masks came off. I recognized a few faces, but most of the guys around me were unfamiliar.

"Thanks," I said, trying to smile like I meant it. "Is it always this intense when you bring someone new in?"

"Ya know, that was new," Stewart said from beside me.

"Yeah, it was really cool, though," Lance said. "I felt it, too. Like, I dunno, we were about to save the world or something."

"I think saving the world would be a lot more like being scared shitless, you know?" I said. Lance and Stewart laughed and Stewart put his hand on my shoulder.

"Well, we're your brothers now, fellow Highwayman," Stewart said. "You should have been one of us all along, being the Seeker."

"Is that like, automatic membership or something?" I asked.

"No, but it should be," Stewart said. "The Regiment was formed by a Seeker. But it's been years since there was one who was a member."

"Well, now there is," I said. "Hey, are you going into Boston this weekend?"

"Don't have much choice," Lance said. "My father wants me to come home tomorrow morning, but I'll probably be stuck at the house all weekend."

"Me, too," Stewart said. "My father hired extra bodyguards for the weekend. I should have had him just hire you," he finished with another clap of his hand on my shoulder. I put a smile on my face and looked around. Everyone was gathered in a tight group, and I noticed a coupel of folks glancing out into the dark. Someone had brought a cooler out, and I headed for it, but all they had brought was beer and more beer. I took a swig and resigned myself to a little control loss and some forced small talk. Fortunately, most of it was about something I actually knew things about: magick.

If I had been a Sentinel, or even on good terms with them, I could have had at least thirty people arrested for violating the first and fifth Laws of Magic, regarding free will and invading another person's thoughts. For that matter, as I listened to Lance talk about how his father had inflicted a curse on a rival that slowly devastated his health, only to offer to help 'cure' him in exchange for a favorable deal, I was reminded of the Ninth Law of Magick, not using magick to rule or using it to profit from the suffering of others.

My salvation came when someone started crashing through the brush nearby. Wands came out, mine included and pointed toward the noise until Ginger emerged from the darkness. As a handful of unsteady wands came down, she headed for Lance and Stewart.

"Baby, what the hell are you doing here?" Lance demanded.

"You guys have got to get out of here," she said without preamble. "The Sentinels are making a sweep toward the lake." Lance went pale, but it struck me that she had addressed Stewart instead of her boyfriend.

"Scramble, everyone," Lance said. "Leave the beer and just get to the boats!" There was a flurry of activity as the lights dimmed and everyone headed for the trees. I turned to Stewart, who was looking around as if he'd just realized where he was.

"Come on," I said, heading for the trail we'd followed to the clearing. "We parked over here."

"Our boat's on the wrong side of the island," he said, his words fast and high pitched. "They'll see us the second we hit the water."

"We'll catch a ride with them, then," I said as I followed the last of the Highwaymen toward the trees. Stewart followed me, crashing through the brush like an elephant. We got to the beach as the last of the group was getting on board. Each of the three small boats was full, and the last of them was riding low in the water with the added weight of Ginger. Dressed in sweat pants and a t-shirt, she stood out enough that I realized she had to have come on her own instead of with the rest of the group.

"What are you waiting for?" Stewart asked as I drew up. The people in the other two boats were gesturing to us, even as the third boat struggled.

"They won't make it with extra passengers," I said as I went to the third boat and grabbed Ginger's hand. "Come on." She got out of the boat when I pulled on her arm, and it slid free of the shore.

"We can't leave you behind," Lance said. "Brother to one, brother to all!"

"Yes, you can!" I said. "We're leaving the same way *she* got here. Now go!" He hesitated for a moment, then waved to the other boats.

"So, how *did* you get here?" I asked as the three boats pulled away from the shore. She held up a ring and glared at me.

"This spreads my weight out so that I don't break the surface tension of the water. It won't work for the two of you. Now you've screwed all three of us!"

"Surface tension!" I said. "That's brilliant. Does it still work for you?"

"Of course it does. I wasn't planning it being a one-way trip."

"Okay, go," I said. "I've got this." She whispered something, then turned and took off across the water, her feet making broad round impressions on the surface. Once she was away, I took my wand out and knelt on the sandy beach.

"What are you doing?" Stewart asked as I etched a broad circle in the sand with my fingertip.

"What I do best," I said when I finished the first circle. "Making shit up as I go along." I drew a second circle that would have intersected the first if I'd made it overlap. Instead, I stopped the lines at the edge of the larger circle and drew in some water based sigils.

"That's a...is that a summoning circle?"

141

"Yup," I said as I touched my wand to it and intoned "*Circumvare*." The blue main circle lit up, then the red one that I was standing in. The result was almost immediate.

A tall, slender column of water shot up from the base of the circle, slowly forming into the form of a woman. I felt its will press against the circle, testing my own willpower and evidently finding that it couldn't just beat its way out. As tests went, this one was kind of mild, but I was willing to accept that as long as it could do what I needed it to.

"What is it that you desire, human?" the elemental asked after a few moments. I raised an eyebrow at that, since most lower order elementals were a little more limited in the vocabulary department.

"I need you to make the surface tension of the water strong enough to support our weight in a path that leads to the shore. Once we are there, you are free to return to your home. There is alcohol on the island that you are welcome to as payment for your services."

"A simple enough task," the elemental said. "But I do not need libations. My daughter does not heed my call. Find her and tell her I am waiting for her."

"I can't guarantee that I can complete this task," I said. "I don't even know who she is."

"You have seen her, only you didn't know it. Promise me that you will tell her when you recognize her."

"I promise!" The ethereal wind hammered me for a moment, and the elemental seemed to change shape, sprouting two arms that spread as if in benediction.

"It will be done," she said. I bowed my head and released the circle. Moments later, a section of the lake seemed to freeze in place.

"Come on!" I said as I ran toward the water.

"What if it doesn't work?" Stewart asked.

"Can you swim?" I asked as my foot touched the surface of the water…and stayed above it. It was fairly easy to see the path of the altered water, since it didn't move and it didn't reflect light the same way as the rest of the lake's surface. It felt like running on a thick gym mat, and I could hear the water under it sloshing with every step. Running across the surface of the lake, I tried not to think of what might happen if the elemental decided to renege on her end of the bargain. It was known to happen if an elemental wasn't satisfied with their payment, and I hadn't had much to begin with. I put on a little more speed, and Stewart managed to keep up, but I was glad when we hit the far shore. Solid ground never felt so good. The three boats were pulled up along the shore, and I could hear the sounds of people moving through the woods.

"All right, you're up," I said when I heard Stewart's feet hit the shore behind me.

"Okay….okay…yeah," Stewart panted, then headed off into the brush. I followed him, and it wasn't long before we were catching up to the slowest of the Highwaymen. Then we came upon the rest of them clustered near the trees. A pair of Sentinels were standing between us and the school.

"Crap," Stewart hissed.

"What about the other way in?" Lance asked. Stewart nodded and took the lead, edging away from the school until he got to a ridgeline. Less than a hundred yards further on was a door set in the side of the ridge.

"Masks, everyone," Stewart said. I hastily tied mine on. "Lance, give Ginger your hat. Ginger, keep your head down." Once the last of us were ready, Stewart approached the door.

"Who goes?" a thin, reedy voice demanded from the top of the door.

"Commander of the Shadow Regiment," Stewart said. "Who challenges me?"

A pale green sprite dropped down from above the door, his wings glowing as he spread his arms to the side and back while bowing his head. "I am Pij," the sprite said. "I'm sorry to have inconvenienced you, sir."

"You were just doing your duty, Pij," Stewart said. "Move aside, now, and let us pass. But speak to no one of our passing. We're on important business, secret business. I can count on you to be discreet, correct?"

"Of course, sir," Pij said, his head bobbing. "Not a peep from me, sir!" He drifted to one side, and Stewart led the way through the door.

"Are you sure he'll keep his mouth shut?" I asked as we made our way through the tunnel.

"They haven't let us down since my grandfather was here," he said. "The school was founded by members of the Regiment, so in the eyes of the sprites, we're the same as faculty. One thing to remember, though. Always wear your mask if you're going to invoke the Regiment. As long as we have them on when we deal with them, they're sworn not to reveal our identities, even if they know who we are."

"Important safety tip," I said. "Thanks, Egon." He laughed and went on. Once he reached the school's utility tunnels, he stopped and faced the rest of the group.

"We split up from here. Standard excuses should work, but since the Sentinels are making a sweep, we can also use that as an excuse if we're caught off our floors. Half of you are Hall Captains, invoke that if you feel it necessary. Whatever you do, do not betray the Regiment. Brother to one," he intoned at the end.

"Brother to all," everyone answered, even me. Ginger gave him a long look over her shoulder as Lance led her and a couple of others down a separate tunnel.

"What's the deal with you and Ginger?" I asked once it was just Stewart and me.

"Lance's girl?" he laughed a little too quickly. "Nothing."

"Calling shenanigans on that," I said. "Back on the island, her eyes were on you when she was telling us the

Sentinels were doing a sweep, and when we split up, that look she gave you was pretty damn direct, like she wanted to be going in a different direction."

He stopped and turned to face me. "Damn, Chance, you don't miss a damn thing, do you?"

"More than I'd like," I said. "Stop stalling and spill."

"Okay, look you can't tell anyone this, okay? So, last summer, Lance broke up with Ginger. Everyone thought it was so he could date some European bitch. But it turned out to be a family thing. A cousin of hers talked her parents into getting Lance's parents to force him to break things off. So, while they were split up, Ginger and I got together for a while. But she really loves Lance, and they worked things out. We're still close, and Lance doesn't know a thing. And it has to stay that way."

I help up a hand and nodded. "I get it. Is it always this complicated with you?"

"Most of the time. Okay, so if anyone sees us, I saw the Sentinels, and I came and got you because of last night, okay?" I nodded, and we slipped in through the door in the basement. The first floor was quiet, save for the sound of people in the day room. We glanced in from across the hall and saw Hoshi and a few of the other scholarship kids watching a movie on the television. A couple of the kids were playing around with energy strings and planes, spinning the glowing filaments and making the flat sheets appear and disappear between their fingertips. I gestured for him to go on, and slipped into the room.

I'd been watching for a few minutes, fascinated by how they could make cubes and spheres just shimmer into existence with a gesture, and after a few minutes, I thought I'd give it a shot. I pushed the energy down my arms and into my fingertips, then tried to cup my hand to make a sphere, but all I got a misshapen blob.

"You gotta pull your hand back when you pop a ball, B. B.," one of the guys said from beside me. "It's like

145

makin' a bubble. Throw it out there, let the magick do its own thing." He put his hand up, then moved it forward and back, like a snake striking. I mimicked the movement and he nodded. "Now, pop it there at the end, yeah like that! That's it, B. B.!" he said when a wobbly sphere emerged. "Now try the cube. Do your hand like this," he held his up with his fingers at a right angle to his palm, "and put your thumb here, yeah, like that. Now pop it like that." He opened his hand, then snapped it into the shape he'd just showed me. I tried it and got a shapeless mass.

"Cubes are a lot harder," I said.

"Naw, you just gotta see it right. Balls, they just happen, but when you're makin' a cube, you just gotta see this point over here," he said, with one finger opposite his thumb. "The other one is here," he pointed to the bend where my finger met my palm. "Everything meets out here." He pointed to the imaginary point out in the middle of the air. Suddenly, it made perfect sense to me. The two opposite points on a cube determined everything else, if you assumed ninety degree angles. The next time, a decent cube showed up in front of me.

Once I had that down, I could spin it, warp it or even throw it. Compared to the rest of the folks in the room, I was a clutz, but it was fun.

Hoshi finally pulled me away from the energy manipulators and dragged me to the couch he and Kiya had appropriated. Desiree sat perched at the end, her round cheeks blazing at something. Judging by how she kept not looking at Hoshi or her roommate, I was pretty sure what had her blushing.

"So," she said at Hoshi's goading, "My um, my parents invited...well, they said I could invite any of my friends out tomorrow for lunch at their shop?" Hoshi gave me a pleading look, and I fought down the urge to laugh.

"I was heading in tomorrow anyway," I said. "And I'd love to meet your folks. We could all hang out."

Her smile lit up her face, and she leaned back into the couch. I felt a little bad, because it served as a cover for my original plan to go buy stuff for charms and a replacement TK rod. But I found myself honestly looking forward to meeting Desiree's family and seeing their shop.

Finally, people started drifting out of the room. Some of the guys stopped by the couch and made a casual farewell, and prompted Hoshi and Kiya to get up. Which of course, meant that it was also time for Desiree and I to head out.

"Would you walk with me back to our hall?" Desiree asked. I nodded and we followed Hoshi and Kiya as they walked hand in hand.

"Still don't get what B.B. means," I said.

"Big Brother," Desiree answered. "Everyone saw how you tore out of the study room the other night when Stewart was attacked. You looked like you were going to kill whoever was doing it."

"Well, maybe not *kill*," I said.

"Yeah, kill," she said. "I was in that room. I felt what you were putting off. And everyone here knows you have blood on your hands."

"I keep hoping people will forget about that," I said. "It's not like I try to remind them."

"That's why they remember." She turned and headed into the girl's side of the building, leaving me to consider that little revelation. Suddenly, I needed to hear Shade's voice in the worst way.

Chapter 10

~ Witnesses are messy. They rarely get it right, but no one cares. ~ Altara Geminos, assassin

The livery carriage emerged from the brick tunnel into Squattertown. It was a pleasant surprise to see the neat stone and wood buildings instead of scrap metal and wood lean-tos. The streets and the buildings followed the curves of the landscape, leaving very few straight lines, many either built around trees or beside them. A few even incorporated tree trunks into the architecture, or used the tree limbs to support upper floors.

A handful of sprites and fairies flitted overhead, and I spotted the occasional brownie along the roadside. But more than anything, I saw humans or hybrids. After seeing so many other races wandering the streets of the Hive, it was odd not seeing them here.

The carriage stopped at a station, and the five of us got out. Junkyard's nose was up and he immediately started looking around, for once not marking anything. Even my nose was having a hard time keeping track of the scents in the air. I got out, then turned to offer Desiree my hand. She took her red skirt in one white gloved hand before offering me the other and stepping down smoothly. Without missing a beat, she turned and offered Hoshi her hand. He made an awkward curtsey as he stepped down, somehow making jeans and a blue polo shirt look more dressy than it was. He turned and mimicked Desiree's gesture, which Kiya waved away with mock-dignity. She stepped down as smooth as you please, managing to look more like a normal person than any of us in khaki shorts and a white button down shirt, her braids a dark veil across her shoulders.

"We'll take Apothecary Lane over to Talismongers Way," Desiree said, pointing to a side street. "It isn't the shortest route, but it will take us past more shops." We followed her as she led the way down the winding street. True to its name, Apothecary Lane was mostly alchemical or herbal shops. A few blocks later found us turning right onto Talismongers Way.

Only one word did the street justice: sparkly. Gems and raw stones were on display in windows, silver and gold necklaces dangled from awnings. Booth after booth filled the spaces between shops, offering supplies for the more hands-on, do-it-yourself approach, while the established shops tended toward the convenience of completed work. I stopped at a stall to haggle with a shrewd little man for a silver bracelet, then headed a few booths down to pick up some charms and gemstones from an even shrewder gnome for one of my Enchanting class projects. I also found a self-heating kettle for Mom, and an amulet that would animate a stuffed animal for Dee. Hoshi, on the other hand, picked up a little heart amulet and promptly gave it to Kiya. My fingertips brushed the vial on my chest as she smiled and kissed him.

"Aren't they cute?" Desiree said softly. The smile on her face looked genuine, and it was infectious.

"It's not natural," I said.

"Says the boy dating a werewolf," she laughed. "They're really good for each other." I looked at her, and wondered for a moment why the Universe was so unfair. Desiree was genuinely pretty, and she was the kind of girl a smart man *should* have wanted to be with. But most people wouldn't see past her weight. They couldn't see the grace in her movement, hear the smart, caring girl I'd come to know, or see the intensity she put into everything. Even watching her roommate kiss one of the most sought after boys in school, she seemed honestly happy for them.

"Just so long as he doesn't get any prettier," I said, trying to cover the sudden turn in my mood. "Then he'll be bad for her self-esteem."

"Don't," Desiree said, shaking her head. She looked at me with a wistful smile.

"Don't what?" I asked.

"Don't feel bad for me," she said. "I've never been all that interested in boys. Or girls, either."

I narrowed my eyes at her and cocked my head a little. "How did you know what I was thinking?"

"I didn't. I knew what you were feeling. Frustration, anger, pity…and a little bit of attraction. Aww, thank you." She leaned forward and kissed my cheek, leaving a slight tingle in the wake of her full lips. "It's okay, Chance. I just don't find all that many people attractive, I guess. Gram says it's pretty normal for cambions to uh, bloom late that way."

"Well, at least I'm not the only person not on the hunt," I said.

"Come on," she said as she grabbed my hand and pulled me down a side road. "I'll show you something I *do* like." We came out by a sign that read Blackkettle Ave. and my nose was inundated with the smell of spices and cooking meat. A low haze hung just above our heads, and I could see bundles of herbs dangling outside a few shops, while another displayed enough cutlery to embarrass Jack the Ripper. Boxes of red, green, and yellow produce in various shades were piled on tables out in front of buildings and under equally colorful awnings.

"Food?" I asked, more than a little confused. "Who doesn't like food?"

"No, you dork," Desiree said as she held a hand up. "Cooking!"

"Ah. I was afraid we were about to walk right into a stereotype or something."

"The fat girl substituting food for love?" she laughed. "No, but I do know my foods and moods. It's not all just chocolate and wine."

In front of us, Kiya laughed. "Ain't that the truth!" she called back over her shoulder. "But you can't go wrong with chocolate."

151

Beside me, Desiree closed her eyes and took a deep breath in through her nose, then let it out with a contented sigh. "This is what I want to surround myself with, this smell, every day. I want to start a magickal confectionary shop, and sell memories and moods baked into the best dishes you've ever tasted."

"Is that even possible?" I asked.

"It is for me," she winked at me and took a sideways step as she held up her gloved hands and waggled her fingers. "Empathy can go both ways with me. It's another reason I wear these all the time."

"What about...?" I started, putting my hand on my cheek where she'd kissed me.

"With mental shields like yours?" she said and made a dismissive sound. "It's like licking a brick wall. I can feel what's going in in there, like being able to see a light bulb in a cage, but I can't feed on it or change it with a little kiss unless you let me."

"Well, if you ever need to, I've still got a lot of excess anger you can snack on."

She stopped and looked at me with narrowed eyes for a moment before breaking into a smile. "You're the first person who's ever said that and meant it," she said. "With most guys, it's a come on."

I tapped my temple. "I have a big bunch of nightmare fuel up here I'd really like to get rid of. Better it helps someone in the process."

"Either way, it's good to have a friend who means it. Come on, I can smell Gram's French Onion Casserole from here. She turned and trotted to catch up with Hoshi and Kiya, leaving me to follow. Junkyard followed her without waiting for me, so I ended up bringing up the rear.

Our destination was just around the corner, Devilish Charms. It was a two story building with an open shop floor on the first story. Rings and amulets filled cases all through the shop, and judging from the number of people

152

browsing, business was good. Desiree led us past the counter and up a set of stairs in the stockroom to an equally open upper floor. The front half was home to a kitchen that took up one corner, a dining table the stretched along the back wall and a sea of soft furs with islands of cushions taking up the front half of the room. A hanging chair draped in blue and purple cloth was in the corner to the left, and the front of the house was almost completely open. Thick panels were folded up in groups along the opening, with a railing of woven wood running about waist high across the front.

The kitchen was busy, too. Three people moved back and forth between tasks that were as esoteric to me as magick was to most cowans. Two of them had to be Desiree's parents. Her father was a taller, whipcord version of his daughter, his face narrower but with the same general shape, especially around the eyes, while her mother was a little shorter and possessed of the same nose and chin. The other woman, though, showed their demonic ancestry the most, with a pair of tiny black horns and all black eyes. Shortest of them all, she was also the prettiest. Her round face was lighting up the room with a smile that I figured I'd need sunblock for if I spent too long around her. Her body was round in all the right places, which on her, was pretty much every place. Her long, black hair had two streaks of gray running back from her temples, and there were laugh lines at her eyes and cheeks that only made her prettier.

"Oh, sweetheart!" she cooed as soon as she saw Desiree. "It's so good to have you home again." She enveloped Desiree in a hug before she pulled back and held her at arm's length for a moment. "Let me look at you, dear."

"Hi, Gram," Desiree said, her own smile getting a few degrees brighter.

"Oh, that school's not so good for you. Just look at that aura. So many dark spots, little hurts. Oooh, but what's

153

this? Is that a bond?" The older woman laughed, then looked over at Hoshi, Kiya and me.

"I've made some friends, yeah," Desiree said to the empty space where her Gram had been. Suddenly, all three of us were caught up in a fierce hug from her Gram.

"You... you three are good for her. Come, sit! Tell us all the things our little darling girl is too embarrassed to!" she said as she ushered us to the table.

"Mom," the other woman said. "You're embarrassing her!"

"Shush you," Gram said. "That's the point! But, let me at least get the pleasantries out of the way. I'm Gram. You must be Kiya, yes? So, you're the pretty one, Hoshi. Oh, I forgot how beautiful you fox children are. Which means you," she turned to me with narrowed eyes, "are the demon's apprentice."

"Chance," I said as calmly as I could manage. "My name is Chance."

"Feh," she said with a wave of her hand. "Names are given. Titles are earned." She put her hand on my chest, right over my heart. "Especially the ones we don't like. Now, help me make my Desi blush. Tell me what she doesn't want us to hear."

"Oh, you should have seen it in Conjuring last week," Kiya said, evidently eager to get the first salvo in. "We were trying to weave light and turn it solid. So, everyone in class does theirs, and they mostly just scattered. Desiree did hers, and when she went to make it solid? Pure peanut butter! It was hilarious!"

"And delicious!" Desiree chimed in.

"Thing was, hers was the only one that actually turned into anything solid. She earned extra points for our house."

I listened as Hoshi, Kiya and even Desiree told stories about her time at the Academy so far, but my gaze was constantly pulled toward the window, because my thoughts were definitely not in that room. Somewhere along the

154

way, her parents introduced themselves, and I remembered her father's name was Paol, and her mother was Silk.

"Your thoughts are still in that awful place," her Gram said to me at one point. I looked up and realized it was just her, Desiree and me at the table. Hoshi and Kiya were being insufferably cute in the kitchen with Desiree's parents, and the room had gotten quiet.

"Yeah, sorry," I said. "I'm being a terrible guest."

Again, the hand came up to wave my comment away, but the expression on her face was softer. "Tell me what's eating up your attention."

"There have been these attacks," I started.

"I know. Skip to the juicy stuff."

I glanced to Desiree, who nodded. "Okay, so the school is warded, and I've figured out how to defend against their new attacks. But with all of the students scattered to the four winds today..."

"You won't be able to save anyone if something happens," Gram said.

"You make it sound like I'm doing this for my ego or something."

"Did you offer to show the Sentinels how you protected your friend?"

"Um, no, I didn't even think of it." Suddenly, the chair I was in felt less comfortable, and I had to fight to keep from squirming in my seat.

"Did you think to ward the school with your special spell?"

"It doesn't work like that," I said. "I'd have to cast...and close... one huge circle. I can barely handle a thirty-foot circle, and that's only if it's permanently inscribed."

"Then the world is safe from one boy's ego for today," she said with a wicked grin. "But think, too, about what this means for the person casting these hexes. You say this is new magick for them?"

155

"Yeah," I said slowly. "My mentor and I think they're experimenting...and all the attacks came from close to the school..."

"Which means..." she prompted.

"That they can't hit anyone unless they're close to them or they've marked them, so if they did try to attack someone this weekend, we'd know where, and eventually, who, they were."

"So, perhaps there will be no attacks today, and you can enjoy your time with friends. And tomorrow, with everyone back at the school, plus parents and mentors...it would not be wise to attempt anything then. So now, rest, have fun, eat well. Your tasks will be waiting for you when you return." She patted my hand and got to her feet.

"She meddles," Desiree said with an affectionate smile. "She says it's what grandmothers do."

"She's good at it," I said. "I hardly noticed. And, I do feel a little better." She grabbed my hand and led me to the kitchen. About an hour later, the random bits and pieces had coalesced into a casserole that tasted like a cross between beef stroganoff and French onion soup.

We left near sundown with full bellies and for me, a little lighter spirit. The carriage took us in through the same side gate we'd been shunted through on registration day. Private carriages were waved through ahead of us, but we were stopped by the Sentinels and ordered out at the gate.

"What's going on?" I asked as the carriage was searched.

"Wands," the stone faced Sentinel answered. I handed mine over and watched as the Sentinels examined it closely using a flat plane of blue energy held between his fingertips. All of our wands and talismans were inspected and returned, then the lead Sentinel pulled a circular brass frame out that held a series of quartz and blue and white stones. At a distance, I couldn't be sure, but I was pretty sure the blue and white stones were sodalite. When Jane

Dearborn's face shimmered into view in the center of the frame, I was sure that was what it was. They spoke briefly, then the Sentinel came over to us.

"The rest of you can go," he said. "Fortunato, come with me." Junkyard hopped down with me and we watched my three friends stare back at us as the carriage pulled out of sight. As soon as they turned the corner, I was hustled into the guard shack, and the other Sentinel produced a gray cloak from under the counter.

"Um, guys, what's going on?" I asked as the second Sentinel slipped out the door.

"I'm Sentinel Graves," the first one said as he shook the cloak out and handed it to me. "Put the cloak on and follow me. Keep quiet and don't do anything to give your position away. You'll have to send the dog back to your room or something."

"Wait a minute," I said. "Am I in some kind of trouble or something? Because this doesn't exactly feel like I'm under arrest, but it sure as hell isn't normal."

"It's for your protection, kid. Dearborn doesn't want anyone to know where you're going or what's going on with you. Your dog is the only one on campus, so it will look strange if I'm seen with it." His tone was even, but I could tell by how he cut his words short that he wasn't happy about me stalling. I fished the bit of broken CD out of my pocket.

"I've got this," I said as I tucked the charm into the knot of the yellow bandana around his neck. "Follow him. *Iam vides me, tu nescis modo,*" I whispered to activate the spell on it. Junkyard shimmered out of sight, and I stood up. As small as he was, it could cloak him pretty effectively. With a flourish, I slid the cloak over my shoulders and pulled the hood up.

Graves reached out and took the clasp between his thumb and forefinger. "*Furtim,*" he said and the world went hazy around me. Without another word, he took off at a brisk jog, and I had no choice but to follow him. He led us past the side of the school and around the back of the last building, then kept going through the sparse woods behind the campus until he emerged near an old stone building that was wider on top than on bottom. Once the blockhouse was visible, he angled toward it, slowing to a stop at the door and holding it open for a split second longer than he needed to. I slipped past him and took a step to the side like Dr. C had taught me while he let the door close behind us.

As my eyes adjusted to the dimmer interior, I began to make out details. The room was long and broad, with a set of four tables in the middle. Low bunk beds were set against the wall, most of them apparently in use, with benches set beneath high windows around the walls. A wide fireplace dominated the wall to my left, taking up a section that looked like a primitive kitchen. Off to the right, a steep staircase led to the upper floor. Sentinel Dearborn looked up from her plate at the table as I pulled the cloak off.

"Told you he'd keep up with you," she said.

"Well, shit," Graves said the moment he saw me. He reached into his pocket and handed her a bill, then shook his head and headed for the fireplace.

"What was that about?" I asked her as she approached.

"I ordered him to set a hard pace when he brought you back," she said. "After Blue Hole, I knew you'd be able to keep up." I nodded, recalling the frantic mile and half run through the woods, trying to beat a dozen Sentinels back to a borrowed car.

"And he didn't believe you?" I asked.

"Well, I might have left out the part about Blue Hole. Anyway, I'm glad you're safe. There's been a new development."

"What's happened?"

"I think I should just show you, first. Come on." She went to the stairs, leading me up to the second story. Single beds with desks and dressers lined the walls, with a pair of large tables in the middle and a curtained off area with the metal bottom of a tub showing beneath it. A smaller pot-bellied stove was set near the end of one of the tables. The table closer to me was covered with a heavily pinned map but what grabbed my attention and wouldn't let it go was the lumpy sheet draped across the second one. A trio of sprites hovered in one corner of the room, and as I looked, Ren swooped down to land near me.

"You didn't do this, did you?" he asked, his voice tight.

"Do what?" I asked. For an answer, Dearborn pulled the sheet away from the far table, and I nearly lost my lunch. Three sprite bodies were lined up on the table. The only way I could be sure they were sprites was by the wings, though. Their small skulls were completely deformed and their upper bodies maimed almost as badly, as if someone had grabbed them and squeezed until bones broke. I staggered and gagged, fighting to keep my stomach from revolting.

"I *told* you he wouldn't have done this," I heard Ren say as I held myself up against the nearer table. I'd seen death before. Powers knew I'd even handed out a little. I'd seen some pretty horrendous things, like my first mentor's body ripped into bloody chunks. But seeing these tiny bodies so badly mangled…it was like the aftermath of someone abusing a puppy or a kitten. Sprites were among the most inoffensive of the fae I'd ever run across, and seeing them killed so violently hit me harder than I expected. The sound of cloth moving reached my ears over the sound of my own retching, and I finally managed to get my stomach under control again.

"They went missing the night of the last attack," Dearborn said. "So you were either a suspect, or you're in danger yourself."

"Why am I still under suspicion here?" I asked. "Hell, I not only helped defend the last victim, I just about led you straight to the real perps."

"You were also the one who said there might be more than one person involved," Dearborn countered. "And as far as we're concerned, it's a damn good working theory."

I rolled my eyes and shook my head. "Yep, that's me. Too clever for my own good," I said.

"You're also the next logical victim."

"Assuming I'm not actually involved."

"Assuming that, yes. This would be the best time to strike at you."

"About that," I said. Everyone in the room stopped and looked at me. "One, so far, they've shown that their range is shit. It's new magick, so it only makes sense."

"Are you sure it's something new for them?" another one of the Sentinels asked.

"I've worked the other side of this," I said. "This is new magick for *anyone*. Souls are only supposed to be able to be given by a binding ritual. The whole thing works like promises. You can't make one for someone else. There are a few creatures that can 'steal' a soul, but there's never been a spell or a ritual for it."

"Until now," Dearborn corrected.

"And we're still not sure of what happens after. But, second, I'm their biggest asset whether I'm on their side or not. No matter what happens, I'm the first person people are going to look at. It makes no sense for them to get rid of me. Besides, tomorrow, all the most powerful wizards and masters on the east coast are going to be on campus visiting their little darlings. Pretty much the worst time ever to launch an attack." I took a step back from the table and looked at them, daring them to find fault with my logic.

160

"You're still not leaving the blockhouse until dawn," Dearborn said after a few moments. "Make yourself comfortable." Damn. Logic trumped by authority. Should've seen that coming from an adult.

Chapter 11

~ Only by the Strength of Men can a woman's wicked ways be mended. ~ Rev. Bill Horton, Pentatite minister.

When the transit field faded, I had a pleasant surprise and an unpleasant one waiting for me. The pleasant surprise bounded through the gate, bounced into my arms and kissed me like she hadn't seen me in a month and a half. I kissed her back just as hungrily. Shade had never felt so good in my arms as she did just then, but I also knew I said that a lot. Her warm body pressed against mine made monkey brain wake up and grunt about too many layers of clothing between us. Even if she was just in a pink tank top and jeans, there was not enough skin touching.

"Enough of the kissy face crap," the unpleasant surprise grumbled as he walked past us. So of course we stopped right away…a few seconds later.

"Damn it's good to see you," I told Shade when we came up for air. Her eyes were smoldering and green when she opened them, a sure sign her wolf was stirring.

"God, I missed your kiss," she breathed. She tilted her head back and bared her throat. My teeth found the pale flesh of her neck and she let out a gasp that became a long sigh. "And I missed that."

"You two coming, or are you just going to mount her right here?" Sinbad asked. We turned to face him, neither of us feeling a bit of guilt. He wore his usual, a black jacket and a motorcycle t-shirt with jeans and black boots. His white hair and flaring moustache were as thick as ever, if anything, he'd let his hair grow a little.

"Who says *he* was going to mount *me*?" Shade said with a wink as we caught up to him.

"Personally, I don't care," Sinbad said with an amused sounding grunt. "You can go at it any way you want, but we got business to take care of first."

"Hey, uh, not that I'm not thrilled to see you, babe, but where are my mom and sister?"

"On Draeden's jet, with Corwyn," Sinbad answered. "Draeden wanted to come out and see how things were going."

"Damn it," I said. "He's going to think I owe him now."

"It can wait," Shade said as her nostrils flared. "I think our business just came to us." Her eyes darted left and right, and I saw the two large men heading our way. Both had amber eyes, and I could see the more pronounced canines as their lips peeled back. Around us, people were scattering. A woman emerged from the thinning crowd to my right, her yellowed eyes on me.

"Don't let them see submission," Sinbad said softly. "Remember, pup, it's all about display with us. But you show 'em you mean business, boy. They can take it."

I nodded and stepped forward, palming my wand as I did. Off to one side, I could see one reach a hand forward to grab Sinbad. He slapped it away and his left hand flashed forward to punch him in the throat. Shade closed with hers, and I blinked to bring my aura sight into play.

To most Weres, the average human is soft, squishy and good with ketchup. We don't even make good chew toys, and we're certainly not much of a threat. But add magick, and the whole equation changes. In my aura sight, I watched as the line of red extended toward me, the approaching Were's intent broadcast by her aura. The split second her hand moved, I put my wand up and said "*Obex!*" Instantly, a telekinetic shield formed in front of me. Her fingers crumpled against it, and I dropped it in favor of my favorite use of the telekinesis spell.

"*Ictus!*" I yelled, and the bolt of pure force sent her flying into the air. "*Ictus!*" I called out again, and caught her at the top of her arc, sending her even further. I turned to see how Sinbad and Shade were doing, more out of curiosity than any real concern for their safety. Shade was an alpha, and Sinbad...I'd learned a long time ago that men and women like him were old for a reason. Shade had her knee between her guy's shoulders and his right arm at an unnatural angle. His left hand was slapping against the floor, but she showed no signs of letting up.

Sinbad, on the other hand, had his by the throat and had forced him to his knees. "You dare try to lay a hand on me, pup? I'm a prince among the Clans."

"We didn't know," the man choked out. "We were just told to teach you a lesson and bring you back to face the Elders." His face held the look of a man who was experiencing fear again after a long time. Both of the Weres they held down were well dressed and neither one looked like they'd missed a meal in a long time. The crowd behind me let out a gasp, and I turned to see my opponent coming back over the roof tops. Wands came out as she jumped to the ground and started my way.

"I'd think twice," I said as I pointed my wand at her. She stopped a few steps away and dropped into a ready stance.

"You won't beat me with the same trick twice, little boy."

I raised my hand and said "I find your lack of faith disturbing." Moments later, her eyes went wide as the band of telekinetic force closed enough for her to feel it around her throat. It was the only spell I knew that had an English casting phrase, and I had to do my best Darth Vader imitation to pull it off. It never failed to catch people by surprise. "It's a good thing I don't use the same trick twice. Now, behave yourself or the next time I hit you, you'll need a passport to get back home." Her hands went to her neck, and I stopped the spell's constriction short of actually cutting off air.

"This is Were business," the woman said. "Leave and I'll forget you interfered."

"You threw the first punch at me, lady," I said.

"The Clans have gone far astray, if this is how they conduct their business," Sinbad said. "You will take us to the people who gave you your orders so that they can give me a direct apology." The woman paled, and I looked over to the man Sinbad held. His face was ashen as well. Shade let her man up as Sinbad released his hold.

"You sure it's a good idea for me to come with?" I asked.

"You're her *gothi*, kid," Sinbad said as he wiped his hand off on his pant leg. "You need to be there as much as she does."

"The things I do to take you to Homecoming," I said as I released the spell. Shade just chuckled and put her arm around my waist.

"I'm worth it," she said, her voice breathy in my ear.

"Damn straight."

"This is about a dance?" the were I'd released asked.

"That's pretty much the size of it," Sinbad said. "Your Clan Elders are getting all worked up over two kids goin' on a date." The girl made a noise of disgust, and one of the guys growled.

"It isn't for us to judge them," the third man said.

"It is for me," Sinbad said. "Now, get your asses in gear." The three Weres all but jumped, then nodded toward a black van parked in an arched tunnel. Milk crates were set on the floor, most upside down, but one was filled with the usual kidnappy stuff: duct tape, and black cloth hoods.

"You were going to black bag us?" I asked. "Seriously? *That's* the best the elders could come up with?"

"It works well enough," one of the men said.

"It's overdone," I said. Sinbad got in on the passenger side, and Shade and I took the two milk crates behind the seats, leaving the other two to sit on the bare metal of the floor.

"Drive," Sinbad ordered. We emerged a few seconds later on the streets of Boston, and the driver headed toward

166

the water. Eventually, we pulled up near a restaurant that advertised "Fresh Seafood!!" under the faded sign of The Wheelhouse. A large fishing boat was docked behind it, and a taller building butted up against the left side.

"Where were you supposed to take the kids?" Sinbad demanded.

The driver pointed toward the larger building. "The processing plant," he said.

"Let's go then." He got out and opened the side doors for us. "You two stay here, and be real quiet." He closed the doors without waiting for their nods and turned toward the packing plant. We went in through a pair of double doors and found ourselves in a mostly empty room. A conveyer system snaked its way through the room, but most of the other machinery was gone. Most of the room was dark, with shafts of light coming down through regularly spaced skylights. In one of the pools of light, a pair of chairs waited near a metal cart.

"Make yourselves comfortable, kids," Sinbad said with a nod toward the chairs. He turned toward the Were with us and pulled a shotgun out of his duffel bag. "You. Go get your bosses. And play it cool or I'll blow a hole in you big enough to drive through. You got it?" The Were nodded and backed away.

Shade and I went to the chairs and sat down. She slouched forward while I let my butt slide forward and crossed my arms over my chest. After a moment, she looked over at me and put a hand on my forearm.

"Have you been working out?"

"Fencing club," I said and curled a fist up to show the new definition my forearms were taking. "And pistol club. So I've been working a lot on my wrists."

"Are you still running?"

"Every morning, now," I said. "I'm also in the cross country club. Did you try out for cheerleader?"

167

"No," she said. "But I did join the tennis team. The rest of the pack is staying away from face-to-face competition, just like we talked about over the summer. Cal wanted to play baseball, but it's still too risky."

"You said you hated tennis," I said.

"I do, but Mom loves it. I figured it'll keep her out of my hair over you." She leaned in and kissed me.

"Get your heads in the game and shut the hell up," Sinbad hissed. Shade squeezed my hand and leaned forward again, her eyes blazing amber. I pulled my wand from my jacket pocket and palmed it so that the tip was laying against the bottom of my forearm. Sinbad had faded into the shadows, and I heard voices approaching.

"No, sir, we caught him completely by surprise," our guide was saying to someone.

"I suppose it's for the best," a deeper voice replied. "Even the young ones can be arrogant little pricks, though. I'm going to enjoy watching him squirm." Our guide emerged from the darkness with an older man in a black suit and a white shirt. Silver touched the hair at his temples and dotted his hair everywhere else. "What the Hell is this? I said I wanted them bagged and bound."

"Change of plans," Sinbad said as he emerged behind them. The sound of the shotgun's slide being worked was like a thunderclap in the open room.

"Reginald," Eugene said. "So, the prodigal bastard comes slinking home, hiding behind children."

"Cut the bullshit, Eugene. You were planning on torturing the girl with silver. And judging from the smell, she's not the only girl you've put to the knife down here."

"You expect me to let some upstart bitch go wandering around in my domain unchecked?" Eugene turned to face Sinbad. "You expect me to let her walk in here unclaimed and not take her for my own?" Beside me, Shade bared her teeth, and the older were stiffened. He shot her a glare before he turned back to Sinbad.

168

"She's a kid, Eugene," Sinbad said.

"That's irrelevant. She's an unclaimed female in my territory. It's my right!"

Shade growled and got to her feet. "I'm not a trophy," she said through clenched teeth. "I'm not a prize. And I will gut any man who tries to take me."

Eugene took a step forward, his eyes glowing gold. "No wolf walks through this town without swearing loyalty to me alone. Especially not some uppity bitch who thinks she's an alpha."

"Sable, Shade, can the bullshit and the posing, both of you!" Sinbad snapped. I got to my feet and went to Shade's side. The look on Sinbad's face was as closed to concerned as I'd ever seen him, and that made my gut clench up.

"I'm not posing," Shade said.

"If you know what's good for your pack, you are." He gave me a pointed look as he put an arm across Eugene's chest. That he'd broken and called Eugene by his pack name, Sable, told me how important it was to get things back under control.

"Shade, don't try to kill the man," I said as I wrapped my left arm around her shoulders. "He hasn't tried to do anything stupid yet."

"He's made the threat," she growled and looked at me with a mix of pain and anger in her gaze. "And no one stopped him."

"You did," I said, meeting her gaze. "You're the alpha here. And I will follow your lead. But we need to avoid bloodshed here if we can. Something isn't right."

She relaxed against my arm. "And you're my *gothi.* I'll take your advice."

"What the hell is going on with you, Sable?" Sinbad demanded. "You're more territorial than a vampire."

"An apt description, Reginald," another voice said. It filled the room, even though it sounded no louder than someone having a regular conversation. A thin man walked

169

into the light, his pale skin almost translucent under the filtered sunlight. The room went cool and damp like the inside of a grave as he looked from person to person with flat, expressionless eyes.

"You've got to be shitting me, Sable," Sinbad said. He pushed Sable away and leveled the shotgun at him. "You're in bed with suckface here?"

"Sinbad, please," Sable said as he raised his hands and shook his head.

"I assure you, it's as distasteful to both of us as it is necessary," the thin man said. "Distasteful necessity is something I believe you're well acquainted with." Even without the physical clues, like how he didn't breathe, the dank, grave-like aura that he gave off set monkey brain to screaming in my head. Between my screeching thoughts, one word kept blazing across my thoughts. *Vampire!* Well, that and *Run!* But, like the idiot I tended to be, I stood my ground. Shade was right there, and I wasn't about to leave her side.

"Why is it so *necessary?*" Sinbad asked.

"Something was hunting us," Sable said. "Vampire and were alike. We couldn't fight it; we couldn't even see it. Only a couple survived the attack, but not for long. Their Anima had been ripped away by something they couldn't see or fight, and they died within hours."

"What about your people?" Sinbad asked. "Did they give you your souls back or some shit?"

"That which infuses us is profoundly different from the Animus that your kind are so dependent upon," the vampire said, his voice cultured and condescending. "For simplicity's sake, it can be said to serve similar purpose. As a rule, however, we do not survive the initial attack."

"How do you know it's the same thing then?"

"My people are more social. When the attacks occurred, there were witnesses each time."

170

"You son-of-a-bitch," I said softly, but even across the room, tall pale and cadaverous picked it up. "You know what kind of magick they're using." The sound of air hissing in through his nose carried across the room as he straightened and looked down at me.

"Who gave you permission to talk, boy?" the vampire sneered. He made a gesture, and I felt the compulsion splatter against my newly strengthened mental defenses.

"You must have a defense against it," I went on, and he took a step back. "Otherwise, there would be no reason for the alliance between you. And you kept it to yourself."

Sinbad turned to Sable and gave him a hard look. "Is that true?" Sable just gaped and shook his head.

I took a step forward and pointed at the vampire. "You left everyone else to deal with this on their own, while you had a way to stop it. Who else did they target? Who else lost people while you cowered behind your own defenses?"

"Watch your mouth, boy," the vampire said. "It's about to get you killed."

"And yours just got you seriously dead," Sinbad growled. The vampire turned to face him with a frown and found himself looking down the barrel of the shotgun. "Kid's one of mine."

With his eyes on the shotgun, he was a fraction of a second too slow to react when I brought my wand up and called out "*Arripio!*" Bands of telekinetic force wrapped around him before he could do much more than bare his fangs. Sable turned to Sinbad and gaped for a moment as the shotgun swiveled back to bear on him.

"Wait!" Sable cried out. "The boy was right, we did have a defense! But we never knew about the others until after it was too late to help them."

"Shut up!" the vampire snapped. "The boy was guessing." The vampire struggled against the spell, and I felt sweat break out on my forehead as I fought to hold him in place.

171

"And the first thing you did was threaten him," Sinbad said. "If you thought you had a chance, you would have denied it first."

"And you really shouldn't have threatened my *gothi*," Shade said as she emerged from the shadows behind the vampire. His sneer turned into a gasp of pain as she put one arm around his throat. "I really like having him around."

"Your advantage is temporary," the vampire said, then hissed as Shade moved slightly.

"That's the first inch of two feet of oak I have at your back," Shade hissed. "Threaten my boyfriend again, and I'll give you more than just the tip."

"But what will you do now?" the vampire said. "Kill me, and the head of Clan Hrovingr? It's well known that you were being brought here. Oh, you might escape, you might even make it back to that cesspit you call home. But war will come for you and your mongrel packs, and you will watch your city burn."

"No, I won't dirty my hands with you," Shade said with a chilling tone in her voice. "I won't need to. All I have to do is walk away. You'll be alive...or whatever things like you are. And while I'm walking, I'll be talking, telling whoever I meet that you knew how to stop the attacks months ago, and choose to keep it quiet, outside of the wolf packs. Or was it just one clan? Either way, if you think you're going to deliver a war to New Essex, I'll deliver ten to your doorstep. And when the wizards get wind of it? How bad is *that* day gonna be, baby?" she turned to ask me.

I grinned. "Extra crispy."

"And how do we avoid our mutually assured destruction?" he asked.

"I'll ask some questions, and I won't tell anyone where I got the answers," I said. "Shade and I will go to homecoming, like normal kids do. And pretty much no one else dies."

"Save your questions, then," the vampire said. "I already know what you want. But do please unhand me, girl. If we're going to be civilized about this, let us dispense at least with the appearance of violence, shall we?"

Shade let go of him and stepped back, and Sinbad lowered his shotgun. "Start talkin'," the older Were said.

"Very well," the vampire said. "Whoever is behind these attacks, they are using a form of Muvian blood magick. It can be countered with the blood of the intended victim's line. Thus, Sable was able to ensure the safety of his clan with his own blood, as I was able to ensure the safety of my broodline with my own blood. I doubt your wizard families are so closely connected."

"Good luck getting them to use Muvian magick, too," I said. "Okay, so we know it's Muvian blood magick. That gives us a place to start."

"As to allowing a rogue wolf to simply walk into our lands without swearing at least temporary fealty to us, or paying us some sort of tribute…" Sable let the sentence fade as Shade favored him with a snarl.

"Have completely forgotten the Ways of the Clans?" Sinbad asked.

"I AM the Clan!" Sable countered. "My word is Law, above reproach. And any wolf who doesn't like it is free to challenge me."

"That isn't our Way," Sinbad said as he raised the shotgun. "If you've forgotten the Clan Laws, then I've been gone too long."

"You don't dare kill a Clan Alpha in cold blood," Sable said.

"You aren't a Clan Alpha," Sinbad smiled. "You never beat me in challenge. This Clan is still mine if I want it. So challenge me, Sable. Take this Clan from me." Sable shook his head and backed away.

"I don't have to," he said. "No one knows."

"They do now," Sinbad said. The Were who had brought Sable to us stepped into the light, and the two from the van joined her. "Shade, Chance, go outside. This is Clan business, and you aren't Clan." I nodded, and we headed for the door. This had the sound of politics, and that almost always got formal and stuffy. And the last thing I wanted after more than a month away from Shade was formal. Besides, we had a van and a few minutes to ourselves.

Chapter 12

~ No man will follow me because another tells him he should. Let him follow me because his heart tells him he must! ~ George Washington, "Brother to Magi"

Shade's face was still red, and I figured mine was at least a shade darker, but Sinbad seemed to be done talking about catching us making out. Of course, none of it kept us from finding a way to touch each other. Shade's arm was draped behind the passenger seat in the van, and her hand was inside the neckline of my shirt, her fingertips warm against my chest as she played with the little vial around my neck. I laid my head against her forearm as I pulled my own cellphone out and dialed Dr. Corwin's number again.

"Chance, excellent timing, we just landed," he said when he picked up.

"Dr. C, I found out what kind of magick they're using," I blurted.

"Oh, the flight was okay, a little bumpy, thanks for asking," he said, his voice heavy with sarcasm. So, tell me, what kind of magick are they using?" In the background, I could hear Mom and Dee talking, and further away, Draeden's deeper voice.

"Muvian blood magick. Sound familiar?"

"A little," his voice went cold. "Etienne used something similar, didn't he? But how does a vampire trying to use life force to bust open a portal to Hell relate to this case?"

"I don't know, it might not, but there are a lot of similarities. Depends on what this group is doing with the souls they're taking. But evidently, there's a way to defend against it. We're almost to the airport now. We'll go into detail then."

Minutes later, Sinbad was pulling the van into a parking spot outside one of the private hangars. A sleek black jet was turning into the open doors facing the runway as we came in the smaller doors opposite. No sooner than it

175

came to a stop, the hatch was opening, and my little sister pretty much exploded out the opening. I had a brief moment to notice that she was like a foot taller before she was trying to tackle me. I just had time to drop a little and brace myself so that her flying tackle was more like a flying hug.

"Oof!" I said, overdoing it a little bit. "Ohhh, I missed you sis." For a moment, all I could see was black curls, and there was a high pitched sound in my left ear that slowly resolved itself into my sister's voice.

"Missed you too!" she said as she pulled back. When she wasn't moving at high speed, I could see that she'd grown maybe a couple of inches instead of a foot. "Is Pyewacket keeping you safe?"

"He's doing a great job," I said. "Even with the homework part." Mom and Dr. Corwyn were a few steps behind her, and I barely got to my feet before I was caught up in a hug from Mom. She seemed smaller, even though she made my ribs creak with her hug. It was when I shook Dr. C's hand that I realized that Dee wasn't the only one who had put on a little extra height.

Finally, Draeden made his appearance. He looked as neatly pressed as he always did in a charcoal gray suit with a pale blue shirt and burgundy and silver striped tie. There was a little warmth in his cold blue eyes, and his lean face cracked into a narrow smile. His staff tapped against the concrete as he walked toward us, the round crystal atop it catching the occasional glimmer.

"Well, Mr. Fortunato, the Franklin Academy seems to be suiting you well enough," he said as he stuck his right hand out. With most mages, I got a tingle or a slight spark. From Draeden, all I could feel was the low hum of contained power as I shook hands with him for the first time.

"Can't say that I'm really that happy to be there, but…" I said.

176

"It's where you *need* to be right now, and you know it. Wizard Corwin says you have some new information on that case. Let's discuss it in the car, shall we?" he said as he gestured toward a long black limousine parked inside the hangar.

"Let's," I said.

"You folks have fun with that," Sinbad said. "Me and Shade have to get back to home."

"Already?" Shade and I protested in unison.

"Already, kid," Sinbad said. "We gotta let Sable save some face here. Don't worry, you'll see your girl at homecoming. Now kiss 'er goodbye so we can get the Hell outta here." We didn't waste time needing to be told twice.

"Your lips are puffy," Mom said as I got in the limo.

"You've got kissy face," Dee added smugly.

"Give it time, munchkin," I told her. "You'll get your first crush and then I'll have my revenge."

"As endearing as this moment is," Draeden said, "we have very little time for, shall we say, unguarded conversation. Now, tell me what you know, Mr. Fortunato." He steepled his fingers together and tilted his head to the side.

I laid it out as quickly as I could, the attacks on the vampires and werewolves, the blood magick defense, and the experimental nature of the attacks at the school. "None of this is on the record or official," I said to finish.

"Perhaps not," Draeden said slowly. "But there is a great deal that can be done in the interests of keeping this information on the far side of that line. Your work has already yielded results. I can't say I'm disappointed."

"I'm thrilled," I said flatly. "So, can I enjoy the day with my mom and my sister?"

"There is one more item that needs to be addressed, Mr. Fortunato. I sent you here to be educated. I sent you here to learn some discipline. I expected a certain amount of chaos on your part, but I did *not* send you here to do the work of the Sentinels. So, if you find anything else, I fully expect that it is to be an accidental discovery that is reported to the Sentinels immediately, as opposed to some clandestine investigation you conduct on your own. Am I making myself abundantly clear?"

"Right," I said. "Get out of the Meddling Kids business. Bad for my health, and not good for my grades, either. Got it."

Draeden turned to Mom and Dr. C. "Is he always like this? I can't tell if he's taking this seriously or not."

"Even I don't know if he's taking you seriously," Mom said in a voice col enough that I thought the windows would frost. "Especially since about six months ago, the Council was one vote away from killing him."

"Not our finest hour, obviously," Draeden said. "And one that we shouldn't be forgetting. But I was also one of the votes in his favor, and at the moment, leaving your son at the Franklin Academy goes against my better judgement. By the same token, Chance," he paused and leaned toward me, "I'd be lying if I said I wasn't glad you're there."

"Well, that makes one of us." The car stopped for a moment, and the rear window hummed as it went down to reveal a Sentinel peering into the car. After a brief exchange, we were rolling into the campus.

"Enjoy your afternoon," Draeden said as the car rolled to a stop. "I'll be leaving in a few hours for Seattle. I've already arranged for a carriage and passage for you via the transit ring back to New Essex." We got out to find ourselves in front of Chadwicke Hall. A group of parents and students were milling about, and a staffer approached with a clipboard in hand. "Ah, it looks like you're in time for the tour."

"I wanna go!" Dee said. "Can we go and see Chance's school?"

"Of course we can," Mom said. "That's why we're here." We hustled to join the group, which seemed to consist mostly of scholarship students, if the clothes were any clue.

Ninety minutes or so later, and I had a new appreciation of Mom's genius level parenting. Dee was beginning to flag, her seemingly endless nine year old energy finally reaching its limits. We ended up at Chadwicke Hall again, in the main dining hall. A line of refreshments awaited us, and no one seemed shy about taking advantage of it. A little food and juice seemed to completely recharge Dee, and she was chattering away as we headed for Jefferson Hall.

Hoshi and Kiya were lounging on the steps along with a lot of other kids. Energy strings were being spun and thrown into crazy shapes.

"Can you do that?" Dee asked. I put my fingers together and willed a little magick into my hands, then pulled them apart with a sheet of purple energy between the rectangle formed by my thumbs and forefingers. Her face lit up as I pulled my hands apart to stretch the plane out further, then imagined her face inside it. She laughed with delight when her own face appeared, and I twisted my hands to break it into a hundred little connected triangles that fluttered away like purple moths. As she chased the rapidly fading energy moths, I made a pair of dark blue energy strands and started to spin them, then threw them along their own planes of momentum so that they seemed to stop spinning and go straight up, then did it so they flew sideways before I pulled them back. I did a few more tricks before I dispelled the energy strands.

"You mean like that?" I asked.

"Yeah!"

"Nope, totally can't do anything like that." That earned me a punch in the arm. "Help! Help, I'm being oppressed!" I cried out. Dr. Corwin and Mom laughed, evidently both getting the line.

"Well, your studies are obviously going well, even if they're being misused," Dr. C said in mock disapproval.

"What can I say?" I shot back. "I'm working real hard on that whole misspent youth thing. Maybe I should follow your example and head down to Padre Island over Spring Break to impress the coeds down from UT?"

"Maybe you should introduce us to your friends?" Mom said, looking toward Hoshi and Kiya. Desiree had joined them, her red gloves standing out against her black t-shirt as she smoothed unseen wrinkles from the stretch satin. "They've only been watching us since we walked up."

"Oh, yeah," I said. "Mom, this is Kiya, the pretty one beside her is my roommate Hoshi, and this is my friend Desiree. Guys, this is my Mom, the dark haired little whirlwind is my sister Dierdre, and this is my mentor, Dr. Corwyn." A chorus of greetings answered my introduction. I looked around for a moment before speaking again. "Hoshi, where's Junkyard?"

"Playing with Ren," Hoshi answered. He flicked his hand toward the open end of the quad. I turned to look that way to see a group of sprites come flying around the corner about three feet off the ground. Their wings were purple with exertion, and a moment later, I saw why. Junkyard came tearing around the corner with Ren on his back, leaning into the turn as he gained on the sprites. His legs churned as he sped up and started passing the low flying fae. Ren let out a yell as they overtook the group of sprites, which got higher in pitch as they barreled toward us. The sprites passed us in a buzz of wings, with Junkyard's feet thudding in their midst. He pulled ahead of the group a few yards later and kept going, not slowing down until he had passed between a pair of trees near one corner of the quad.

As Ren and Junkyard came trotting back toward us, the other sprites flew up to them, and I could see Ren handing each of them something, then they scattered.

"What was that all about?" I asked as Ren rode up with a smug look on his face.

"Just a little race," Ren said. He flitted into the air and dug into his pouch, pulling out a lump of something. At the sight of it, Junkyard's tail started whipping back and forth and he started dancing in place. "Who's the fastest dog in the whole wide world? Who's the fastest? Junkyard is! Yes he is!" He tossed the little lump into the air, and Junkyard went still, then leaped up and caught it in his jaws mid-flight. For a moment, all he did was chew and wag his tail.

"Who is this?" Mom asked.

"This is Ren," I said. "Ren, this is my mom, my little sister Dierdre and Dr. Corwin, my mentor. Ren…works for the school."

"Are you helping my brother?" Dee asked.

"Wellll," Ren said slowly as his face scrunched up and his wings turned a pale green. "I uh, I help take care of Junkyard and I run errands for him sometimes as a favor."

"It's okay, Ren, they know what we're doing."

"Oh!" he said. His wings turned a bright pink and he dropped down to eye level with Dee. "Yes, I am helping your brother." There was no mistaking the pride in his voice, or the way his chest puffed out.

"Ren!" a high pitched voice called out. Ren's wing's went dark green as he rose higher and turned to face a red-winged Egle as he streaked toward us.

"Exactly what is the meaning of this?" Egle demanded as he held out a little round poker chip with something written on it.

"It's a task token," Ren said.

"I know what it is. I know what they're used for, too."

"Oh, well then there's no need for me to explain anything…right?"

"Except how so many sprites turned up with tokens for *your* tasks and complaining how you cheated them," Egle

181

bellowed. "Gambling is forbidden. Cheating is enough to get your wings torn off."

"Hey! You leave him alone!" Dee said. "He didn't cheat. He won that race fair and square!"

"Young lady, I appreciate your candor," Egle said. "But that doesn't change the fact that Ren was gambling. And, most likely cheating."

"I wasn't cheating," Ren protested. "I even handicapped myself."

"So you admit you were gambling," Egle said.

"Along with the rest of your staff," Dr. Corwin said. "I think I'm going to have to speak to the headmaster about your leadership."

"What?" Egle said, his wings going a sickly brown.

"You did say that a lot of your sprites showed up with those tokens, which means that they were gambling, too," Dr. C said in a chilling monotone. "Now, if you're only going to punish Ren, it seems to me that you might have your own racket going…one he got in the way of. If you're not involved, then it certainly doesn't speak well of your leadership, or this school. So, you can either drop the matter entirely, you can address it fairly and discipline *everyone* involved, or I can take my concerns to the headmaster. It's up to you."

Egle's wings were a dark, sickly green by now. "Well, perhaps I can overlook this one infraction. But no more schemes like this, Ren. I assigned those tasks to you. I expect you to get them done as assigned in the future. And I'll speak with the rest of the staff about this." He rose into the air, his wings going from green to a dark red before he flew off. Ren turned to Dr. Corwin and rose to his eye level.

"Thank you so much, sir!" he gushed. "If ever you need anything, just ask, and I'll either do it or get you someone who can!"

"You're already doing exactly what I'd ask," Dr. C said with a smile.

Ren turned to me, his wings darkening a little. "I'm sorry…" he started.

"You little hustler," I cut him off with a smile of my own. His wings fluctuated between pink and green. "I can't say I'm proud of you, but I know if Junkyard didn't want to race, he wouldn't have. But I am impressed."

"You are?" he asked, his wings turning pink again as his face lit up.

"Yeah. It was the kind of thing I might have done back when I worked for the other guy. But I'm curious, what did you feed Junkyard a minute ago?"

Ren grinned and pulled another lump from his pouch. "Nothing special, just pemmican," he said as he handed it to me. "Dried meat, fat and fruit mixed together. I add in a little peanut butter or maple syrup for flavor sometimes. It isn't bad for him, I promise. I eat it all the time." I pulled a little piece off and tried it. Savory and tart at the same time, the peanut butter made it even better.

"Can I try it?" Dee asked. Ren pulled a third bit of it from his pouch and handed it to her. Her face lit up as she chewed it, and she immediately stuffed another piece in her mouth before she turned to Mom. "Mom, Mom! You've got to learn how to make this stuff!" She handed the rest to Mom and turned back to Ren. "Do your wings ever get tired?"

"I often wonder that about human legs," Ren said. "But when I get tired, I simply land for a bit, much like you sit down." As if to demonstrate, he flew over and landed on Dee's shoulder. Her smile got bigger; I was definitely going to have to do something nice for Ren. As he chatted with Dee, the doors to the hall opened, disgorging Stewart and Rebecca, leading four people that I guessed were their parents. Stewart led the group down the steps toward us.

183

"Dad, this is the boy I was telling you about," Stewart said with a gesture toward me. One of the two men with him, a tall guy with steel gray hair, stepped forward and offered his hand. Much like when I'd shaken Draeden's hand, I felt the hum of restrained power when our hands touched.

"Randall Hampton," the older man said with an almost genuine smile. "I want to say thank you for saving my son's life. That's a debt I don't think I can ever fully repay."

I shook my head. "A good man doesn't keep score like that. And I'm trying to get there."

"Corwin, right?" the elder Hampton asked Dr. C. "I've heard of you. You're doing a good job with him. Still, Chance, if you need anything, anything at all, don't hesitate to ask."

"Chance, I thought I knew every pretty girl here. Who are these two ladies?" Stewart asked.

"This is my mom," I said. "And this is my sister, Dierde."

"Your sister," he said. "Is she the one who…" he let the question trail off, but made a thrusting gesture with his index and middle finger. "With an iron-cored wand at that?" I nodded, and he turned to Dee. "You know, I wish I could be here when you decide to come to the Academy." He put a hand to her shoulder, and she squirmed out from under his touch.

"Mom says I can be anything I want," Dee said. "So I'm going to be a Time Lord. Only I'll be a Time Lady, instead."

"Well, you still have to go to school," Stewart said. "And if you're anything like your brother, I certainly hope you come here."

"I might," Dee said with her chin thrust out. "Or I might not." Stewart laughed and turned back to Mom.

"She's a lot like her brother, and I mean that as a compliment, Miss..?"

"Murathy," Mom said. "Or you can call me Mara, if you like."

"Well, Mara," Randall said, "We were about to go enjoy the Parents Day banquet. Why don't you and Chance's friends join us?"

"We'd be delighted," Mom said. "Maybe now I can learn what my son has been up to from an unbiased observer."

As Dee started toward us, Stewart reached out a hand toward Ren. "Get off her, vermin," he hissed. Ren flew up as Dee gave Stewart a glare that he missed as he turned to walk behind her. As Dr. Corwyn and I hung back, Ren fluttered above us.

"Draeden got me the unredacted files for the two students from last year, plus the most recent ones," he said. He pulled out a thumb drive and handed it to me. "I haven't had a chance to go over them, so you're likely to know more than I do pretty soon. If you do find anything new, let me know right away."

"Gotcha," I said. We hurried to catch up.

"Mom, can Ren come stay with us?" Dee was asking as we drew close.

"I wish I could," Ren said, his voice sounding genuinely sad. "But I belong to the school, Miss Dierdre."

"People don't belong to other people," Dee said.

"Sprites aren't people," Rebecca said with a laugh.

"They are too!" Dee countered. That made Stewart, Rebecca and their parents laugh. I could see Dee's temper starting to get the better of her. It was amazing how much it resembled Mom's temper slipping.

"Sis," I said, gesturing for Dee to come over to me. Ren landed on my shoulder.

"I'm gonna kick that girl's butt," she hissed.

"No, you're not," I said. "What's going on for Ren and the sprites isn't cool, but you have to choose your battles. Most people think that sprites deserve to be slaves. Kicking butts isn't going to change their minds about that."

"What will?"

"I don't know," I said. "All I can do is treat Ren and the other sprites like people, and hope someone follows my example for now. You don't have to like it."

"I just have to do it," she finished for me. "I know. And I *don't* like it."

"Me, either, sis," I told her as I gathered her into a squirming hug. "And I'm proud of you for that."

"And if I could," Ren said, his voice soft and quivering with emotion, "If I had a choice, I would swear myself to you two and your family, whether I was slave or free."

"You'd never be a slave to me," Dee said. "Okay, Chance, I'll drop it for now."

"For now," I agreed. We turned and headed back to the group.

"Is there something you want to say, young lady?" Rebecca's father asked as we approached.

"Not unless you're apologizing for laughing at me," Dee said. The man started to turn red, but the elder Lodge put a hand on his arm.

"Let it go, Saunderson," he said gently. "She's just a little girl, and she does have a point. We all laughed at her idealism." He turned to Dee and inclined his head with a refined dignity. "Miss Dierdre, you have our apologies for laughing at you."

"Apology accepted," Dee said. If she sounded a little smug, I figured she'd earned it.

186

Chapter 13

~ Don't make a bad day worse. Better to destroy a good day; the fall is greater. ~ Prectil the Jester, demon of harmful mirth.

My phone rang as I waited by the transit ring for Shade to arrive. Dr. Corwin's number was on the screen when I pulled it out of my jacket pocket, so I answered it right away.

"Any progress on the case?" he asked.

"Not really," I said. "It's such a mix. Lodge, Cargill and Hampton were all from powerful Boston families, but Hart, she was a scholarship student. Lodge and Cargill were almost off the charts in terms of magick potential, while the other two were…Hart was above average, and Hampton is mediocre at best. Three guys, one girl. No correlation between birthdates or astrological signs. All three guys looked pretty much the same, but Hart was dark haired and dark eyed. Could be a pattern there, but I don't have enough info to say for sure. The only thing I know for sure is that whoever is doing this has access to the school's tunnels. My gut tells me that they're mages, sir. Dark, twisted and evil as Hell, maybe, but they're mages, I'd bet my life on it."

"I'm inclined to agree," Dr. C said. "But at least one of the attacks was different, the one on Hampton. They were experimenting with piercing wards. With Lodge and Cargill, we know they stripped them of their souls. But we don't know about Hart. We don't know if her disappearance is even a part of it, do we?"

"No, we don't," I said slowly. "We don't even know if there's a crime scene. If it is, it would have been the first. But there's a *lot* of info missing from her file. When we take her and Hampton out of the equation, we get two very powerful students who got their souls stripped."

"Okay, I'll tell Draeden, and ask him to have the Sentinels look into Hart's case. Meanwhile, keep your eyes open and be careful."

"Every day, sir," I said. "Every damn day."

"Did the formal suit still fit?" he asked. I looked down at the black, formal cut jacket and vest I wore. With the tie in the school colors, and matching cuff links, I had to admit, I didn't look bad, and it was more comfortable than I expected.

"I had to have Hobart do some alterations on it," I said. "I'm a little taller than I was a couple of months ago."

"Well, I'm going to let you go. Shade just got onto the transit platform. For tonight, let all of this go, and try to be a teenager for a while. Enjoy the dance."

"I'll try, sir," I said as the announcer called out the transit from New Essex. There was a flash of blue, and the passengers appeared. "I'll definitely…try."

Shade was easy to spot among the more casually dressed people on the platform in her dress. Shimmering green silk draped over her right shoulder and hugged her body down to her hips, where the skirt flared slightly, falling lower in back than in front. Green stockings covered her legs, with matching green heels with ankle straps. She hadn't seen me yet, and her head moved left and right as she scanned the crowd, revealing that she'd pulled her hair back in front and braided it together at the back of her head. Her make-up accented every line of her face, making her full lips look even more kissable and her gray eyes stand out from across the room. People crossed in front of me as I went to get her attention, and when they had passed, I could see that she had closed her eyes and tilted her head back. Her nostrils flared as she tested the air.

"Shade," I said, pitching my voice at a normal volume. Her eyes snapped open and she turned to face me. When she caught sight of me, she smiled. Nothing else in the world seemed to matter. That smile was for me. This goddess of beauty was happy to see *me*. The why didn't matter. She stepped off the transit platform, danced through the crowd and into my arms. Her lips touched mine, and fire and lightning seemed to dance across every nerve.

"Hey, there handsome," she whispered. "You busy tonight?"

"Never too busy to show a beautiful woman a good time," I said as I nipped at her neck.

"I'll bet," she purred. "Let's get out of here before my boyfriend shows up."

Someone cleared their throat behind us, and we turned to face Sable. He was flanked by a pair of hulking Weres, and his expression was one of cool disdain.

"Have you forgotten our agreement, little pup?" he asked.

"I sent you word of her arrival," I said.

"The word of a mage," he said with a casual wave of his hand. "Less than worthless among the Clans." He held his hand out, presenting a thick golden ring with a huge ruby set in it.

"It's the word of my *gothi,* Sable," Shade said. "He is Pack, and he spoke for me at my command."

"Those aren't the Clan's laws, pup. You will follow all our ways while you walk in our lands."

"Not part of the agreement, *Eugene,*" Shade said. "I respect your ways, you respect mine. I sent you word through a Pack member. My *gothi* is Pack. That's *my* law. So I'm not kissing your ring and asking for mercy. I *am* going to a dance with my boyfriend. If you want to challenge me over something so inconsequential, we can do it *after* Homecoming."

"I see why my brother's hair is white now," Sable said with a low rumble of a laugh. "He's welcome to you. I think I'd prefer to deal with your pet mage after all. At least he knows his place."

189

"Don't mistake his good manners for submission, Sable," Shade said with a laugh. "You haven't seen my *gothi* fight."

"Has anyone?" he sneered as we walked past him.

"No one who's still alive," Shade countered. We left him silent and fuming as we headed for the carriage I had waiting. Once we were inside, I took my jacket off and Shade snuggled into the crook of my right arm. Her right hand splayed out on my chest, and her fingertips found their way between the buttons of my shirt to find bare flesh. She moved to let my hand have access to her dress, and after a moment, I looked down at her in surprise as my fingertips encountered nothing but soft, smooth flesh.

"Are you wearing a-"

"Nope," she answered before I could finish the question. "That's not the only thing I'm not wearing."

"You mean..."

"Maybe," she teased. "If you play your cards right, I'll let you find out for yourself."

"And how do I play my cards right?" I asked.

"Dance with me," she said, her eyes suddenly soft and searching. "Every dance. Just remind me that you love me. And...the usual."

"You can say no any time, Shade. Any time. I'll never push it."

"What did I ever do to deserve you?" she asked.

"A neurotic warlock with anger issues and a shitty attitude? I'm not sure any sin is worth being stuck with me. But I wonder who thought I deserved to have you in my life."

"A damaged werewolf with intimacy issues? Probably some capricious jerk of a God who thought you needed extra special punishment."

"See, we're perfect for each other."

"Yeah, equally screwed up," she giggled.

190

"That's why I fell in love with you," I said. "I love how your broken parts fit with mine." We rode in silence after that, our hands slowly exploring, and just enjoying being in physical contact for more than a couple of minutes.

When the carriage slowed, I put my jacket on, and grabbed the little plastic box that had Shade's corsage in it. She let me fumble with it for a couple of minutes before she took it and put it on herself. Moments later, we were getting out near the doors to Chadwicke Hall. Music thumped from inside, and Shade pulled me toward the dance floor. For a couple of hours, I alternated between looking like a spastic idiot and trying to occupy the same space as Shade during slow dances.

It was Hoshi and Kiya who ended up stealing the spotlight, though, during the dance contest. Shade and I didn't even bother to try, mostly because she would have been hopelessly handicapped with me as a partner. Slowly, the judges tapped out couple after couple, until only Lance Huntington and Ginger were left facing Hoshi and Kiya. The two Boston kids had moves that screamed ballroom dance training, but in the end, they were just not equal to Hoshi's dramatic flair and Kiya's balletic grace. It was close until Hoshi lifted Kiya into a handstand over his head. Everyone went wild as they stood there, holding the pose for a moment. Then Kiya lifted her left arm as Hoshi swung his right arm away in a matching move. They twisted slightly, and then slowly, as the last notes of the song started to play, twisted a little and bent their arms so that their faces met in a kiss.

Exhausted, Hoshi, Lance, Stewart and I ended up sitting out the next dance as the girls took the floor. Rebecca and Ginger tried to keep up, but they were eclipsed by Shade's natural agility, Kiya's athleticism and Desiree's sensual grace. They danced through three songs, finally deigning to grace us boys when a slow song came on.

"I like them," Shade said as she slid into my arms. "Your friends, I mean. Those other two have sticks jammed so far up their twats I'm amazed they can turn their heads."

"That's an image I can do without," I laughed. "But you're right. I'm glad you like them."

"They're fun to dance with. I could have used a few girls like them on the cheer squad last year. But, the next slow dance, you should ask Desiree to dance with you." She slowly turned us so I could see Desiree shaking her head at one of the Hall Captains, a tall blond boy with the typical aristocratic good looks. He laughed and walked away, but Desiree didn't look amused.

Desiree, Hoshi and Kiya joined us when the next fast song came up. After a few minutes, Hoshi started marking time the exact same way I did, imitating every move I made with a serious face. Of course I laughed, and it became a game to do the same few moves in unison for a few minutes while the girls danced circles around us.

When another slow song came on, Shade nodded to me and left the floor. I caught up to Desiree as she went to follow and touched her arm, careful to make sure I hit the glove instead of bare flesh. She turned to face me, her face set in a frown until she recognized me.

"Would you care to dance?" I asked. She smiled and slipped her hand in mine.

"I know you have an ulterior motive," she said softly as we started to sway together.

"Figured you would," I said. "Does it bother you?"

"The ulterior motive? Not from you."

"What makes me so special?"

"It's not your *only* motive."

"Busted," I laughed. "Just don't tell my girlfriend."

"What could I tell her that would hurt either of you?" she asked. "That you think I'm attractive? Or the part where you feel the same way about me as I feel about Kiya?"

"I thought my shields were better than that," I said, though my shoulders seemed to relax on their own now that I didn't feel like I had to hide the fact that she really *was* attractive to me.

"Your thoughts are. But your feelings…way different. It's nice to know someone thinks I'm pretty without trying to make a conquest of the fat chick."

"I am *never* playing poker with you," I said.

"Probably a good idea. You might control how you react to your feelings, Chance, but you have no control at all over how strong they are. And with you…they're strong." She laughed for a moment. "All of them are that way."

"Well, offer's still open, if you ever need some extra anger to feed on."

"Here's hoping I never get *that* hungry," she said with a laugh. "But thank you. For getting me, for being my friend as fiercely as you are. For enjoying dancing with me. I think I might actually like it here now."

"Me, too," I said, finding I actually meant it. I was still going to miss the Hell out of my family and friends back home, but it was actually starting to get tolerable here. The song's last notes faded, but another slow song came on, and we kept dancing. After only a few moments, someone tapped me on the shoulder. I turned to find myself facing the blond guy who had been bothering her before.

"Excuse me, I'll be cutting in here," he said, and slid his arm between Desiree and me.

"No, you won't," Desiree said. "I'm enjoying this dance with my friend."

The guy stopped for a moment, then looked at Desiree before he turned back to me. "Dude, chill," he said.

"Not my call," I said. "You heard her, she doesn't want to dance with you."

193

His head turned to me, then to Desiree. "Slut," he hissed before he turned on his heel and walked off. I moved to go after him, but Desiree's hand on my shoulder stopped me.

"Don't bother," she said softly. "I'm used to it."

"You shouldn't *have* to be."

Her full lips curved into a smile, but her eyes were sad. "Just dance with me." This time, she seemed to press closer to me, and she laid her head against my chest. The song came to an end, and we stepped apart, then headed for where Shade was laughing with Hoshi and Kiya.

"You two skipped a slow dance?" Desiree asked.

"Well, you get this much hotness out on the floor, and people will start to get self-esteem issues," Hoshi said.

"Erik Bradley zeroed in on Shade, here," Kiya said. "We ran interference."

"I told you, I would have been fine," Shade said.

"It wasn't you we were worried about," Kiya said seriously. "He's got a rep for taking things too far, and his family tends to do a lot of cleaning up after him. Lawsuits are the nicest thing they're known for."

The call went out for the last dance, and Shade and I hit the floor with Hoshi and Kiya on our heels. Desiree even wandered out, her hips swaying slowly as she danced on her own. I tried to focus into that one moment, to keep the night going forever, smiling as I remembered how many other times I'd wished for the same thing. After wishing for so many nights to just pass as quickly as possible, it was one habit I never wanted to break.

Eventually, the song did end, and the lights came up. Shade kissed me as reality came back to plague us. "This was my first school dance," I said.

"We missed all of last year's dances, didn't we?" Shade said as we joined the others in heading for the door.

"No way," Hoshi said. "*This* was your first dance?" We stepped outside and into the cooling wind

194

"You poor thing," Desiree said. "How did you like it?" She came around in front of Shade and me and walked backward so she could face us.

"It was really cool," I said. "I had a lot of fun. What's the next dance?"

"I think it's the Sadie Hawkins dance," Kiya said, then shook her head.

"Isn't it the Winter...Formal?" Desiree said haltingly. She stopped in her tracks, her face pale in the starlight.

"It's...it's....what's going on?" Kiya asked. Hoshi tried to hold her up, but she sank to her knees.

"Oh, no," Desiree said. "Chance, no..." she moved toward Kiya but then sagged into me before she made it a step. To my left, Hoshi was calling Kiya's name. I took a calming breath and closed my eyes, then opened them with my Sight, knowing already what I was going to see.

Two red tendrils of energy were attached to Kiya and Desiree, right over their heart chakras. I tried to muscle Desiree next to Kiya, and Shade added her strength. Out on the grass, I couldn't draw the circle I needed, but it wouldn't be the first time I'd cast an unsupported circle.

"*Circumvare!*" I yelled, forcing every ounce of magick I could muster through my body as I tried to visualize the Lemurian sigils. As the circle flickered into existence, Shade grabbed Hoshi and pulled him free of the space it would cover. For a moment, it held, then the two tendrils broke through it again.

"*Circumvare!*" I screamed into the night again. "*Cleniklopoc toklilt holktar!*" I added in Lemurian, trying to add an extra layer to the barrier. Both fell after only seconds, and I tried again. In front of me, Desiree and Kiya stirred as the wind kicked up around me. I reached a hand out and grasped one of the tendrils. I cast again, and this time, I felt the presence on the other end.

You can't save them.

"You can't have them!" I screamed in defiance.

Yes, we can. Alone, you might save one, but you're too weak to make the hard choice. You're too weak, you're going to fail them both. " Desiree struggled to her knees and looked down at Kiya, then got to her feet. The wind screamed around us, forcing Shade and Hoshi to the ground.

"Circumvare! Circumvare!" I yelled as the energy tendril burned across my palm and into Desiree's body, but she looked at me as if she didn't feel it. She slowly pulled one of her gloves off and stepped close to me.

"They're right, you can't save both of us," she said as she slowly raised her bare hand. "And you love too fiercely to choose." She turned her face to look at a place over my shoulder and raised her voice. "You think you're going to break him by making him choose or fail, you miserable piece of shit? Well, I'm not going to let you!"

"Des, no!" Kiya cried. She clutched at Desiree's leg as her friend closed the distance between us and put her hand out toward my face.

You can't stop us. We'll take who we want.

"To Hell with you! *I* choose who you get," she said as her hand caressed my cheek. "I choose me. Save Kiya, Chance. Save Kiya." She pulled her foot free of Kiya's grasp, then took one labored step outside the circle, then another. The energy filament was ripped from my hand as she turned to look at me, the wind whipping her hair back from her face for a moment. She smiled at me, and in that moment, I knew what she'd just done. Her body glowed, her soul suddenly visible for a moment, then it was ripped free of her mortal form, whipped away by the strand of unholy energy. She gasped, then her eyes rolled back in her head and she went limp. Time seemed to stretch out as I watched her body fall to the ground. I couldn't hear anything, couldn't see anything but my friend in that moment.

196

Time roared back into place and hammered my senses. My left hand was in agony. *"Circumvare!"* I roared, and this time, the circle held. The energy strand hammered against the shield and I could still feel the other presence on the far end.

You can't beat us. Stop interfering, or the next attack will be far more personal.

"It's *already* personal," I snarled. The pain searing across my palm helped me focus on the circle, and I took the agony and channeled it into the my magick. Suddenly, the attack stopped, and the wind died down to a stiff breeze seconds later. Shade's head came up, and she rolled off of Hoshi as I knelt by Kiya.

"Oh, God, Des," Kiya sobbed as she stumbled to Desiree's limp form. "What have you done?"

I didn't say anything for a moment, but I knew. I'd seen it in when she smiled back at me.

She had let herself be taken because she knew what I'd do. In the end, she knew I was going to come for her. She knew that when I did, I'd bring the wrath of Hell with me.

"What did you do?" Kiya repeated, her voice raw as she knelt over her friend.

"She doomed them all," I said, my voice sounding flat in my own ears. "Hoshi, go get the Sentinels."

"They're already on their way," he said.

"Chance!" Stewart called out as he ran up from one side. "Are you all o-" he stopped as his feet went still a few feet away. "Oh, no. Oh, God, I'm so sorry."

I looked over at him as the anger in me seemed to flicker and die out, along with every other emotion. He stood there, his hair sticking out, flecks of green sticking to his pant legs, and it barely seemed to register in my head that I knew who he was. I looked ahead of me, to Jefferson Hall. Only yards away. If we could have made it there, would I have been able to stop the attack? *Could* I have stopped it at all? The sound of feet pounding up behind me

197

brought me back to the here and now, and I looked over my shoulder to see a trio of Sentinels run up. The lead pulled a pair of spellbinders out as he got closer, and I just held my hands out.

Stewart's protests were just so much empty noise as the silver manacles closed around my wrist, and Hoshi's objections died when I shook my head. Even Shade's gentle touch on my arm couldn't break through the numb static that was shrouding everything. Even the throbbing in my hand was a distant sensation. I let them lead Shade and me away, with Hoshi and Kiya being escorted by the other Sentinel. More people came, two with a stretcher, and a tiny bit of comfort blossomed for a moment. At least they weren't going to leave Desiree laying in the grass.

Nothing seemed to matter until I got to the Blockhouse, and found myself facing Sentinel Dearborn.

"How many?" I asked as she opened the spellbinders.

"Six," she said. Her voice sounded as flat as my emotions, and that alone stirred something. She looked as numb as I felt. "I guess we can count ourselves lucky it wasn't seven."

"Were they all…" I started to say, but I wasn't sure of how to ask the question.

"All of the attacks were the same. Multiple victims, away from thresholds, on terrain where it would have been impossible to draw a strong circle."

"Are they all … dead?" Shade asked.

"No," Dearborn said. "So far, all of them are alive. As far as we've been able to tell, the attacks were very precise. Not as much psychic damage as previous attacks. As much as I hate to say it, they learn fast. They knew the best time and the best way to strike."

"This was a show of strength," Shade said as she looked around the room. My head came up and I followed her gaze. The Sentinels, while still moving with purpose, all seemed to have closed in on themselves. Their backs weren't as straight, and the all moved a little slower. They had been beaten, and they knew it. So had I.

Shade took a slow breath, then brought her head up. As she did, her shoulders came up, and her back straightened, lending her an inch or two of height. Her chin came up, and even though she was an inch or two shorter than me, it was as though she was looking down at me from a much greater altitude.

"They need you to think they're stronger than they really are," she said. "They need you off your game to buy time for whatever's next."

"In case you missed it, they pretty much kicked all our asses out there. I'd say they're exactly as strong as we think they are," Drummond said, his voice heavy.

"If they were, they wouldn't have stopped with six, or seven or ten," Shade said.

It took me a minute for my brain to catch up to her, but when it did, I had a hard time containing my enthusiasm. "The Battle of Britain!" I said. The whole room turned to look at me with varying levels of confusion showing. "After France fell, Hitler's warlocks couldn't break the British sea wards, and he still needed the Tunguska Artifact to finish the Grand Summoning. So he tried to make everyone think that Britain was beaten. He basically kept hitting them with his newer air power to make them surrender without having to actually invade! That way he could turn the bulk of his army and his warlocks toward the Russian front and ignore Britain. It's the same here. They must have hit some kind of limit, or need to do something else!"

"Or both," Shade said. "If they were as strong as they want you to think, they wouldn't have stopped. They would have kept on until they had everything they needed, and we'd be watching something a lot worse happen right now."

199

"This isn't bad enough?" one of the Sentinels next to Dearborn asked.

"Evidently not," Dearborn said. "And I'm not going to give them the chance to show us what worse looks like. Miss Cooper's right, this was a display of strength. It was meant to demoralize us, to put us off balance and keep us from interfering with something important. Our job is to find it."

"Ma'am," another Sentinel said slowly. "With all due respect, she's just a kid."

"No, Jaspers," Dearborn said. "She's an alpha werewolf. She understands threats and displays of force a lot better than most people. And she's right. If they *were* as strong as they want us to believe, then they wouldn't still be hiding. Drummond, get those patrols back out there. I want every inch of those woods scoured before daybreak. Coordinate with the sprites."

"Um, can I go?" I asked, holding up my manacled wrists.

"No," Dearborn said. She pulled out a metal rod and tapped the manacles. They opened with a click, and I felt my skin tingle as magick coursed through me again. "You're still officially a suspect. Miss Cooper is free to leave, though."

"Boy, do I know how to show a girl a good time or what?" I asked as I took her in my arms.

"Well, it's never boring with you," she said. "But I should go. I'm supposed to be staying at Wanda's tonight, and if I know my Mom, she'll call around my normal curfew to make sure I'm actually *with* Wanda. Besides, I need to make another stop on the way back."

"Okay," I said, disappointed that our night was being cut so brutally short. "The carriage driver will take you back. I'm going to miss you."

She leaned in and kissed me deep, her hand reaching around to grab my butt cheek. "I already miss you," she

200

said as she took my right hand. We walked to the door, and she slipped her hand around mine and put my palm to her own bottom for a split second, hiding the movement between our bodies. Every other thought left my mind as she let me know exactly what she was wearing under her dress.

We stopped at the door, and she turned to face me again. "Love you, baby" she whispered. "Be careful. Please."

"I will be," I whispered back. "And I love you." We kissed again, then she stepped back, leaving cool night air where her body had been pressed against mine. I watched her disappear into the darkness, and slowly regained the ability for coherent thought. I turned back to the room and recovered more sanity with every step I took toward the table.

"So, how long am I staying with you guys this time?" I asked.

"Long enough to have that left hand taken care of, and for the Headmaster to approve your release."

"I thought you guys only answered to the Council," I said.

"It's an advisory role, but one that the Council wants us to take *very* seriously."

"As if having Polter for a boss wasn't bad enough," I muttered. Dearborn didn't answer, and I didn't blame her. Another Sentinel came over and inspected my hand. There was a red streak across my palm, and my fingers were swollen and pink, but other than that, the damage didn't seem to be too bad. She pulled a tin from her pouch and smeared a thick, green ointment across my hand, then wrapped my hand from just above my thumb to the tips of my fingers in white gauze.

"Keep this hand immobilized like this for the next two days. That should take care of it. Have the infirmary change it tomorrow afternoon and Monday morning," the Sentinel

201

medic said. "You might see some streaks under the skin. Those are normal, and they'll fade by Monday night." I nodded and wandered over to a bench along one wall while she put her gear back in her pouch. Since I had the bench to myself, I stretched out and tried to relax a little. I wasn't sure how long the emotional numbness was going to last, but I figured when it wore off, I was going to be hard to get along with.

Somewhere along the way, though, my body decided 'relax' meant 'take a nap.' The next thing I was aware of was Professor Kenneson's voice nearby. "It's telling enough that he didn't save a more deserving student, like Winthrop, but he only managed to save one of the two," he was saying quietly. "That practically begs for sympathy while making him look like a hero. The truth is, the boy is barely competent, and we both know his loyalties have never truly shifted. These demon lovers aren't capable of changing. Once a demon's thrall, always a demon's thrall. That's just reality, and no amount of political correctness is going to change it."

"I'm not convinced that you're right," Caldecott's voice replied. "The boy has proven himself through an Ordeal and his conduct. He may not be a model student, but he's certainly not involved in this." I opened my eyes and slowly turned my head to see them standing a few feet away from me, both in their school blazers. They were facing away from me, and everyone seemed to be giving them a wide berth.

Kenneson sighed and shook his head. "Sir, demons only take thralls from those who already hate the rest of humanity. They reinforce that hate in them from the moment they accept their oaths. They're fundamentally incapable of integrating with civilized society. Whether this boy is directly involved in this or not, he has an agenda that runs counter to everything we hold dear here. He may not be a *part* of this plot, but I can assure you, he supports it. If

202

you can't charge him with something, at the very least, for the sake of our benefactors' peace of mind, expel him." I sat up and made my way over to them, letting the sounds of the rest of the room cover my approach. Caldecott had his hand to his brow, his eyes closed and his lips pursed.

"When did you become an expert on what demons teach their slaves?" I asked. Both men started, and Kenneson took a step back.

"Mr. Fortunato," Caldecott said. "I'm not sure how much you overheard, but you can't take things out of context here."

"I heard enough. Don't worry, it's nothing I haven't heard before. I'm used to it. So, can I go now, or are you going to kick me out to make the important people happy?"

"You're not going to be expelled, son," Caldecott said with a smile that bordered on sincere. "You're free to go. And I want to commend you on your efforts last night. Miss Marlin's parents were very grateful."

"I can't take credit for that, sir," I said. "Desiree stepped out of the circle so I could save Kiya. If you're going to be saying good things about anyone, then Desiree is your hero."

"You did your best son," the headmaster said. "No one can ask more."

Except my best wasn't good enough. If there was one thing I was learning from my first semester at the Franklin Academy, it was that there was no A for effort. Only results mattered. So far, I was coming up short in that department.

Chapter 14

~ Make your friendship such that no man regrets knowing you, and your wrath such any man would regret wronging you. ~ Master Ben Franklin, "Wisdom for the Magi"

"Mister Fortunato," Professor Kenneson said, forcing me to look up from my textbook.

"Yes, Professor Kenneson," I answered.

"If we Miss Marlin was not able to *afford* yellow orchid petals for her summoning, what *cheaper* substitute might she use?" he asked, putting a less than subtle emphasis on the words that reminded everyone in the class that Kiya was poor.

"Sunflower petals would be ideal," I said. "But any yellow flower petal would do, sir. The color is what is most important." I thought about telling him that sunflowers should have been the first choice in the formula he gave us, not an alternative. I wanted to point out to him that fire elementals would have found the symbolism more appealing. But I'd grown either wiser or weaker in the three weeks since I'd overheard his conversation with the headmaster, and I kept my mouth shut.

"Correct, but only just. I want one thousand words on what would make sunflowers an adequate substitute on my desk by Wednesday. You can all thank Mr. Fortunato for this little exercise in expanding your minds. Dismissed." There was a collective moan as we put our books away, but no one seemed ready to take it out on me. I didn't even catch so much as a dirty look on the way out.

"Mister Fortunato," Kenneson said as I walked toward the door.

"Yes, Professor?"

"I understand you checked out several books regarding conjuration last week."

"Yes, sir, I did," I answered.

"Do you have any of them with you?"

"Yes, sir," I said as I pulled the two I had from my pack. He took them from me and set them on his desk.

"Let's see what we have here...*Foundations: A History of the Grotto*...and *Spirit Allies: A Biography of Silas Caldecott, Esq.* I believe I'll be holding on to these. I've already suspended your library privileges." He leaned forward as the dull fire of anger fought to rise inside me. "I don't know what your agenda is, young man, but I will personally see to it that it fails. It's a foregone conclusion that you will never graduate from this school, so checking out library books relating to my class will do you no good. In your shoes, I would quit sooner rather than later, and save myself the time and embarrassment that overstaying my welcome further would inevitably bring."

"May I ask you a question, sir?"

"You can ask," he said with a smug smile.

"Does that ever work? The veiled threats, I mean."

"Every time," Kenneson said.

"And it would have a few weeks ago," I said. "But not today. And especially not now." The professor stood up and narrowed his eyes at me.

"You'd do well to take me seriously, young man."

"I've been threatened with worse by things a *lot* scarier than you," I said, my voice calm. "Most of them are dead. I'm pretty sure you don't want me to take you *that* seriously." I turned and kept going to the door, with Junkyard trotting at my side.

Ren flew up almost as soon as I cleared the entrance to the Grove. "I got what you need," he said. His wings were gold with excitement and he bobbed in place instead of hovering steadily. "But we only have a couple of hours. If that."

"I won't need it for that long," I told him as I headed for my dorm. "What about Hoshi and Kiya?"

"I just saw them heading into the woods. I figure they'll be consoling each other for a few hours."

"At least," I said. "Two less people to keep a secret. Okay, meet me in the tunnels at eleven. I still some appearances to keep up, and I need to talk to Lucas and Dr. C."

"Okay," Ren said. He flew away, then stopped after a few yards and flew back. "I know that this whole situation is bad. If I seem...enthusiastic, it's because I finally feel useful again. I just wanted you to know that. Because...I'd like to consider myself your friend, if that isn't too much."

I smiled. "You *are* my friend," I said. "And I'm yours. Don't worry, I get it." His wings turned bright gold as he rose a couple of feet, and without another word, he turned and flew off.

After dinner, I went to my room and set down the extra plate I got for Hoshi on his desk, then turned my laptop on and hit the call button on Lucas' program. It did its digital dance number, and Lucas' face appeared after a few moments. The background was unfamiliar, but I recognized the classical music his grandfather usually played in the background.

"Hey, Lucas," I said after he greeted me. "Where the Hells are you?"

"We're at the bookstore. We're remodeling the upstairs store room. Dr. C's here, too." Dr. Corwin leaned into the picture and waved.

"My place is being watched," Dr. C said. "But that has nothing to do with your case. We went over the case files for the last attack, and we noticed the same thing. Every victim was particularly strong, magickally. Your friend Desiree? Her empath ratings were just about off the chart, and she was actually getting stronger. Kiya...no one understands the sources of her power, but she's pulled off some amazing things, especially with water based conjurings and spells. The windstorm the night of prom? They traced that back to her. The other five fall into the same category. Lots of potential power in all of them, usually focused in one element or one particular type of magick."

"So our only standouts are Stewart Hampton and Josie Hart," I said.

"Given the nature of Hampton's attack, he was just a convenient target to experiment on. And we still don't know if Hart's disappearance is related, but the Sentinels also came up dry in finding the rest of her academic files. Did you find anything about her on your end?"

"Not directly. Ren found out that her room hadn't been assigned this semester, so he's going to go check it out tonight."

"But you're not going to the girl's wing after hours, right?" Dr. C asked. Beside him, Lucas gave him a sidelong look, then turned to me with an expectant smile.

"No one is going to see me in that dorm at all tonight," I said. "Unless things go sideways and I have to go in to save Ren's ass or something like that."

"If I thought it would make a difference, I'd tell you to be careful," Dr. C said. "Just don't get yourself expelled, at least."

"Last thing I want," I said.

"Good. I need to go take care of an unwelcome guest right now, so give me at least until tomorrow evening before you call and let us know what you found." He got up and left.

I'll explain in a little bit, Lucas typed in the message field. *Don't go anywhere for a few, okay?* I nodded and he cut the connection. A few minutes later, the screen lit up with an incoming call, and Lucas' face appeared when I hit the green answer button.

"Okay, so what's up with Dr. C?" I asked.

"We're dealing with a little something of our own here," he said. "There's a priest missing and a bunch of rogue vampires in town. Dr. C thinks the two are connected, and so do a few other players, but the Council can't stick its nose in."

"So who's watching Dr. C's place?" I asked.

"He thinks it's a faction of vamps who like what the rogues are up to."

"So, is he going to jump in the middle of all that anyway?"

"Not exactly," Lucas said slowly.

"Lucas," I said, trying to make my tone as stern as Dr. Corwin's could be. "What's going on?"

"Well, remember how last time shit went down with the vampires, and you got sort of invited to interfere?"

"Thraxus owed me that," I said. "But what about it?"

"Well, you'd be his natural choice for this, but you're out of town, soooo…"

"So?"

"He kinda told me to deal with it."

"WHAT?" I yelled. "How did he *kind of* tell you to deal with it?" I demanded when I got control of myself.

"Well, there's a detective in the Missing Persons section who got assigned to a related case. And I guess an anonymous tip pointed him to me as an informant."

"That's Thraxus style, all right, but I still don't get how you know he *told* you to get involved."

"I was getting to that. He walked into the store a few days ago and started talking about a breach of etiquette. He said that, if he wanted to, he could kill me right then and there for interfering at Inferno, and the Council couldn't touch him for it because I wasn't part of the invitation. Chance…." He stopped and looked down. When he raised his head, his eyes were blazing. "He threatened to kill my grandfather first."

"Lucas, I'm sorry," I said. All of the anger drained out of me, and I felt my hands and face get cold. "This was my fault. I never should have let you get involved in any of this."

"No, Chance," he said, his voice sharp. "*You* tried to warn me the first time, but *I* made the decision to get involved. This is on me, no one else. If you want, I'll let you shoulder half the guilt, but that's where I draw the line."

"You drive a hard bargain, dude," I said through a tight throat. "So, is there anything I can do to help out on this?"

"Funny you should ask," he answered then leaned closer to the camera.

Half an hour later, I was pretty sure I'd told Lucas what he wanted to know, but I wasn't so sure he had everything he *needed* to know. I was really only certain about one thing: Thraxus and I were going to be having a talk the next time I was back home.

With all of that done, there was really only one thing left for me to do, and that was catch some sleep before I broke a dozen different rules in the middle of the night. I changed into my gray sweatpants and hoodie, then laid my blanket down on the floor and grabbed the quilt Mom had made for me and snuggled under it. It was the only thing I could sleep under that was heavier than sheets, and autumn in Boston was pretty, but damn was it cold compared to what I was used to. My biggest worry was actually getting to sleep.

Help me.

I came awake with a gasp, and found myself reaching for something, with the memory of a girl's voice in my head. The room was dark, with only a few slivers of moonlight slanting in gray across my empty bed. A warm, wet tongue licked my right cheek, then Junkyard's furry mass leaned against me from behind.

"I'm okay, buddy," I said as I got my bearings. "Just a weird dream. Guess it's a step up from a bad dream, right?" My phone showed I only had a few more minutes before the alarm I'd set was going to go off, so I cancelled it and slipped my shoes on.

Hoshi was asleep on his bed, the plate on his desk only half eaten. I shook my head as I slipped my backpack on. His eyes were puffy, and I could see his cheekbones even in the soft glow of the moonlight. Even the guilt I felt over not being able to protect Desiree had settled to a muted ache over the past three weeks, but it was evidently still hard for Hoshi and Kiya.

As Junkyard and I slipped out into the hallway, the familiar flip-flop in my stomach reminded me of why I seemed to be doing okay: I was doing something. I wasn't sure if sneaking out in the middle of the night to investigate a missing student was what the counselor had *intended* when she told me to find a healthy outlet for my feelings, though. Oh, well, it was just one session.

The basement was quiet and dark, like always. A whispered "*Lumio*" brought a soft glow to the tip of my wand, and let me thread my way silently to the door into the tunnels. Ren was waiting on the other side with a bundle of blue cloth. His wings shown gold as he fluttered in the air near the door.

"Quick, put it on and hide," Ren hissed, thrusting the bundle at me. "The command is '*occulto.*' Someone's coming!"

I shook the bundle out to reveal a Sentinel cloak, and with a flourish, swung it across my shoulders. "Junkyard, center; Ren, on Junkyard." Sprite and dog moved quickly, with Junkyard sliding between my knees and Ren descending to sit on his shoulders. "*Occulto,*" I whispered, and the world went hazy like before as the cloak's chameleon spell activated. Footsteps sounded from behind us, and I crouched in the corner of a small alcove.

Moments later, a Sentinel and someone in a staff uniform stopped a few yards away and consulted a piece of paper.

"Yes, that's Jefferson Hall up ahead. We're fine," Professor Talbot's voice reached my ears.

"So, where does this one go?" an unfamiliar voice asked.

"Out by the old chapel."

"Well, that explains something," the Sentinel said. "We chased some kid in a mask out that way a few days ago, lost him near the chapel. He must have known about that tunnel."

"Oh, those idiots," Talbot said with a short chuckle.

"You know who they are?"

"Not exactly," Talbot said. "At least, not individually. You probably ran across a Highwayman. They're nothing to worry about, just a bunch of rich boys playing at being in a secret society."

"Not a fan, huh?" the Sentinel asked.

"I was never a member," Talbot said. "So I have no idea what they do. I just get the same briefings the rest of the faculty get when they show up. We should be almost to Jefferson Hall."

"Jefferson…let's see," the Sentinel said. "Hampton, Nakamura, Fortunato and Marlin. Three of them have been targets. And the fourth…well, you know what they say about him."

"Yes, I do," Talbot said. "But only an idiot shits where he sleeps The evidence to support the theory isn't very strong, either. Mostly circumstantial. Let's press on." They turned toward me and started walking, leaving me to sweat as they passed within a couple of feet of me. I stayed still until the sound of their footsteps faded, then took off the way they came from. Ren led me past turn after turn, only stopping when he reached our goal, a thick door that looked almost exactly like the one we'd left at Jefferson Hall. We slipped into the basement, and with a gesture, I sent Junkyard to the door while we headed for the stairs. If things went sideways, at least he could slip out and pee on something.

Minutes later, we were on the third floor, pacing quietly down the hall. Ren hovered just above my right shoulder, his wings crystal clear now. I counted the door numbers, then stopped near the end.

"Where is it?" I whispered, looking to my left.

"It's right here," Ren said, pointing to a blank section of wall. I frowned as I realized that the part of the wall he was pointing at should have been only a foot to my right, but Ren was floating about ten feet away. I shook my head,

"Wait, you can't see it, can you?" he asked.

"Not yet," I said as I shrugged my pack off. I unzipped it and pulled out the enchanted mirror. With a slow turn, I scanned the wall in front of Ren. For a moment, nothing happened. That wasn't unusual. Like most concealing spells, this one was hard to get past. But my little focus worked on a principle that most illusions ignored: reflections. Dealing with two different perspectives for the same viewer, the reflection wasn't altered by the chameleon spell. However, this one didn't shimmer and change. It took me a moment to realize that it was already showing me the correct image.

"This isn't an illusion," I said. "It's a *neglenom* spell." Of all the mental manipulation spells, the *neglinom* charms were the ones I had the hardest time with. I willed my mental defenses into place before I turned my gaze back to the wall, and the hallway stretched a little to reveal the door to room 312.

"They aren't strong enough to work on fae," Ren said smugly.

I shook my head. "It wasn't cast with fae in mind," I said.

"Of course not," Ren said. "It would have been an exercise in futility."

"Whatever," I said. "Did you remember to grab the key?"

"Oh, sorry I forgot to tell you. I mean, I remembered to grab the key, and I would have, but it wasn't there! Even the master key for the room was gone."

"Someone really didn't want this room to be used, did they?" I asked. Once again, I unslung my pack, this time reaching under one of the titanium plates that ran down the middle of the back panel to detach the set of lockpicks I stored there.

"Wait," Ren said. "This door has active wards."

"Crap!" I hissed. "I don't have time to take them down."

"Don't worry, I've got this." With that, Ren sped down to the far end of the hall. Moments later, the door clicked open, and I was treated to the site of my sprite friend hovering on the other side of the threshold. "Wards only work on the outside, right?"

I nodded. "So how did you get inside without setting off the wards?" I asked.

"Oh, that was simple. Through the mail box. The school wards those, and I work for the school."

My senses were still buzzing a little, so I put my hand up to the invisible line that ran across the opening. Slight pressure met my fingertips, and I stopped. "The wards seem to be negated, but...there's a threshold here."

"Well, that's strange," Ren said. "And kind of inconvenient. Hey, wait... please, come in." The pressure against my fingertips disappeared.

"How did you...?"

"I work here," he said with a broad smile. "No matter who sets the threshold, the building belongs to my masters."

"And a servant can act in the name of his master," I said as I stepped into the room. It also explained how he could negate the wards on the door. In theory, he could

214

have opened it from the outside as well. I closed the door behind me and brought my wand out. "*Lumio pallide caeruleo*," I said softly, and a pale blue light filled the room.

The first thing that came to my attention was that someone was spending a lot of time here. The bed on the left side of the room was unmade, and several plates were stacked neatly on one corner of the desk next to it. The other bed was piled with clothes, and the desk on that side of the room had a thick book on it, and something that made my blood run a little cold. Set in the middle of the blotter on the desk top was a metal plate inscribed with familiar looking runes and sigils that seemed to crawl across its surface.

"What in the Nine Hells is that?" Ren asked as he went to hover near the desk.

"Muvian," I whispered as I pulled my phone out. "At least, I think it is."

"Don't you mean Lemurian?"

"No, I mean Muvian," I repeated as I brought the camera up and tried to focus it on the metal tablet. "The language Lemurian is descended from." The camera wouldn't focus, and when I turned the lens away from the tablet, afterimages kept writhing across the screen. It wasn't until I switched the camera off that they disappeared.

"That was creepy," Ren said from over my shoulder. I set my pack down and pulled out my sketch pad and charcoal. No sooner than I'd laid the paper against the tablet, the writing seared itself against the paper, and I had to pull it away to keep the page from bursting into flame.

"So was that," I whispered. The larger book was written in what looked like Greek, and it cooperated much better when I focused the camera on the bookmarked pages.

"Hey, Chance?" I heard Ren say from behind me.

"What?" I hissed.

215

"I found the rest of Josie Hart's file." I turned to see him holding a thick manila folder with the school logo on it. One of the closets was open behind him, and I could see something on the door that made my stomach drop. I stepped past Ren and snapped a picture, then took the file from him and stuffed it into my backpack.

"What are you...oh, crap," he said. His wings glowed a pale green as he saw what was on the door behind him.

I'd seen the same thing once when Dr. Corwin worked as a consultant for the New Essex County Sherriff's Department over the summer. Detective Collins had a name for it, and I found myself parroting his words.

"God, I hate the murder wall." Printed photos were tacked to the inside of the closet door, and eight of them had a red X across them, all of them familiar faces. Desiree, Sterling Lodge, and five other people who were lying in the school's infirmary, and one who was in a morgue somewhere. Hoshi's picture was up there, and so was Kiya's. Off to the side was another picture, and Ren floated over to it, then turned to face me, his wings almost white.

"Chance," his voice wavered. "That...that's your..."

"Family," another voice finished.

I turned and leveled my hand, hissing *"Eximo!"* almost by reflex, releasing the power stored up in my ring. A dark figure dodged out of the way of the weakened kinetic bolt, and I ended up blowing the window out into the darkness.

"Fulmen!" the dark figure spat, and I threw myself down on the floor as a thick blue spark arced across the distance between us and struck the closet beside me. I reached back and grabbed a handful of clothing in the closet and flung it in front of me. Hangers and fabric filled the air, and the next bolt jumped from wire hanger to wire hanger, bending away from me and finding its mark in the wall socket.

"Go!" I yelled as I scrambled toward the door. Ren darted for the gaping hole where one window used to be,

216

and the dark figure sidestepped to block the doorway. My right hand found the handle of my backpack, and I came up in a crouch. For a moment, I faced off with the mysterious figure. Small and definitely feminine, she held her wand in her fist like a knife. Behind her, the hinges of the open closet door glowed a bright red that was fading to a cherry color.

"I should have killed you first," she said. "But you're such an idiot, and you did everything we needed you to, up to now."

"I've been saying the same thing myself," I said. "The idiot part, I mean."

She snorted and raised her wand. "Well, you're going to die stu-"

"*Ictus!*" I yelled, catching her midsentence. She ducked, and I turned and threw my backpack out the window. "*Obex!*" I followed up as she pointed her wand at me from the floor. Her next bolt stopped short of my flesh by a couple of feet, though I could still feel the hair on my arms stand up.

"Nowhere left to go, warlock," the girl said. "Except down." I looked over my shoulder at the gaping hole in the wall, then back at her as I grabbed the skull and crossbones amulet around my neck. "*Percutiens malleo*," she said, and an invisible bus hit me.

I was briefly aware of the magickal backlash as the massive blow shattered my shield spell and the world went white. Wood splintered and more glass shattered as I became weightless.

"*Scutum sphaeram*," I choked out as I felt myself tumble through the air, and white flared across my vision again like a nuclear blast as I forced more magick through my already overloaded energy centers, using the amulet to create a simple shield all around me. A spike of pain seemed to go through me from my forehead to my fingertips. Then something hit me across the back and my body was tumbling as I figured out what had just hit me: this little thing called the planet. My ears were ringing, and the world kept tilting around me. Finally, the spell gave out and dumped me onto the grass. I staggered to my feet, then the world went sideways on me as the ground kicked me in the ribs with swift follow-up to the side of the head.

"Chance!" Ren yelled from somewhere nearby. I heard the buzz of his wings in the whitewash that was my world.

"Junkyard!" I called. "Junkyard, get my backpack, and get the hell *out* of here!" In the distance, I heard Junkyard's bark and a whine.

"I'll be okay, buddy," I said. "Now, go!" I struggled to my knees and pulled the cloak off, then wadded it into the smallest bundle I could.

"Get this back where it belongs," I said as I held the cloak out blindly.

"You're all messed up," Ren said. "People are coming."

"Do it!" I snapped. "Now!" The cloak was lifted from my grasp in a clatter of wings, and I was suddenly alone again. I heard footsteps from one direction, and the sounds of crickets and frogs in the other. I swayed to my feet and stumbled towards the sounds of wildlife. With the backlash ripping through me, I was down to two basic concepts: cover good, people bad. Wildlife meant trees and brush, and trees and brush meant cover. My body barely did what I wanted it to as I tried to make my way to the woods, my arms flailing in the general direction I intended, my feet only hitting the ground because gravity said so. But for all I knew, I was heading straight into the arms of the people who wanted to kill me. Then, the ground dipped away from me, and I ended up barely avoiding a total faceplant. Something sharp scraped at my forearms and cheeks when I tried to sit up, then someone had me under the arms.

"Easy, *gothi*," a rumbling voice said as they dragged me along.

"Who...who are you?" I asked as my body started to shake from the magick overload. Some of the attack must have leaked through and started to damage my nervous system.

"My name is Roland," he said. He stopped and hoisted me like a rag doll. "I am champion of Sable's clan. Your alpha asked us to watch over your school after the last attack."

"A-a-a-asked?" I managed through chattering teeth.

"Well, she threatened to reveal Sable's negligence if he didn't." He made a noise that sounded like an amused avalanche, then came to a stop. Nearby, I could hear the sound of water rushing over rocks.

"S-s-sounds...right," I said.

"Take a deep breath and hold it," Roland said as he shifted his weight. "This is going to be a little jarring."

The next thing I knew I was under water. *Cold* water that kept pounding me and twisting me around. I hit something firm. My legs straightened and pushed against whatever I'd hit, and suddenly my head was clear of the water. I took a gasping breath as more water pounded down on my shoulders. My vision went from white to clear with painful swiftness, and the spike of pain in my head subsided to a dull fire.

"Gah!" I yelled as I tried to step free of the cascade. My feet dragged against the bottom, but I managed to get clear and turn around. In the moonlight, I found myself facing a waterfall, and on the bank, a werewolf in its hybrid form. The amused rockslide sound came again, and I waded toward the shore. I flicked my hands to get some of the excess water off before I pushed the sopping strands of my hair away from my face. I shifted to the Sight and watched as my aura slowly reasserted itself after being dowsed with water. As it did, it felt like someone was taking sandpaper and scrubbing every square inch of skin along the way.

219

"I...apologize for the shock," the werewolf said. "It was the only way to get rid of the excess magick fast enough to prevent damage to your body."

"Yeah, you just sound all broke up about it," I said as I made it to the bank. "Damn. My wand is gone, my phone's probably ruined."

"I have your phone. The sprite grabbed your wand. You have other concerns though."

"Like getting back to my dorm without getting caught," I said. "And getting the info I found tonight to the right people without putting my own ass in a sling."

"Among other things, yes. There are people searching the grounds. Your odds of making it back are...slim, to say the least."

"You wouldn't happen to know of an old chapel on the south side of the grounds, would you?"

"I would," Roland said with an expression that might have been a smile on a human, but showed way too many teeth on a hybrid wolf's face. Without a word, he turned and trotted into the brush again. I followed as best I could, and figured out really fast that I hurt in a lot of places. He made just enough noise that I could follow him, but no more.

In the distance, I could hear people moving around, calling out to each other, while sprites zipped around above them. Lights glowed among a group of people gathered by one of the buildings, and windows glowed as people turned on lights. Up ahead, Roland was waiting next to a small stone building.

"I smell a trail leading here," he said, pointing at a thick wooden door set at an angle next to the building's foundation. He held out a hand and dropped my cellphone and a crumpled bit of cloth into my waiting palm. I tucked the phone into my pocket, then shook out the cloth to reveal the Highwayman mask. A few seconds later, I was slightly more anonymous and shivering.

"Thank you," I said. "I owe you big time."

Roland shrugged. "Sable's plan never sat well with me," he said. "This is the kind of thing we should have been doing all along. Now, go. I'll wait here for a bit, and if anyone comes near, I'll lead them off."

"Don't wait too long on my account," I said. "They'll do their best to catch you."

"They can try," he said before he slipped into the brush nearby without another sound. I pulled the door open and made my way down the steps, descending into darkness at first. My cellphone screen lit the way well enough, and I found a corner a few feet in. I stepped around it to find myself facing a pair of sprites hovering at eye level. They took one look at me, then both looked away.

"Is the way safe, little brothers?" I asked, trying to sound serious and solemn.

"The way is safe, sir," the one on the right said.

"Good," I said. "I'm on business with the Shadow Regiment. No one must hear of my passage here."

"Yes, sir," the other sprite said. "No one will hear it from us."

"Good work." I slipped past them and opened the door. The tunnel went straight, and before too long, I was at the intersection where I'd seen the Sentinel and Professor Talbot earlier. And just a few yards away was the door to the basement of Jefferson Hall. I was in the right building, but now I had one more problem: explaining my wet sweats. I crept up the stairs and peeked out into the hallway. The lights were on, and the occasional person moved deeper in the hall, but this section seemed relatively quiet. Across the hall, I saw another door. The green plastic placard on the door read "Laundry."

Before I could chicken out, I slipped out the door and across the hallway. The other door was unlocked, and I was inside before I could even think about regretting it. From there, it was a matter of finding my own mesh bag and stripping down, then putting my slightly dirty but much dryer clothes on and replacing them with my wet sweats. I pulled the mask off and slipped it into my pocket, hoping no one noticed my hair was still damp and my shoes squished when I walked. Rather than put the shoes back on, I just carried them, and headed for the stairs at the far end of the hall.

When I made it to the third floor, the halls were clear, but I heard voices down in the main lounge. I tossed my shoes into my room with a wet sound and found Junkyard waiting for me. My backpack was at the end of my bed, and his tail thumped against it once before he came over and bounded up to lick my face.

"I'm glad you're safe, too," I said as I wrapped an arm around his neck and hugged him. "Come on, we need to see what everyone is up to." We padded down the hallway to find Stanwicke at the door, looking stern.

"You're late," he said as I heard names being called out behind him. "Where were you?"

I pointed down to Junkyard. "Had to take him downstairs. I didn't think it was a good idea to let him go anywhere on his own right now. I came as soon as I heard." He looked down at Junkyard, who favored him with an open mouthed canine grin and a wagging tail.

"All right, go on in," Stanwicke said. He stepped aside and let me into the room. Almost everyone from our side of the hall was there, and Stewart was reading down a list of names. They were already in the K's, which meant mine had probably already been called, and my absence noted. I stood there in my bare feet on the hardwood floor and shivered as I sent the files on my phone to Lucas with a message to get the pics to Sentinel Dearborn anonymously.

"And Fortunato," he finished. "Better late than never. Okay, that's everyone accounted for. Go back to your rooms. We'll make sure everyone's family knows that they're safe." As everyone filed toward the door, he gestured to me to wait for him. Hoshi winked as he walked past me.

"Junkyard, potty," he whispered as he passed me.

"Yup," I answered. Then he was out the door, leaving me alone with Head Boy.

"I'm not sure if I'm relieved or disappointed Hoshi was telling the truth," he said.

"I'd be happier with relieved," I said.

"Well, so far, you've been the only person who seemed to be able to get ahead of them. When I heard there was a magickal duel over in Lincoln Hall, I hoped you'd found something out, or maybe even caught them in the act. And if this was you, I need to know so I can cover for you." I had a split second to make a decision. I wanted to trust Stewart, but something nagged at me and made me reluctant to add more people to the circle. And when in doubt, my tendency was to keep secrets instead of share them. I could reveal it later if I needed to.

"I wish," I said. "I didn't even know what had happened until you said something."

"Officially, you still don't." He nodded toward the door, and I headed out. Halfway down the hall, I stopped, my heart in my throat, when I saw the Sentinel standing guard outside my door. Hoshi was facing him, looking up at the man's unwavering chin. That could mean only one thing.

My room was being tossed. Again.

"Great," I muttered under my breath. The Sentinel moved aside, saying something apologetic as I approached. Sure enough, my room looked like a grenade had gone off in my closet and a tornado had hit my desk. There was one other bomb waiting to go off in my room, as well.

Sentinel Dearborn.

Her normally bland expression had been replaced with a scowl that I felt like a physical impact, and her whole body looked smaller, like she was compressing herself to keep from exploding. "I assume you can account for your whereabouts for the past two hours or so?" Her voice crackled with anger, and I took a step back.

"Over there, by the bed, until all this started," I said as I pointed. Technically, true. My starting point and her starting point just differed.

"Are you telling me you had nothing to do with this?"

"Depends on what you're talking about," I said. Again, total truth. "Am I supposed to have blown something up? Killed someone? Summoned a demon? Stolen important government secrets? You've tossed my room, what, three times? You've taken me in to question me *every* time something happens, and so far, I've been *clean* every time!" My voice rose as I went, unspoken frustrations suddenly carrying a lot of weight. "How do I convince you that I'm *not* the monster here?" For a moment, I felt the heat crawling up my face, and my heart started to pound, and then, as if getting it off my chest was enough, the feeling faded, leaving me feeling drained.

Dearborn looked around, then at me, and gave a short little laugh and a nod. "Guess you're right about that. Truth is, this seemed more like your style than any of the other times. But…you're here, no one saw you leave or come back. For that matter, no one seems to have seen much of anything."

"What did happen?" I asked.

"Looks like someone got into a fight over in Lincoln Hall. In a room no one seems to remember being there. It started a small fire, blew out the power and blew out an entire wall, along with one of the people involved."

"Well, that last part sounds like me," I agreed. "But I don't start *small* fires."

"That's true," she agreed. "Anyway, I was kind of hoping it was you, and that you'd turned up something useful."

224

"Believe me, if I had something useful, you'd have it as soon as I could get it to you."

She gave me a level look, then smiled as she nodded again. "I'm sure I would. And I'd tear you a new one for interfering with my investigation."

"You wouldn't give me letter of commendation at the same time?" I asked.

"Not even if you blew the lid off the whole thing and delivered the culprit to me on a silver platter. This isn't a Saturday morning cartoon or an action movie. You don't get both at the same time. Now, clean up this mess." She swept out of the room, leaving me to face the mess her people had made. I started grabbing clothes and throwing them in the general direction of the closet until Hoshi gave me the all clear from the door.

"Okay, how did they miss the files?" I said as I reached for my backpack.

A rustle of fabric came from over my head, and Ren shimmered into view on top of the curtains as he held out my chameleon charm. The file was bent into a tube under his other arm. He hopped off the curtain and drifted down, his wings a soft yellow.

"You're welcome," he said as he handed the folder over to me.

"Thanks, smart ass," I said as I opened it. "But we can't keep this. I need a photocopy of it, then we need to get this to the Sentinels pronto."

"I'll have it for you by morning," Ren said. "They'll close the admin office downstairs before long, and I can use the photocopier there. I can even send it to the Sentinels via intracampus mail. Who do you want to send it to him?"

"Make it Headmaster Caldecott," I said. "That way she'll open it fast."

"You got it!" he said.

I turned to Hoshi. "Thanks for covering for me. I'm sorry I didn't say anything to you, but I figured if you didn't know about it ahead of time, you couldn't get in trouble for not reporting me."

"Like I don't owe you big time for not telling anyone about me and Kiya breaking curfew all those times," he said. I shrugged and grabbed a t-shirt off the floor. "Seriously, man, it's not all..." he made a hip thrust and added a couple of moans. "She's taking this really hard. And the counselor's no freaking help. They want to send her home and have her see a certified psychic counselor. She doesn't want anyone poking around in her mind. The only person she trusted that much is in a coma right now."

"I might know someone she can talk to," I said. "There's a cambion Shade and I go talk to sometimes, when we're really screwed up."

"There's not a lot of good options for her, man," he said as he flopped onto his bed. "She lost all her friends from before because of her *gift*," he said, using air quotes on the last word. "So going home isn't really an option, but staying here is hell, too. I found her yesterday by the lake. She told me she kept on seeing herself wading into the water, that the water was calling to her. What if I'd gotten there a minute later?" I stopped and turned to face him.

"She said it was calling to her?" He nodded and I felt my face crease into something resembling a smile. "Your girlfriend might not be as cray-cray as she thinks she is," I said.

Chapter 15

~ The bad guys always make it personal. ~ Caleb
Renault, protagonist of the Blood and Honor series.

I usually hated waiting. It ground away on my nerves, and most days, while I could do it, I was Hell to get along with afterward. To make it seem less like waiting, I sat under the bare branches of an alder tree beside Jefferson Hall with my legs folded almost into the lotus position, and tried to finish visualizing the matrix for the new defensive spell in my head. Going to apprentice level casting was a huge change for me, since now I had to include hand gestures as well as the spell's matrix, and learn to associate that matrix in my head with the complex design of it. That usually meant more words, with each word of the spell creating part of the matrix in the magick focused part of my brain. I almost had this one down, all that was missing was what I was doing right then: practice. The last sigil was always the hardest for me, since I had several others floating around in my mind's eye. I carefully imagined it as if I was drawing the semi-circle with a pen, etching it out with infinite care in my mind, and hovering the imaginary pen over the exact center point inside the half-circle before carefully dropping it to make the last little mark to close the spell matrix. As the entire set of sigils glowed in my head, I heard the sound of paws on dry grass, then a growl and teeth closing on something hard.Sounds of disappointment and a couple of laughs and jeers reached my ears as I brought myself up out of the trance, holding the image as I recited the words of the spell. Finally, my eyes opened, and I saw a red disk incoming. With the spell complete in my head, I could reach up and catch it, then flip off the squad of upperclassmen who were looking disappointed. Junkyard dropped a bright green one at my feet.

"Good boy," I said as I pulled a piece of pemmican from the baggie at my side. He sat down, and I tossed it in

227

the general direction of his mouth. His head moved so fast, I wasn't sure if he actually caught it, or if he vacuumed it out of the air. Either way, it last all of a microsecond.

"Hey," I heard Kiya say from behind me. Hoshi hovered over one shoulder and nudged her forward. "Um, Hoshi says you might know about why I keep wanting to go down to the lake?"

"Well, he knows more about it now than I do," I said.

"I know names," Hoshi said. "Not much more, and even that's a guess. Nearest I can find, you're being called by the Abantubomlambo, the River Folk. The Nguni shaman claim them as their teachers."

"So, I'm…not trying to kill myself?" she asked. Her eyes flicked back and forth between us.

I shrugged. "You still could be, but I don't think you're trying to drown yourself. I talked to a water elemental a few weeks back who told me to let her daughter know she was calling to her. I figure, with what Hoshi told me, you're that daughter."

"It would explain why your evocations are so hard to do, and why your conjurations are so unpredictable," Hoshi offered.

"It would explain a lot of things," Kiya said, her voice almost inaudible. "So, how do I do this?"

"Go to the lake," I said. "And listen." I hoped it was that easy, but by now, I still wasn't sure of anything. "Take Hoshi with you. I think the rest will come to you."

"You're not coming?" Hoshi said.

I shook my head. "No, I have another promise to keep."

Kiya took Hoshi's hand and pulled him away. "Please, let's go do this. I need to know." He let her tug him toward the lake, only sparing one look at me before he turned and went with her.

Once they were out of sight, I stood and dusted off my jeans. Junkyard looked up at me and made a sound in his

228

throat. "Yes, it's that time again," I said. He trotted over and picked up a purple Frisbee, then brought it back and dropped it at my feet. When I tilted my head, he put a big paw on top of it and dragged it toward himself.

"You want to keep it?" I asked. He barked and wagged his tail. "Sure," I shrugged. "Why not?" He followed me into the dorm and to my room, where I found Ren waiting with a package and a handful of fresh flowers in his arms. Mom's neat, swirly handwriting was on the outside of the rectangular cardboard box. I cut it open to find a cone of paper that held flowers from Mom's garden and a sachet with fresh herbs. Dee had enclosed a letter of her own, her wobbly cursive handwriting a rebellion of its own, since her school refused to teach it. There was a bag of homemade cinnamon fireballs, and a plastic bag with dried apple and pear slices. I set those aside, pleasures for later, after I saw to what was important. I took the flowers and the herb sachet and headed for the door with Ren and Junkyard on my heels. Like every time I made this trip, I didn't hurry across the quad. The cool air, the setting sun, even the fall decorations in peoples' windows were things to be noticed, savored. Appreciated and held onto as I stopped at the door to Barton Hall, the school's infirmary. It took me a moment to make myself go inside. That part never got any easier.

The nurse on duty nodded to me as I passed, and the Sentinels at the door to the long term care ward gave me a cursory look through their goggles before letting me pass. Then I was among the fallen, and in front of the person I'd failed. Every bed was swamped with huge bouquets of flowers and balloons and cards. Desiree's was no exception, though there were more flowers, more cards and fewer Mylar balloons. There were also candles, pictures and small stuffed animals. Extravagance gave way to sentiment at her bedside.

She'd lost weight, and it made her face look gaunt, robbed her of even the semblance of peace as she lay there in front of me. They had covered her up to her shoulders with the sheet to keep people from touching her by accident. For a while, all I could do was sit there. Ren landed at the foot of her bed, and Junkyard sat beside me.

"Hey," I finally said. "I think I finally caught a break. I can't go into it here, but I think I found one of the people behind this. And, I think we figured out what's going on with Kiya." I scrubbed my hand across my face as I struggled to keep my voice from cracking. It was always harder at first, but it never got easy. "We think she's got a spirit trying to reach her, something from her family's ancestry. Turns out, she might be more shaman than mage." The rest was mundane, stuff I knew we had all missed being able to talk about at meals and between classes. But it was important that I say it. Finally, I ran out of little things, and I only had the really big stuff left, the things that seemed to be too big to make fit into words. The things I wanted to say, but hadn't been able to.

As I sat and tried to figure out what was going through my head, a nurse came up. "Do you mind if I take her vitals real quick?" the little blonde woman asked from beside me. I shook my head, actually glad of the distraction for a few moments. The nurse pulled her arm out from under the sheet and took her pulse, then checked the machine beside the bed and the IV bags. Finally, she turned to me and smiled.

"You're here more than any of her friends, even her roommate," she said. "And her vitals always get stronger after you've been here. You must care about each other a lot."

"She's a good friend," I said. "And I don't have a lot of those. But...she doesn't seem to have an off switch when it came to caring about people. She just *does*, as hard as she can."

230

The nurse nodded, and patted Desiree's hand. "I hope you don't mind a little unsolicited advice. Touch has healing properties of its own. And every time you're here, it seems like you leave with a lot unsaid. Don't worry about the words. She's your friend. She'll know what you mean."

I looked up at the nurse, at her pale blue eyes, and wondered why she was telling me this. Did she know something I didn't? She smiled, and it lit up her eyes. Then she looked down at her watch, her page boy cut sliding forward to obscure part of her face. "Well, that's almost the end of my shift. Put her hand back under the sheet before you go?" With that, she slipped past me and out to the hall. I turned back to Desiree.

Why the hell not? I thought. I reached out and took her hand in mine. Immediately, the harsh edge of grief seemed to dull, and the ache of sadness seemed to lift just a little. All that was left was the warm glow of affection for her. My free hand came up to my face as I finally realized what it meant to me to call someone a friend, how much I cared for that small group of people. I took a long, shuddering breath, overwhelmed by what I was feeling. It was the same fierce devotion as I gave to my Mom and Deirdre. To me, my friends were as close as family, one and the same as far as my heart was concerned. And that list was small. Dr. C, Lucas, Wanda, Junkyard (yes, even my dog), and now, Desiree held that place in my heart. There were other people I cared about, sure. But these few, they were family to me.

"Des," I said, my voice cracking, "I need you to get better. I need you to beat this. Hell, I just need you. You're my friend, and I don't want to lose you. I'm *not* going to lose you. I will move mountains and shake the gates of Hell if I have to. So you hang on. Please. Be there when all this is done. You help me be a better person, and all seven Heavens know I need that." By the time I was done, my voice was stronger, and steady. I tucked her hand under the

231

blanket and got to my feet. Ren flew over to the table and laid his flowers down, and I set mine next to his. Junkyard reared up and put his paws on the side of the bed, then gently laid the Frisbee down across her legs. Tears welled up in my eyes at the gesture. Hells, even my dog loved her. I kissed her forehead before I left, feeling oddly lighter.

I was halfway across the commons when my cheap cell phone pinged to alert me that I had a text. I pulled it out of my pocket and slid it open.

>>*Call home, little hero. I want you to hear this.* ##

I didn't hesitate. I cleared the text screen and hit speed dial for Mom's number. The first thing I heard when she picked up the call was Dee screaming in the background.

"Chance, what's going on? Dee just started screaming and thrashing!" Mom said.

"Mom, get her to Dr. C's place *now*! You need to get her into the big circle upstairs!" Even as I closed the connection on my phone, I had the one Shade gave me out and I was dialing as I ran across the quad.

"Hey baby…what is it?" Shade's tone went from sultry to business in nothing flat.

"I need you to get to Dr. C's place pronto," I said. "Someone is attacking Dee, and I think I know how to stop it."

"Got it. Who else do you need on this?"

"Lucas and Wanda."

"I'll make sure Wanda's there. Tyler, saddle up, I need you to go to-" She cut the connection midsentence, and I smiled. That was my girl, all business when it counted. Next on my call list was Lucas.

"Hey, dude, what's up?"

"Get to Dr. C's place on the double. Someone's trying to hurt Dee. I'm going to need you to show him a symbol to protect her."

"Shit! Okay, I'm on my way." I heard the screeching of tires as Lucas hung up. Last but not least was Dr. Corwin. He answered on the fourth ring.

"Chance, this is a little premature-"

"Dee's being attacked, sir," I said, finally letting some of the desperation I was feeling come through in my voice. "Everyone is heading to your place, I need you to get her into the circle and do the defensive spell."

"Chance, I can't."

"What do you mean you can't? This is my *sister* we're talking about."

"I'm not at home right now."

"It's gonna take everyone a few minutes to get there anyway-"

"Chance, I'm in San Francisco."

"What the hell are you doing in San Francisco? Shit! This can't be happening! Lucas, Wanda, and Shade are still warded to get in right?"

"And your mother and Deirdre," he added. "I can have-" he was saying when I cut the connection. The stairs went past two and three at a time, then I was on my floor and ignoring Stanwicke telling me not to run in the halls. My sneakers slipped as I tried to stop, and I ended up sliding past my door by a few inches before I could stop and push my way in.

It took me precious seconds to grab a pen and a few sheets of paper from my mobile bookcase. I leaped across the room and frantically started drawing out the defensive ward. When I was halfway through, I hit the call button on my laptop, and Lucas answered right away.

"Almost to Dr. C's place," he said as soon as he answered.

"Okay, good," I said, trying to breathe a little slower. "Once you get there, use the key above the kitchen door to get in and head to the attic."

"Okay, I'm pulling to his place now. Wait, I don't see his Range Rover."

"Yeah, slight change of plans there. Tonight the part of wizard is going to be played by you."

The sound of a door closing came over the speakers, then I heard footsteps. "Dude, I'm not a mage."

"You've got some talent," I said as I heard the door unlock. "So you're gonna have to be mage enough."

"Okay…mage enough…not a lot of options, huh?"

"Only one." I heard his feet on the stairs, and his breathing got heavier and faster.

"I think they're here," he panted. "I hear…Shade's bike…and your sister. God, she sounds like she's being skinned alive!" I could hear Dee's screams in the background.

"Okay, you haven't practiced casting a circle, so we're going to have to do this the hard way. Are you in the attic?"

"Yeah. Um, what's the hard way?"

"We'll get to that. See the big workbench on your right? There'll be a bunch of little paintbrushes and some pots of ink. Grab one of the smaller brushes and a bottle of ink. Wait, get a second brush, you're gonna need it. There's also a box of lancets somewhere. Grab those."

"Chance, we're here, I have Dee," I heard Shade say in the background. I wiped the excess moisture from my eyes and willed myself to keep my voice calm. I laid the completed ward down in front of me and turned my camera on, then tried to hold my shaking hands still enough to get a clear picture of it.

"Okay, baby," I said, certain she could hear me, even over Dee's frantic cries. "Take her to the center of the circle and sit down with her. Is Wanda there yet?" I hit the button, and the flash went off, but when I looked at the image, it was blurry and overexposed.

"Almost," I heard her say. "Tyler's about a block away." My fingers shook as I turned the flash off and tried again.

"Okay, got the ink and a few brushes," Lucas said. The new image was still blurred.

"Okay, hang on one," I said as I took a deep breath and centered all my excess energy into my core. My hands stilled and my heart rate slowed a little. I held the phone over the page and tried to snap another picture. This time, the image came out clear. I immediately sent it as a text. "I'm sending you an image, Lucas. I need you to draw it between Dee's shoulder blades *exactly* as it is in the image."

"I'm not an artist," Lucas protested. "Wanda's the one who can draw."

"You don't have to be," I said. "It's just a couple of circles and some funky symbols. You've got this."

"What do you need me to do?" Mom's voice came over the speaker.

"I need you to help Shade hold Dee still, Mom," I said, my voice shaking. "I need you to help her get a handle on the pain and fight." I scrubbed at my eyes and fought to keep my shit together. What I *wanted* was something to hit. A target. I typed away on my phone's surface, frantically entering in instructions for Lucas.

"Wanda's here," Shade said, her voice calm and strong. "Where do you want her?"

"In the circle. Listen up guys, I'm sending a text. Once you cast the circle, we're going to lose signal, so I need you to be ready. Lucas, you ready to draw?"

"Yeah," he said, his own voice quavering. "I just need to get her shirt out of the way." There was a tearing sound and Mom's voice came over the line.

"There," she said. "Now, Deirdre, hold still, very still."

"Momma, it hurts!" Dee sobbed, and I had to wipe away fresh tears of rage and frustration.

"Dee," I said. "Listen to Mom. I'm going to try to stop this, but Mom needs your help," I said over the phone. "You can do this, sis. You have to. Please, just listen to Mom and do exactly what she tells you. Hold still so Lucas can help me protect you."

"Take my hand, sweetie," Mom said. "Hold on tight, but don't move."

"Do it, Lucas," Shade said. Nearby, I heard Wanda's voice begin to chant, and Dee whimpered.

"First circle, done," Lucas said, his voice steady now. "Outer circle. First symbol...second...third...fourth and fifth...last symbol between the circles. Okay, moving to the two below the circle."

"No, Lucas," I said quickly. "Get the second brush. Shade...give him your vial, babe."

"What's that?" Mom asked.

"It's Chance's blood," Shade said.

"What? When did you...never mind," Mom said. "Lucas, do what you need to."

"Do the first symbol in my blood, Lucas. Wanda, there should be some lancets next to Lucas or somewhere in the circle. Mom, I need some of your blood, too. Just a few drops."

"Got it," Wanda said. "This shouldn't hurt at all."

"First symbol done. Do I clean the brush or something?"

"No, it's fine. Do the second symbol quick. Then...you're going to have to use the lancet to put three drops of your blood on the outer ring of the circle."

"That's...the hard way, isn't it? Okay, second symbol done. Okay, Wanda, do it."

"Tyler," I heard Shade say. "Catch." The next thing I heard as the sound of plastic hitting flesh.

Then Dee screamed.

Up to that moment, I thought her sobs were the worst sound I would ever hear in my life. But the scream that she uttered now was pure agony, unbridled and unrestrained, a pure note of torment that sounded like it was being ripped from inside her until her lungs were empty. It wasn't the high pitched squeal of a skinned knee, but the full throated wail that defied comfort. I knew that sound. I'd made it plenty of times myself. Even over the phone, I could hear the ragged, gasping breath she took, and cringed when she let out another scream that slowly dwindled.

"What is that?" Lucas asked.

"Deirdre!" Mom cried.

"No, let her go," Shade said, her own voice suddenly uncertain. "That's the attack. Chance, the energy strand is inside the circle, but it's…it's like it isn't hurting her any more. She's standing up, and there's a kind of barrier around her. Dee, what are you-"

The next sound that reached my ears was an animalistic howl of pure hate.

"Oh my God!" Shade said. "She grabbed it, just like you did! She's pulling on it and-" The connection went, but a heartbeat later, the world went white outside my window, thunder cracked and boomed across campus, and my windows rattled. My mystic senses buzzed as energy flooded the air.

"Way to go little sis!" I whispered as I felt the feedback wash over me. Nothing in the world could have prepared Dee's attackers for the pure wrath of a ten-year-old. I *really* didn't want to be one of her foes just then.

I dialed Lucas again, and Tyler picked up.

"Is she okay?" I demanded. In the background, I heard incoherent noises, and my heart jumped into my throat. "Is anyone hurt?"

"Yeah, they're all fine. Here, Dee wants to talk to you," Tyler said.

"Chance? Are you okay?" Dee asked, sounding like a ten-year-old again. A tired ten year old, but a ten year old all the same.

237

"Yeah, I'm fine, sis. Are *you* okay?" I asked. My heart was racing, and I suppressed the urge to laugh.

"Yeah," she said, her tone defiant. "Thanks."

"Good. Whatever you did, you sure kicked their ass. I'm glad you're okay. Do you remember where you felt it first?"

"Yeah, my shoulder started hurting. But Chance, you've gotta help those people. I could feel how much they're hurting them. You've gotta help them. And one of them wanted me to tell you something."

"They had a message?"

"Yeah, the pretty one with the dark hair. She said to search your feelings, stupid. But, she didn't mean it like she was being mean or anything."

"Thanks, sis," I said. "Can you give the phone to Lucas?"

"So, was that mage enough?" Lucas asked a moment later.

"Mage enough, brother," I said, suddenly unable to say more. "Mage enough. Can you put me on speaker?"

"You're on the air," Lucas said a few seconds later.

"Thank you, everyone," I said. "I can't say it loud enough or hard enough. Thank you." I sniffled and someone giggled.

"Thank all of you," Mom echoed. "You saved my little girl." Her voice cracked, which made the tears roll down my face as well. The surge of emotions I'd felt earlier welled up inside me, and I leaned back in my chair.

"Chance?" Dee said in the awkward silence that followed. "Are you gonna kick their...butts?"

"Yeah, Dee," I said. "They picked on my little sister. You bet I am."

"Whatever you do to them," Wanda said, her soft voice laced with steel, "they deserve it, and worse. So...I lend you Her Fury." I sat up straight at that. If *Wanda* sounded pissed, then someone had just earned a special place in

238

Hell. There was a rustling as someone took the phone, and I heard Shade's voice next.

"Be careful," she said. "I need you to come back to me."

"I will," I said.

"You better. I love you."

"And I love you."

"Chance, sweetie?" Mom's voice came.

"Yeah, Mom."

"Son, just let the Sentinels handle this. You're coming home just as soon as I can get up there and pull you out of that awful place. So start packing. And we're going to have a long talk about some of the things you and Shade are doing, young man. But…I'm so proud of you."

"Thanks, Mom," I said.

"You're not going to let the Sentinels handle this, are you?"

"Would you?"

Mom sighed. "Not at your age, no. And if I thought I could…no, I'd handle it myself."

"Love you, Mom," I said before I closed the connection. My emotions were starting to get all tangled and sentimental, but what I needed just then was the cold rage that had helped me beat Dominic King and Dulka and every other threat to my family, not this upswelling of affection for everyone close to me. I shook my head as I tried to reach for the anger that was usually so close to the surface, but it was like trying to blow up a tire with a big hole in it. No matter how mad I tried to get, the feeling just seemed out of reach.

"Search your feelings," I said. "Right, there's some useful advice. Why can't it be something simple like, 'the bad guys are here, go beat them up' or something like that?" I said. Then I stopped and frowned. I couldn't tap my anger, but I was getting all caught up in love. One of the primary emotions cambions couldn't feed on. But I was

239

a veritable buffet of strong primal feelings that she *could* feed on. The strange emotional numbness I'd been wallowing in since homecoming wasn't grief. It was almost like exhaustion.

She'd taken one of her gloves off to touch my face right before she stepped out of the circle. Somehow, she'd been feeding on me the whole time.

Search your feelings, stupid. Desiree had done more than sacrifice herself to save Kiya. She had given me a direct line to her attackers.

Finally, I could go on the offensive.

"Check, assholes," I growled.

Chapter 16
~ Know the mind of your enemy. Use his own thoughts
against him. ~ The Left Hand of Death.

If anyone ever wondered why wizards act like assholes
sometimes, it's because we have to keep secrets all the
damn time while still having to be as honest as we can.
When Hoshi finally made it back to the room, I had to stop
working on the divining spell that was supposed to help me
find Desiree's soul.

"You look a little worse for wear," I said as he closed
the door behind him. His lips were swollen and there was
grass in his hair and all over his jeans.

"No, I don't," he said. "I look amazing. You're just
jealous because I pull this off without even trying."

"Your shirt's inside out," I pointed out. He looked
down at his torso, then hastily grabbed the hem of his shirt
and pulled it over his head.

"Great, next thing you know, everyone will be doing
that," he said as he pulled his shirt back down.

"So, how'd it go?" I said, trying to sound casual. "With
the water spirit, I mean."

"I'm...not sure," Hoshi said, his expression going
serious. "I mean, I think it went good. There was this
shimmery place in front of her that she talked to for about
an hour."

"But?" I said. There was a hint of loss in his voice.

"She's probably not going to stay at Franklin. She
talked about having to go gather her tools. Walking the
Earth is how she described it. Can't say I blame her. It isn't
like she's learned much that's really helped her here." He
sat down on the bed, for the first time since I'd met him not
smiling.

"She's a shaman," I said as I took the desk chair on his
side of the room. "This place trains wizards. I can't see

how Franklin would have much to offer her. For that matter, I'm not even sure what it offers you."

"Same thing it teaches you. Technique. But yeah, not much on the whole how to live with a fox spirit inside me, or how to control my *kitsunebi*. Mostly it's been standard wizard stuff."

"That's a load of crap," I groused. "You need better training than this."

"There is no *better* training than the Franklin Academy," Hoshi said with a smile. "Says so right in the brochure." I rolled my eyes and made a face at that.

"Yeah, right."

"Seriously, my dad thinks I'm just not applying myself, and my mother keeps telling me that I need to get all the superstition my aunt taught me out of my head."

"Dude, you turn into a fox! I've watched you change." I shook my head, unable to believe his parents could be so blind. "Your mom's a kitsune! How does she...never mind, I shouldn't ask." Hoshi's face was a mask of hurt, and I knew I had walked right up to a line and stomped around a little on the other side of it. Face burning, I got up and walked to my side of the room.

"You know, later on, when you try to apologize for this, I'm gonna tell you that you didn't do anything wrong," he finally said. "I just wanted to get that out of the way before you said something and things got awkward."

"I had no business saying that," I said.

"Man, you just say what I've been thinking my whole life. I just never did actually say it."

"I'm not real sure I even did."

"No," he said. He sighed and leaned forward. "My dad's Japanese but Mom's Chinese. Chinese kitsune aren't as...popular as Japanese. Their name, *huli jing*, it's like calling a woman a homewrecker in Mandarin and Cantonese. So my mom didn't tell my dad she wasn't human until after I was born. He didn't deal with it very well. So she does everything she can to act like she's human. I'm not sure if sending me here was to pretend I was a mage or to get me out of sight so Dad would forget."

"Or both," I said.

He nodded and leaned back. "You know what I want to do? Call my mom's best friend and see if she still wants to teach me. If she'll still talk to me."

"Is she a kitsune, too?"

"Yeah. Mom stopped talking to most of her kitsune friends right after I was born, but she made her best friend my *kai ma*."

"*Kai ma*?" I asked.

"It's like a god mother," he said. "She asked me if I wanted to learn what it meant to be kitsune one day when I was like nine, but Mom told her no."

"Well, there's only one way to find out," I said. "Call her and ask."

His phone beeped at him, and he smiled when he checked the screen. "Kiya," he said as he held the phone up, then turned his attention to tapping out a reply. I left him to that and went back to my clandestine plans.

My phone buzzed in my hand, waking me from the fitful sleep I'd been in. I turned it toward my face to see the time, and breathed a sigh of relief. In place of my usual horrors, I'd dreamt at least twice that I'd woken up late, and I'd awakened several times afraid of that very thing, only to check my phone and discover it was still early. The heavy quilt slid off my legs as I got up, still in my cargo pants and black t-shirt. Junkyard raised his head and looked at me from the bed.

"Need you to stay here this time, buddy," I said. He lowered his head to his front paws and gave me the sad puppy eyes, but I shook my head and grabbed my leather jacket and my combat boots. The hardwood floors were cold even through my socks as I slipped out into the hallway. Once I had my coat on, I headed for the stairwell. I didn't put my boots on until I was out the front door.

Ren flew down and landed on the stone as I was tying the laces on the second boot, his wings muted. "I hate fall and winter," he said. He pitched his voice softly.

"Fall isn't so bad in Missouri," I said, my own breath misting in the cold air.

"So, how do you plan on finding…by the way, *what* are you even looking for?"

"Souls, one in particular. That's been what these people have been after this whole time. But it didn't really hit me that I might be able to find them until I figured out that Desiree was still feeding on me." I pulled one of the little gemstones from my pocket. I'd attached a length of string to it to make it into an improvised pendulum.

"Really?" Ren said. He lifted into the air and followed me down the steps. "What does that have to do with being able to find them?"

"It means that they're not consuming them yet. They're storing them." The pendulum hung straight down for a moment. When I sent a flow of magick through it, it began to spin in a slow circle.

"But how do you track someone else's soul?" Ren asked.

"You don't. I'm tracking *mine.*" With nothing but my own energy to work from, the stone started to swing in narrower circuits, until one end of its arc pointed across the quad, straight at the Denham Building. "Come on," I said.

I took off at a jog across the quad, my boots making only the slightest bit of noise as I ran. Ren flew ahead, his wings a whisper in the predawn air. When I got there, he had the door open for me, and I slipped inside. This time, when I dropped the pendulum, the stone began to float the moment I ran magick through it.

"What the…" Ren said, then went silent as it pointed up and to the right.

244

"Okay," I said under my breath. "That rules out secret rituals in the basement."

"I would have known about those," Ren said. We took the stairs up to the second floor, and the pendulum still shot upward. It did the same on the third floor. On the fourth floor, the angle was more shallow, but it still pointed up.

"Ooookay," I whispered. "How do we get into the attic?"

"This way," Ren said. He flew down the hallway and stopped at the door of a classroom. "I'll be right back." He sped off, and I reached into the pocket of my jacket to grab my chameleon amulet. I watched the world shimmer once I activated it, and then settled down to wait. A few minutes later, the door clicked open, and Ren zipped out into the hallway. I turned my head toward him, and the world came back into focus. I followed him into the room, and he zipped straight back to the supply closet. Four classrooms fed into the diamond shaped room, with doors opening onto two different hallways. Ren pointed to one wall, where I could see a wooden ladder affixed. I climbed up the ladder and pushed the thick wooden hatch up. It moved with surprising ease, and I grabbed my wand in alarm.

When no one attacked me, I stuck my head up into the room, and saw that the hatch was on a counterweight system. Ren rocketed past me as I climbed up, returning just as I was standing up straight.

"Over here," he said, then zipped off toward a door. I followed, and found my hand hesitating at the door knob. My heart was beating faster and the bottom seemed to fall out of my stomach as I felt the adrenaline surge through me. When I moved my hand another inch toward the door, every finger began to shake and curl up like claws, and my skin felt like it was trying to crawl up my arm. For a split second, I considered opening my mystic senses, but just making myself aware of them made my stomach turn.

245

"You feel it, too," Ren said from over my shoulder. "What in the Nine Hells is it?"

"Nothing good," I said. My fight or flight reaction was getting worse, and I was having to concentrate to keep my breathing steady. *Great,* I thought. *Fight or flight, and I can barely touch the part that says 'fight.'* "I need something positive, something Desiree can't feed on, so I can make myself open this door."

"Like positive feelings?"

"Exactly."

"Not exactly familiar territory for you, huh?" Ren mused. "Well, let's see, there's confidence, faith, love, compa-"

"Wait, go back," I said. "Confidence…"

"Faith and love."

"Faith and love," I said. "She lent me Her Fury." Wanda's Goddess had lent me Her wrath once. I couldn't tap the anger, because it had to come from outside of me, but the motivation came from something Desiree couldn't feed on. Love. Every amazing, terrible thing that I'd ever done, I realized, had come from that. I'd survived the fight with Dominic King to free Shade and the rest of her Pack. I'd pulled the trigger and killed him to save my mom and my sister. Defied the entire Conclave to save Wanda. And I'd put myself back in my father's and Dulka's clutches to protect my friends. And right now, my friend's soul was on the other side of the door in front of me.

Now, the hard thing was going to be using my hand to open the door, instead of my foot or a magickal battering ram. Flesh still crawling, I reached for the door knob and turned it, ready for any chamber of horrors that might be waiting for me.

The room on the other side was…tidy. Clinical. A circular table had been set up in the middle of the room. Thirteen crystals were set into smaller circles on the outer edge of the table. Seven of them glowed. A set of three

246

chalkboards were mounted on the far wall, covered in writing. The two on the left and right were magickal formulae, while the one in the middle held only one thing on its green surface: a circle. Chalk dust marred the board where parts had been erased and redone. A writing desk had been set up between the chalk boards and the circular table, and I could see metallic sheets laid out on it. On the right, jars held alchemical agents and tools, and on the left…

"Mammon," I said as I walked toward the altar.

"He's bad, right?" Ren asked.

"He is the horror Sleeping C'tolsh Moloch serves," I said as I pulled my phone out. "He was what was waiting in the Abyss when the Morning Star was cast into it."

"Wow…he's been around for a while. But shouldn't you be careful about saying those names out loud?"

"Maybe," I said as I took a step back from the altar. Now I had several pictures of it, I turned and snapped one of the blackboards and the central table. As much as I wanted to lay waste to the altar, I still had other problems to deal with. Like how to get seven souls back into their bodies. "He was cast into a prison after the Light Bringer took over the Nine Hells. Him and all the things that served him. You can't summon him; not even with a full circle, a sacrifice and a lawyer."

I turned my attention to the circle of crystals on the table. Each one was labeled, and each one had smaller crystals set around it. I could feel the power pressing against my mystic senses as I got closer, even with them intentionally dormant. The cards by each soul container were written in a precise hand, with detailed descriptions of strengths, date taken, etc. Everything about them as there, except one thing.

No names.

With all of the info presented, the names had been left off. Each one was labeled Subject, and then a number.

They'd been stripped of as much of their humanity as possible. Truth was, if I were ripping someone's soul out of their body, I'd want to avoid looking at what I'd done, and I sure as the Nine Hells wouldn't want to know who I was screwing over.

An arc of dark purple energy jumped from the crystal I was in front of when I tried to touch it, leaving my right hand numb. I turned my hand to look at it, revealing an angry red welt.

"Their shields too strong, Keptin," I said in a bad Russian accent.

"Now what?" Ren asked.

"I find a way to get stronger." I moved around the table until I found myself looking at a subject who displayed high levels of empathy and Infernal magick. Even in my pocket, I could feel the pendulum tug at my jacket. Now it was time to use some of the minor magicks I'd been learning in Evocation class.

"Manus protegat, et absorbuit," I said softly, then put my now shielded hands toward the crystal. Like before, dark purple energy reached out as my hands got close. Instead of flinching away, I let the variant of the shield spell absorb the energy and put my thumbs and index fingers together, then pulled them apart, creating a sheet of purple in the open space between them. *"Dicere intra,"* I intoned.

"Chance!" Desiree's voice came through. Light purple static formed into a rough semblance of her face. "Listen to me. We don't have much time. I can't fight my way out of this. There are too many of them holding us in. You've got to cut them off from the circle somehow."

"I can try to do that," I said, my stomach suddenly unknotting in relief.

"Good. I'm glad to see you and all, but you've got to know, one of them is planning something, and I don't think the others know about it. I don't know what it is, but I don't think it's good. All I can get is a sense of greed. But if you can break their hold over the circle, I think I can help you restore the souls to their bodies. We just have to…wait…someone's sensed what we're doing. Get out of here until you're ready to fight back." At the far end of the table, I could see a crystal glow brighter, then another.

"I'll be back for you, Des," I said. "I promise I won't let you down."

"I know," she said, and the staticy face smiled. "You don't have it in you." The sheet of energy went blank, and I dismissed the spell, then pulled my hands away.

"Ren, stay sharp, someone might be coming," I said as I hustled around the table, some instinct warning me to avoid the brightening crystals. I had pictures of almost everything in the room, but I still wanted to record what was on the desk.

Thick sheets of vellum were laid out on the writing desk, and I tried to snap pictures of each one. Even without reading the words, I could guess what they were by the way they were laid out: contracts. But I doubted they were offering their own souls in exchange for a damn thing. Once I had pics of the whole desk top, I turned my attention to the raised section at the front. Inkwells and nib pens were scattered across the top, and blank pieces of vellum lay in the empty space below it. I reached below the edge of the desk and pulled. A wide, shallow drawer slid open, and I looked down to see a revolver laid atop sheets of paper and pens. On instinct, I grabbed the gun and looked it over careful to keep the barrel pointed at the ceiling. It was a pretty standard model, and the cylinder swung out when I hit the release just above the trigger. The six rounds fell out into my waiting hand, and I dropped one into my pocket, then closed the cylinder back up and set it as close to where I found it as I could.

"Someone just came in through the tunnels," Ren hissed. "They're between us and the doors."

"Time to go," I said. I hustled to the door and then went past the trap door that went down into the supply room. Set in the far wall was a small window. That was my way out.

"Are you crazy?" Ren hissed as I crouched next to the little white painted frame and pulled out my wand. "Those windows haven't been opened since…well, before the turn of the last century, I think."

"*Libero porta,*" I whispered as I moved the wand in a tight circle. Chips of paint and puffs of dust erupted around the edges of the window, and I tucked my wand away.

"Wizard," I said as I pulled the bottom frame up.

"More like an apprentice. It's still another two stories to the ground. Unless you're a sprite, too, you're still kinda screwed."

I put one leg out the window, then leaned my body out and felt along the rough stone wall for what I wanted. It didn't take long before my fingers found an inch-wide ledge to grab onto. "Nope, still a wizard." I swung out, holding my weight on my fingertips as I reached for the next handhold, this one much easier to see. Then I was in range of the thick conduit pipe that ran electricity to the building. It ran up the side of the building from the top of the breezeway that connected the halls together. Another conduit led to the roof of the next building, and I used it to climb to the roof, then ran across and used the one on the far side to climb down. It was a slow process, but I repeated in once more before I jumped to the ground and sprinted toward the door of Jefferson Hall. As I went, I dropped the other five bullets from the revolver in the grass. Ren flew ahead, and when I reached the door, he had it pushed open an inch to let me in. Junkyard was waiting with him, his tail wagging to greet me.

"Here, take this, and bring it to me after lunch," I said as I handed him the last bullet and my cell phone. He flew off without a word, and I sprinted for the stairwell. I made it up the stairs and across the hall without running into anyone. In the gray predawn light, Hoshi was sprawled across his bed, a manga book next to one hand, mouth open and drooling a little. I figured at least a third of the girls on campus would think he was too cute for words. I wished I could just let him sleep in. It was Sunday, the one day for just that. But someone had attacked my sister less than twenty-four hours ago, and I had just found the lair of the people behind it. And I had seen the contracts on the table. All thirteen of them. Whoever was behind this had a full coven of warlocks behind them. I was in deeper than I had originally thought.

"Hoshi," I said as I kicked the side of his bed. His eyes snapped open and he sat up halfway as he tried to focus.

"I roll to evade," he slurred. "Where's my dice?"

"Wake up," I told him. "I need your help."

Chapter 17

Stewart and Rebecca were sitting together at lunch, the house power couple holding court at the cool table near the front of the cafeteria, right next to the soda fountain. The usual snickers and sly looks started up as I approached, but they didn't last long. On cue, someone got up and went to the soda machine, effectively blocking it for a moment. But when I veered toward Stewart, there was a moment of silence.

"Here to whine about something, thug?" one of the guys at the table said.

"No, I imagine he hears enough of that from you," I said. A low "Ooooh," drifted up from the table, and Stewart glared daggers at the offender. Undeterred, the guy got up and tried to loom over me.

"You got a problem, charity case?" the guy said. He had a good four inches on me, and probably twenty pounds. But his hands were soft and his stance was so far forward that he was almost off balance.

"No," I said, letting a little frost creep into my voice. "Why? Did you want one?"

The guy leaned back a little at my tone. "Don't push me, Fortunato," he said. "Or I'll kick your ass." He took a step as if to go around me, but his shoulder 'accidentally' hit mine. I moved with it, and he stumbled a little before he moved on.

"What's up, Chance?" Stewart said when I turned to him.

"I was hoping to be able to talk to my *brother* tonight," I said. "I need his help."

Stewart's eyes narrowed. "I can arrange that. Is it true what some people are saying?"

"No," I said. "I don't have a tail. Or horns."

"That you're really helping out the Sentinels," he said.

"You know I couldn't say anything if I was," I told him.

"Come on, Chance," he said, leaning forward. "They attacked me, too. It isn't like we're not in this together. Brother to one."

"Brother to all," I finished. I leaned down and lowered my voice. "Okay I may have offered them some advice a couple of times, but it isn't like they exactly trust me, okay? That's why I need my brothers to back me up. I'll lay it all out tonight, I promise. There's just a lot I can't go into in the open. Not everyone can be trusted, you know?"

He nodded and gave me a knowing smile. "We'll take care of it."

"I knew I could count on you," I said as I straightened and walked away. Hoshi caught up to me in the stairwell.

"So, does the Ninja Mage Detective Agency have a special badge or something?" he asked. "Or do we all wear the same kind of hat but in different colors?"

"There's a company trench coat," I said. "And you need to do something crazy with your hair."

"Hey, my hair is perfect."

"I know. It isn't fair. So, are we good?"

"Team Ninja Mage Detective is ready."

"Good," I said as I opened the door to our room. "Now all I have to do is make a couple more surprises, and we're set." Ren was already inside, lounging against Junkyard.

"Are you sure this is a good idea?" Hoshi asked. "There are a dozen Sentinels on campus. I'm sure they could handle this."

"Sentinels are great soldiers, but what they know about Infernal magick wouldn't fill a thimble halfway. And these people are probably on a par with most Council members for sheer power. So yeah, they *might* be able to handle these warlocks, and they *might* be able to stop what they're trying to do. But I guarantee you, it would be a coin toss, and even if they did win, there would be a lot of dead Sentinels."

"And we're going to do better with a bunch of half-trained students?"

"No," I said. "I'm going to do better with a bunch of half-trained students, a sprite and a demon trained warlock…and a clever plan."

"Oh, well, we have a sprite. That's a game changer."

"Don't forget the clever plan," I said.

"How could we possibly lose? Seriously, why are *you* the one who has to fix this?"

"Because the Sentinels don't know how to restore the souls of the victims. Now, I need to make a phone call, then get to work on a couple of things."

It was almost dark by the time I got everything done. I tucked my focuses into my jeans pocket and handed Hoshi a sheet of paper with his part of things outlined on it.

"Why am I doing this again?" he asked.

"Because, no matter what, you know it's the right thing to do."

"Damn, is a little more light-hearted banter too much to ask?" Hoshi said.

"Not any more," I said as I headed for the door. "I need you serious, focused, and on task."

Hoshi swallowed and got to his feet. "Yeah, I can do that."

"Team Ninja Mage Detective, for the win, right?" I held up a fist.

"For the win," he said and rapped his knuckles against mine.

Junkyard and Ren followed me out the door and down the stairs. Tonight, Junkyard wore his harness and pack, and Ren buzzed above him. As we made our way across the quad, Ren banked right and ended up flying beside me. His

255

wings weren't glowing, and he carried what looked like long knitting needles in his belt.

"Here, you better have some of this," he said as he fished something out of his pouch. He handed me two foil wrapped lumps.

"What is it?"

"We call it *tanwuud*," he said with a shrug. "It means fuel for the body, or body fuel. It's pemmican with an herbal extract that cranks your body up to eleven and gives it the fuel it needs to do it all at once. For non-sprites, we usually don't give more than a couple of doses like I just gave you."

"Is it addictive?"

"Only if you take too much of it. And then…not for long. The human body can't handle being cranked up that high for very long."

"Got it. Take sparingly, if at all. How long does it last?"

"About an hour. Please, promise you'll be careful with it."

"Don't worry, I don't plan on taking it unless I really have to. But I also know me…odds are good I will. You know what to do on your end." I stopped and went to one knee so I was on a level with Junkyard. "You go with Ren, buddy. Take care of him, and stay safe, okay?" He let out a short bark, then licked my chin.

"Don't worry, I'll take care of him," Ren said. I stood and nodded, letting them head their way without another word. It was time to get this party started.

Stewart was waiting next to a boat by the lake, his cloak over his arm. "I'm glad you're finally going to let us help out with this," he said as the boat slid off the shore. He pointed to a bundle in the bow of the boat, and I found an extra cloak and a sword. I pulled my mask from my pocket and put it on, then slid the cloak around my shoulders. Stewart guided the boat around the southern tip of the island, and a row of boats parked on the bank came into view. We slid to a stop at one end of the row and got out. I let Stewart lead the way to the meeting place, and found myself amidst the masked group of the Shadow Regiment again.

"Brothers," Stewart said as soon as we reached the gathering. "The way…is not safe. We've known this for some time this semester, but we've been able to do damn little about it. Tonight, that changes. One of our brothers comes to us seeking aid in fighting this evil! Will we fulfill our vows?"

A ragged chorus of "Aye!" answered, and I stepped up beside Stewart.

"Someone has been attacking our fellow students," I said. "We all know someone who was taken at homecoming. Up until now, we've been powerless to fight them because they always struck from hiding." A low murmur rose at that. "We didn't know who they were, and we didn't know how to fight them. But now…now I know enough to let us take the fight to them."

"Do you know who they are?" someone asked.

"Yes," I said. "I know two names. One is Josie Hart, the girl we were told was missing at the start of term. The other," I said, then paused to get control of myself. "The other walks among us, right now."

"Who?" several voices demanded.

"One of the Shadow Regiment?" another member demanded.

"You're gonna need some proof," Stanwicke said, his voice and hair giving away his identity. In my pocket, my phone hummed, the first part of my plan coming together a few seconds late.

"Oh, I've got proof," I said as I pulled the phone out of my pocket. "Right here, though it's proof by absence. See, a few nights ago, I snuck into an abandoned room. Josie Hart's old room, to be exact. She kept a visual record of the victims, past and future. And first off, I saw the photo of Leonard Cargill. But no picture of Josie. I saw pictures of almost every other victim, except one." Silence fell as I turned to face the culprit. "Stewart Hampton." A gasp went up at that, and Stewart scoffed.

"You're out of line, Chance," he said. "I was attacked just like the others."

"That's what it looked like, at first," I said. "But the deeper I looked, the less it was like the others. See, first, you're not on their victim shrine, and second, all of the other victims were talented in some way. Either strong in one element, powerful empaths or just strong mages in general. But you and Josie…you were mediocre at best. Neither of you fit the pattern. And I saw the circle they used to attack you. It was never designed to take your soul. Sure, it might have hurt a little, but you were never in any real danger. Was it supposed to get me to trust you or something?"

Stewart took a step back and flung the hem of his cloak aside and brought up his wand. The tip glowed red, and I could feel the noisome power being funneled into it. "You idiot," he said as he took another step. "That wasn't about gaining your trust, it was to get you to show us how you would defend against our attacks. And you did exactly what we wanted you to do. You showed your hand, and now we can blast our way through your defenses." He pointed the wand at me and uttered something ugly sounding. A black beam lanced out of his wand and hit me in the chest like an elephant on steroids, sending me sailing through the air.

I got to my feet, my movements slow and deliberate, and faced a wide-eyed Stewart.

"How…you can't be…" he sputtered. "We neutralized your defenses!"

I looked down at the glowing red blood ward on my chest, then back at him. "I got new defenses. Now, let's try yours out. *Ictus!*" The kinetic bolt shot across the clearing,

258

but not before Stewart got a shield of his own up. My spell shattered his protection ward like glass and sent him to the edge of the clearing, twice the distance he'd sent me.

"You broke your oath, Stewart," I said as he tried to get to his feet. "That carries consequences. Your magick is broken. You were never that strong to begin with, and you didn't take the time to master technique." He scrambled to his feet as I walked toward him. "It was all there in your files."

"I'm a Hampton!" he yelled. "I *deserve* power, I was *bred* to it! Not some entitled nobody from a tainted bloodline. And not some pampered little shit like Lodge! There was no way he should have been stronger than me!" He flung a fire bolt at me, but it splattered against my telekinetic shield like a bug.

"It's over Stewart," I said. "Shadow Regiment, we have been betrayed by one of our own. Stand with me."

"It isn't that simple," another voice said from behind me. I turned to see five of the Regiment facing off with the other seven. Fortunately, there were more white wands than there were red ones, but the nasty surprises weren't over. Another person had stepped into the clearing, and her wand was also glowing red. "I never made that promise. My magick is intact. And you know how powerful those souls make us."

"Ginger?" Lance said, his voice high and wavering. "You can't be part of this baby."

"Don't 'baby' me," Ginger sneered. "I have bigger dreams than taking your last name. I'm twice as powerful as you'll ever be." Her wand moved, and a red bolt screamed across the clearing to hit Lance in the chest and send him flying into the brush.

"Highwaymen, fall back!" I yelled as more bolts flew. Most went wide as the rest of the Regiment figured out that their shield spells were no match for what they were facing.

259

Only one made contact, and it was a glancing blow, but it was still powerful enough to knock its target flying.

"*Ictus latior!*" I yelled. As the wide TK blast plowed into the line of false Highwaymen, I plunged into the brush. A few steps in, I found Lance clutching his chest but still struggling to his feet. I sent another bolt behind me as I grabbed his shoulder and pulled him to his feet. He cried out, but he stumbled along with me. The other six Highwaymen were staggering to the boats and pushing off.

"Come on, Lance, I need you to drive," I said as I helped him into the nearest boat. "Head for the Grotto," I told him as we slid back into the water. With our three boats out, I sent a series of bolts across the water and splintered the two remaining boats on the shore. "Head for the Grotto!" I yelled across the water to the other boats.

"They'll hear you," Lance said, his voice tight from pain.

"That's the idea," I said as the other boats turned to follow our course. We were almost to the shore when I caught movement on the island's bank. Seconds later, the boat was scraping across the sand of the bank. I got out and went to the back to get a shoulder under Lance's arm, and we hobbled onto the bank together. Moments later, someone else was at my side.

"Hurry," the guy said as he put Lance's other arm over his shoulder. "They iced over the lake. They're running across."

"We're almost there," I said as we rounded the corner. The Grotto was right in front of us, and I shoved Lance and the other guy forward. "Go. There will be someone waiting." I turned at the edge of the circle to face the oncoming assault.

Most of them came on foot, but Stewart and Ginger were flying. It wasn't the superhero style, either, like they were laying flat. This was the full on, upright super-villain stance with the arms out, one leg bent a little. Ginger even had the toe point going on with her straight leg. Hoshi came up behind me, and I could feel the circles activating behind me.

"Here they come," he said. "Trademarked villain pose and everything." The others came to a stop a few yards away, and I took a step backward as Stewart and Ginger dropped toward the grass. They touched down in front of their other comrades and took a step forward.

"I gotta hand it to you both, great form on the entrance, especially you Ginger. And you *really* stuck the super-villain landing," I said.

"You think they're gonna monologue?" Hoshi asked.

"I was kind of hoping they would." Seven wands came up, all glowing red. I raised my right hand, then closed it, and a shimmering field of energy closed in front of me as multiple blasts slammed into it.

"Okay, they aren't fooling around," Hoshi said. I turned and looked at the circles inside the main circle, which was now acting as a protective barrier for us. "Now what?"

"I walk ancient ways," I said as I held my hand out to him. He touched the edge of the circle, then placed his palm against mine. With a thought, I released control of the circle to him. "And you make sure the circle holds."

"Not sure I get that first part."

I found the point I needed, and placed my foot on it. The blasts continued outside, distracting me. "When the founding fathers started this school," I said, trying to focus on what I was doing. "This circle was already here. Only it wasn't just a circle back then." Talking about it helped me keep me focused on my intent, and each footstep glowed as I moved further into the Pattern woven into the circle.

"What...was it?" Hoshi asked.

"The Greeks would have called it a labyrinth. The First Nations each had their own names for it, but they all came down to one thing, the dance toward the Source, what white

261

people called the Great Spirit. Back in the day, like, when Atlantis was still above sea level, aspiring wizards would walk something like this to awaken their power. Shamans among the Native Americans sometimes walked them as part of their path to initiation. But, if a mage or shaman who was already Awakened walked the path…" I stopped talking for a few seconds as I met resistance to my movement. I pushed against it and focused on the moment, on the magick that flowed through me. My foot touched the ground. "If a mage *could* walk the path again," I said, "then it was like they were Awakened all over again." Another attack hammered the circle, and Hoshi turned his attention to it, letting me focus on what I was doing. Energy moved through me, going up my legs and spreading through my chest with every step. As it did, I felt pinpricks like embers in my bones. The body was an imperfect conduit for pure magick. Prolonged casting would eventually exhaust most mages. But for me…for me it started to hurt. Every broken bone I'd ever suffered made me an increasingly less suitable channel for magick. And I'd suffered a lot of broken bones.

The memory of my first night as Dulka's slave replayed in my head, and I grunted in pain as I took another step. He'd started with the bones in my right leg, then moved to my left arm. Back in the present, I winced as I felt those two bones break again with the next step. I felt Dulka flip me over in my past, then his taloned finger scraping at my forehead, scraping at my *brain*. Another step, and I relived the way it felt to have him force my Third Eye open, unable to block out anything mystical, even to the point of experiencing the recent past, present and near future all at once. It had taken me days to figure out how to close myself off from all of that. Like those days, I walked blind, putting one foot in front of the other, every bone in my body burning inside.

Another footfall and I found myself facing the center of the circle, my footsteps glowing white in the meandering path behind me. Only seconds had passed, but I still felt like it had been days. Now I stood in the Source. All magick flowed from it, and it was vast. Even a glimpse of the whole thing pushed the edges of my sanity, but I had to look. In an instant, I felt myself turned inside out, then put back together. Before me lay paths back to the world I knew. One was the same route I'd taken. I would return the same person who stepped in, broken in a lot of places and no better for the trip, all memory of this moment gone. Another showed me the life that could have been, one where my mom won custody of me, and I was never enslaved to Dulka, where I was a normal kid until I met Mr. Chomsky. Other variants played themselves out in front of me, different versions of my life that could be. All of them tempted me.

I took a step forward. The moment my foot moved, I felt an awful, beautiful presence focus on me.

Choose a path.

"I did," I said. "Mine. This is who I am, and as fucked up as I might be, as much as I might want to have a different past, a different life, I can't be those people. I wish I could."

The memory of what might have been will haunt you. You will wish for those moments for the rest of your life. You will always yearn for what you could have had.

"I know," I said as I took another step forward, forging a new path out. "But I need to remember this. I need to remember that I chose who I am, that I turned all the crap that happened to me into something better. I forged myself into this. This is who I am, and it's who I need to be."

It is a good choice. It is not the wisest one, but this is not a moment for wisdom. Go, child of misfortune, return to your world, reborn as you were...and more.

263

My foot touched the edge of the circle, and I was back in the world. Behind me, each of the minor circles inside the main circle was active, each column of magick a solid cylinder of energy, concealing what was inside. Scholarship students stood beside each circle, their hands pressed against it, but each of them also with a hand extended toward the main circle, all of their faces etched in deep concentration.

"It's about damn time," Hoshi said. "We can't hold this up much longer. Are you ready?"

"Are you?" A chorus of replies sounded around me. "Then let's put boot to ass."

Hoshi turned back to face the outside of the circle and put his hands up in front of his face, then brought them down quickly. Outside, the seven warlocks paused for a split second, taken aback by what they saw waiting for them.

Hoshi didn't give them a chance to recover. "Now!" he yelled. Behind me, a dozen circles came down in rapid succession, each revealing what was inside: elementals. Some held one, others held more. Fire blazed, water rippled, air shimmered and massive earth elementals just loomed. Once more, Hoshi led the way, summoning bright green fire around his hands, his *kitsunebi*, something no one here had encountered in a fight. His first bolt took one of the opposing warlocks in the shoulder and knocked him to the ground. Then it was on, elementals moving forward, air and fire spirits rushing to be the first into the fray, the fluid water elementals sweeping to the sides while the rocky forms of the earth elementals started a slow, implacable charge. Surprise turned to fear and rage on the faces of the warlocks, and they let loose with attacks as fast as they could. Then the rest of the crew got in on the attack, unleashing everything they knew how to, some from wands, others from focuses. And still the warlocks held. But in the midst of it all, I saw Stewart and Ginger rise into

264

the air, their heads turned to look over their shoulders. They spared their comrades a look, then met each other's eyes for a moment.

They ran.

"Stick to the plan!" I yelled at Hoshi as I ducked and crab walked below the onslaught of magickal attacks. Then I was clear of the circle. Behind me, Hoshi called out to fall back as I broke into a sprint, then stopped for a moment and dug one of the foil packets of *tanwuud* out of my pocket. Ren was right, it tasted like meat and fruit, but had the consistency of peanut butter. I had barely swallowed the first bite when I felt the surge of energy. My feet seemed to be light as feathers, and I took off, reveling in the feel of the wind on my face. Overhead, I could see my targets floating along, slowly getting closer as I gained on them. Like I had thought, they were headed toward Denham Hall. I hit the top of the slope I was on and saw multicolored flashes of energy lancing back and forth in front of me. Two Sentinels stood with their backs to Denham Hall, squaring off against a single warlock. As I got closer, I could see a third Sentinel laying on the ground. I spared a quick look at the flying duo. They had their arms raised, wands pointed toward the Sentinels. I decided to get in on the act.

"*Ictus stricta!*" I said, sending a narrow TK bolt at the warlock on the ground. On its heels came a blue beam that caught him as he staggered from the impact of my bolt. He went down, and the Sentinels barely got a shield up in time to stop the red beams of Infernal energy coming down at them from above. I sent another bolt skyward, and a barrage of sparkling shards arced up from the line of trees to my right. Stewart and Ginger dodged to either side, then flew to the top of the hall.

A lithe figure emerged from the trees on the right, dark skin glistening, long hair in tight braids bouncing on her shoulders. Clad in a loose, flowing shirt and jeans, Kiya looked like a warrior goddess as she raced forward, a thick, twisted staff in hand. A yellow nimbus surrounded the head of the stave, and it left a glowing trail behind her as she ran.

"Make a hole!" she yelled at me as she turned the staff my way. "Make a BIG hole!"

Suddenly, I was flung into the air. When I reached the top of the arc, I could see that I was going to come down on the roof of Denham Hall. "*Ictus! Ictus! Ictus!*" I yelled as I blasted at the roof in a tight pattern. The hole I left ended up being at least ten feet wide. Then something caught me and lowered me to the floor for a soft landing. I still stumbled when my feet hit the floor. Kiya landed behind me as I got my balance back.

"What are you doing?" I demanded.

"There are at least two of them in there," she said. "Even as amped up as you are, you're no match for them."

"Don't die," I said. "I don't want to have to tell your folks."

"You look after yourself. I've got help of my own." She raised the staff. "On three. One, two.."

"Three!" I said. We unleashed a blast on the wall, not even bothering with the door.

"Well done," a familiar voice said from the cloud of dust. I walked through the hole we'd made.

"Professor Talbot," I said.

"You don't sound surprised. What gave it away?"

"Two things. Your jacket, the day the first attack happened. You didn't have it on when you came to get me, but when you had it on later, it showed splatter from the circle. And you still had your tie on. No one else had taken the time to put theirs on that early in the morning except the hedmaster. Then at the second attack, you were the first there, and you asked if I saw them."

"I asked if *he* had seen them."

"The Sentinels had already hidden me. There was no way you could have known anyone else was there unless you had seen me when I first showed up. But you still looked for me."

"And I thought I covered my tracks so well. I even stood up for you."

"I wondered about that."

"As long as you were free, everyone would be looking at you, instead of actually investigating."

"Professor, why are you wasting time?" Stewart said. "Let's just kill him!"

"He's stalling," Talbot and I said at the same time.

"You're waiting for the Sentinels to arrive," Talbot said.

"And you're waiting for the rest of your coven to get here."

"The Sentinels are no match for us."

"Think again. You're already down by at least six. My group retreated and drew five into the circle and the Sentinels too. They're trapped and cut off from your power."

"Idiot, that only makes us stronger. The fewer of us drawing on the soul stones, the more power there is to go around. Enough of this. Kill them." Stewart and Ginger raised their wands, and I barely got my shield up in time. Their attacks hammered into my shield, and I understood what he meant about them getting stronger. Even in my augmented state, I could tell I wouldn't last long against them. Suddenly the barrage lessened, and I saw the yellow glow of Kiya's staff beside me. They had forgotten about her, and now Ginger was paying the price, having to hold off an attack through sheer will, her red beam striving against Kiya's yellow less than a foot away from the tip of her wand. But with every second, she gained another inch.

"Impressive," Talbot said. "You shouldn't be that powerful."

"I walked the Ways," I said through gritted teeth. "Something you'd know about if you bothered with the history of your own school."

"Then let's see how you handle *me*," Talbot said. With a gesture, he threw a short beam of Infernal energy at me, and my shield collapsed. The blast itself hit me in the shoulder knocked me back through the hole in the wall we'd made coming in. My vision went white for a moment, and when I could see again, there was still a haze of red as the pain in my shoulder caught up to me. The flesh was red and raw there, blistered at the edges. I shook my head and got to my feet. The distance to the next room felt like a million miles, but I forced myself forward.

Talbot, Stewart and Ginger were all drawing from the crystals, red lines of power running from the circle to their outstretched hands. Kiya had lost most of the distance between her and Ginger, and Stewart was adding his strength to the assault, too. Kiya's defense had their beams splashing all around her, leaving scorched lines in the floor, or gaping holes where it had burned through.

"*Ictus latior!*" I yelled. The wide blast wasn't as effective against their shields, but it drew Stewart's attention to me. ""*Scutum sphaeram*," I uttered, just in time to catch both Stewart's and Talbot's attacks. Beside me, Kiya cried out and dropped her assault, bringing up a blue shield a microsecond before Ginger's beam splashed against it.

"You're just like the others," Talbot said as he poured more power into his attack. "Just a self-centered, entitled little brat who thinks the world owes you something. You think you *earned* that power? You think you *deserve* it? That it's your *right*? The others, they thought their last name made them worthy. They thought that they deserved power because they were *born* to it. And they demanded I give it to them, all the while kissing their lily white little asses." I dropped to one knee as I drew on every ounce of

268

power in me, growling with the effort. Beside me, Kiya took a step back, then another, her own shield beginning to falter as it deflected Infernal fire against the floor and ceiling. "Let me show you real power. This is the strength Mammon gives to the loyal."

"If you're gonna do something, do it now!" Kiya screamed. "We can't do this much longer."

"Happy to oblige," Talbot said as he drew his off hand back.

"She wasn't talking to you, asshole," I spat. He stopped and looked to me, then he started looking around the room. After a few seconds, he shook his head and put his hand back out to draw from the crystals. The arc or energy leapt to his palm, then faltered and died. One by one, the crystals went dark, except for Desiree's, which glowed brighter and brighter. The attacks against our shields weakened and then sputtered to a stop.

"No!" Talbot howled. A string of harsh, ancient syllables poured from his lips, and the lines between the crystals started to glow. Desiree's began to weaken as he spoke.

"They're recasting the binding!" Kiya said as Stewart and Ginger joined in.

"Not gonna happen," I growled. "Pop quiz, Professor. Why should you *always* cast a circle on the ground?" Talbot didn't waver in his casting, but his eyes went to me, and something flickered there that I had been wanting to see: doubt. I looked to Kiya, hoping she understood what I meant to do. Whether she did or not, she nodded, evidently ready to follow my lead. I took a couple of steps forward, then dropped to my backside and slid under the table supporting the crystals. Kiya was an inch behind me, and when I pointed up at the bottom of the table, she gave me a wicked grin, and her staff flared bright yellow.

"Aw, hell yeah," she said.

269

""*ICTUS!*" I roared. Her staff and my wand erupted in unison, and the center of the table exploded upward. We stood up to find the crystals floating in a circle around us, and all three of our opponents on the ground near the edge of the room. Now three lines of power were flowing from them to Desiree's crystal, and it was glowing bright enough that I had to shield my eyes. Then there was a loud *crack!* Desiree's crystal shattered, and we were faced with her soul, free of its prison and floating beside us.

Ginger let out an inarticulate scream and raised her wand as Stewart pointed his at me. Kiya and I both let loose. The blast sent them through the wall and flying into the quad. We turned to face Talbot. He raised his hand and uttered something harsh, but even as he did that, Desiree thrust her hand toward him. His spell flared to life around his hand, then faded as Desiree's soul glowed brighter.

"How?" Talbot asked, his voice rising in pitch. "How did you do that?"

"This is an Infernal spell," Desiree said, her disembodied voice crackling with anger. "Fueled by hate. And I'm part cambion. Every time you tapped it, I fed off of you, and I leached more and more power away from you. Until tonight, when I took it all. But he isn't important, Chance," she said, her crimson form turning to me. "We don't have much time to get their souls back to their bodies."

The click of the hammer being drawn back was all the warning we had. Kiya shoved me to one side, then cried out in pain as the gun in Talbot's hand fired. I hit the floor with her on top of me, coming down behind the wreckage of the table. I turned her over, expecting to see a gaping wound somewhere vital. Instead, I saw the gouge along her shoulder. She grimaced in pain, but she was still very much alive. I stood.

"Surprised?" Talbot said as he waved the pistol at me. "Did you think I didn't have more bullets? That I wouldn't *check*? Did you think I couldn't *reload*?"

"No, I counted on you doingexactly that," I said. I held my hand up to reveal the ring on my middle finger. "*Vocare!*" I said. The pistol flew from his hand to mine.

"Look around you," he sneered, sounding way too confident for a man who had just been beaten and disarmed. "This building is on fire, and we've been casting powerful spells close to volatile alchemical reagents. Any minute now, it's going to either explode, or it's going to collapse on itself." I looked around, and sure enough, I could see the flicker of flames from the places where their shots had either missed or been deflected by our shield spells. The alchemical table that we had blasted Ginger and Stewart through was already starting to smolder, and as I watched, blue flames sprang up.

"What's your point?" I asked as my eyes fell on the crystals, the souls of kids trapped against their will.

"My point is, you've castrated yourself by trying to be a hero. You're not going to shoot me, and you can't chase me and save your classmates at the same time. So it really means you only have one option." He turned and looked back at me with a smug grin. "So, farewell, and-"

I pulled the trigger.

Chapter 18

*~ Victory is often a hollow reward. ~ Col. Blaine
Halifax, British war mage*

"You shot me!" Talbot screamed as he held his hands
to his left thigh.

"Yeah, I did," I said as I walked over to him. "I'm still
a little fuzzy on that whole good-bad thing." Somewhere
below us, a muffled thump sounded. "Kiya, grab those
crystals. I've got dumbass here." I knelt beside Talbot and
picked him up, then hoisted him onto my shoulder. He let
out a yelp at that, and I made sure to jostle him a little
more. Ren's super fuel seemed to still be working, and I got
him down the ladder without too much strain. The fourth
floor was already burning, and I would have bet that our
fight wasn't the only one that had caused some damage.
Kiya followed me down the ladder, and Desiree's spirit
simply floated through the ceiling to join us. I headed for
the stairs. Flames were dancing along the ceiling as we hit
the hallway, and the air was almost black from smoke. We
descended out of the worst of it by the first landing to the
second floor, and the air was almost clear as we hit the first
floor. I heard wood groaning, and the building shuddered as
something collapsed above us. The we were at the door,
and Kiya blew it off the hinges. I stumbled into the cool
night air, then suddenly something hot kicked me in the ass
and sent me flying.

My shoulder hit the grass and I slid for another twenty
feet. When I finally stopped, I looked back to see the
second and third floor pretty much gone, and the first floor
now engulfed in fire.

"I am so expelled," I moaned as I sat up.

"Worry about that later," Desiree said. "Come on!"
She floated toward the infirmary, and I got to my feet.

"Don't move, Fortunato!" I heard Dearborn bark. I
turned to see her facing me with her *paramiir* staff leveled
at me. Without thinking, I reached for it, and it flew into

273

my hand. Oh yeah, still magickally amped, too. I threw it back to her.

"I'm not the bad guy here. He is." Her eyes flicked to Talbot, then back to me as her expression turned to one of disgust. "We still have to restore the souls of their victims," I said.

"Go." She didn't have to tell me twice. Kiya and I got to our feet and took off at a run. Around us, lights were coming on in the residence halls, and people were starting to come out into the quad. I heard Hoshi's voice behind me and saw him leading the rest of the scholarship students he'd recruited and the remaining Highwaymen toward the infirmary. The fight was over, but the hard part was just beginning.

The doors to the infirmary were open, the Sentinels on duty facing the quad, *paramiir* out. "This area is off limits!" one of them said in challenge. When Desiree floated past him, he lowered his staff.

"They're with me," she said. "Please, they're trying to save us."

"Let them go in," Buchanan's voice came from behind me. As one, the Sentinels stood down, and we followed Desiree.

She floated in the middle of the room, her hands out toward the bodies on the beds. "I don't know if...if I'm strong enough to do this. If *we* are strong enough."

"The damage was pretty bad," Buchanan said. "I haven't been able to figure out a way to undo it."

"It is not about strength, or knowledge," Kiya said, her voice serene. "This is about life. It takes life to create life, and to restore it." She went to Buchanan and put her hand to his cheek. Her eyes were radiant as she smiled at him. "You love teaching because you see that life in your students." She turned to me. "We are that life, Chance. Not just you and me, but all of us. We have it to spare because we're young. You have to ask everyone for their help, for a little bit of themselves."

I backed away and put hand hands up between us. "I'm not a big one for persuasive speaking. And I'm not all that popular, either."

"This isn't about you," Kiya said. "And trust Mother Wata. You'll find the words you need." She gestured toward the door, and I...I couldn't help but go. Hoshi stepped up behind me as I walked out the door with Buchanan on his right.

"*Volumen sursum,*" Buchanan uttered, and the air in front of my face changed. The quad was quiet. Students were milling around near the doors to their halls, and leaning out windows. I took a breath and hoped. Then I prayed. For the first time in a long time, I asked for Divine help. *Please, help me get this right.*

"Franklin Acadaemy," I said, and my voice boomed, sounding stronger than I dared hope. "We need your help. I need your help. Not for me, but for your fellow classmates. If there was ever a single moment when we could be everything we hoped, a moment we could look back at for the rest of our lives and say that we saved a life, that we were truly human...that we were the best we could be...this is that moment. Your classmates need your help, they need you to be their heroes right now. Please, don't look at me, look at your friends, and do this for them. But I warn you, what we're about to do calls for a sacrifice. It takes life to restore life, soul to restore soul. You'll be giving up a little bit of yourself to help save not just the lives of your friends, but their very souls. That's what makes us heroes. So if you've got it in you to be something better, to be worthy of everything this school is supposed to stand for, then *step up!*"

A few students started moving into the quad, then more. Windows emptied, and more started coming out into the open. Scholarship students and Boston bluebloods came

275

side by side, their faces determined. My chest went tight as I saw more and more join the group in front of me. Kiya came up to stand beside me.

"I told you that you'd find the words," she said. Her hand was a gentle presence on my shoulder, and her smile sounded through in her voice.

"Or maybe they're just good people," I said.

"They are. I will begin here. Help Desiree guide the souls back home." I turned and went in.

"Put the stones on the beds," Desiree said as I walked into the infirmary. I didn't hesitate, and in moments, I had each crystal nestled between the feet of the comatose victims. Desiree stood at the foot of her bed and nodded.

"Okay, looks like we're good to go."

"I'll need to feed from you," she said. "Is that okay?"

"Sure, anything you need."

She pointed to her body on the bed. "Just hold my hand."

I went to her bedside and took her hand out from beneath the sheets. Her palm was warm and soft, and her hand closed slightly around mine. Outside, Kiya began a chant, and after a couple of minutes, Desiree started to glow, her soul turning from red to white. I felt all of the anger drain from me almost immediately, and I had to struggle to focus on things that might keep that emotion alive in me.

"No, Chance," Desiree said. "Let go of that. I need something else now. Something pure. Just go with it. It's okay." I nodded and let the anger go. White energy began to drift like radiant smoke from Desiree, slowly reaching toward the other students until it hit the crystals. The moment it touched the red crystals, they glowed white as well. Vaguely human looking forms floated up from the crystals, then began to descend into the bodies below them.

Sudden relief and joy flooded me. I'd made a promise to make things right a year ago, and this moment was a tangible reminder that I was making good on it. Desiree glowed even brighter and the crystals cracked, so that the tendrils of white flowed directly into the bodies. The limbs began to glow, then the torsos, until finally, their heads and crown chakras lit up. Each of them began to float above the bed, surrounded by the blinding light. After a few moments, it resolved itself into different colors. Oranges, blues, bright pinks, vibrant yellows began to course through the glowing auras as the bodies descended. Then the energy strands were absorbed into the bodies, leaving Desiree standing there in the middle of the room, glowing, her smile as radiant as her body.

"Your turn," I said. Desiree looked at me and shook her head.

"You can let go now, Chance," she said.

"Don't you still need to feed from me until you get back into your body?"

"Not my hand. Of me. You can let me go now."

"What do you mean?" I asked, my voice cracking. "Aren't you…?"

"No, Chance. My body isn't alive any more. Thank you for holding my hand until the end."

"No, Desiree," I said. "No, no, no. Please, not you. You helped everyone else. You're supposed to live."

"My fate was sealed the moment I broke my crystal, Chance. Even you have to know that. It's okay. I knew what I was doing. I made this choice." She floated toward me, beautiful and amazing.

"Why?" I demanded. "Why you? Why not me?"

"Because you still have other duties to fulfill, other promises to keep. I'm going to miss you, and all that might have been between us. You would have been my friend for life. But…part of me will always be with you." Her ethereal hand reached out and touched my cheek. My skin tingled all over as she held the touch for a moment, and thin white glowing strands connected us for a moment as she pulled her hand away. Her hand touched mine, the glowing energy infusing my skin for a moment.

The room glowed around her as she began to expand and lose shape. "Desiree," I said, pleading. "Please…"

"Let go, Chance. Let go of my hand, and let go of me."

I opened my hand, and Desiree's hand fell to the sheets, limp, unmoving.

"She didn't die in vain," I heard someone say behind me. I turned to see another bright presence, then my vision cleared, and it was the nurse who had talked to me the other night. "Sacrifices like that…her friends, her family, they'll all know, they'll all remember. It's cold comfort now, and all you can do is honor her choice, her sacrifice."

Tears rolled down my face unchecked as I shook my head. Something in my soul was missing, and nothing was ever going to fill that hole. Greif, sadness, something full of pain and loss welled up inside me, and came out in a wordless scream. I tried to push all the pain and sadness out in that one agonizing sound, to exorcise that particular demon, and find a place where that hurt didn't exist. And when I got to the bottom of that scream, I found out that there was no place where that hurt hadn't gone. There was no escaping it, no relief from it.

Cheers came from outside. I stood, and found my shield against all the pain. Rage ran through my veins, only this was not the cold, calculating rage I was used to. This was a hot, unthinking fury that was new to me. I scooped Desiree's body from the bed and walked out of the infirmary, suddenly offended that anyone celebrate just now. I carried her to the open doors, and the cheering died when I stepped through. One by one, the faces of my classmates, of my friends, fell as they realized what they were seeing. A part of me felt bad for that, but I felt any sense of blame for them slip away. Then my gaze fell on Talbot. He stood there in manacles, his face set in a frown.

278

His anger pissed me off. I carried Desiree toward him, and the crowd parted before me, cheeks damp as they moved, even among the Sentinels. I set her frail form down at his feet with infinite care, and made sure to tuck her hand under the sheet before I stood to face her true killer.

"She was my friend," I said. "And you killed her." Talbot went pale as he recoiled from me.

"Please, Fortunato, you have to-"

His nose broke under my fist with an almost satisfying sound. "Get up." He struggled to his knees, and I could see his death in his own eyes.

"It wasn't personal," he said.

"It was to me," I said. "Get. Up!"

"Please, stop this," he said. "I know you're upset but… but…"

"Tell me what you want," I said. "Beg me for mercy."

"Sentinels!" Talbot yelped and held out his manacled hands. "I'm in your custody! You can't let this happen." Dearborn came forward and grabbed the chain between the spellbinders, then pulled them free with a yank.

"You attacked his family," she said coolly. "He's within his rights to demand justice." She turned away from him, and every Sentinel did the same, symbolically seeing nothing. A high pitched squeal escaped his lips as he tried to crawl away.

"*Adducite huc,*" I intoned. The TK spell yanked him to me. I held him by his shirt and shook him. "Say it. Beg for mercy."

"Yes, please," he stammered. "You're a good person. Don't kill me. Please, mercy."

"For Desiree," I said, looking down. "For her, I'll spare your life. But that's all I'll let you keep." My hands flared with Hellfire, and his eyes went wide as I looked back up at him. I sent the Infernal flame into his body, feeding it all the hatred and anger I had, relishing his screams. I let it ravage his body, and focused it on his nervous system, burning away tissue as precisely as I could.

He sobbed and whimpered as I finished. "Please, no more." His breath came in pained gasps, and I smiled.

"No more," I said, and pushed him away. He fell to the ground in a boneless heap, the only sound coming from him a strained wheeze. "No more anything. I take from you everything. You'll live, but that's all you'll ever do." I knelt and picked Desiree's body up, then turned and walked away, leaving him paralyzed from the neck down, barely able to breathe.

I could take no pride in what I'd just done, but I could take some small satisfaction. What I'd inflicted on Talbot wasn't justice. I didn't think that could ever happen. What I had done was punishment, nothing more.

It would have to do.

Chapter 19

*~ To comfort them was our desire, but we were called
to silence. ~ Briathos, angel. Unsourced text.*

"While Mr. Fortunato's time here has been beneficial
both to him and to the Franklin Academy," Headmaster
Caldecott said, "it is the conclusion of both this institution
and his family that the Franklin Academy is not the ideal
environment for his academic needs." The Headmaster's
office was pretty full, and as he set the letter down on his
desk, I looked around the room. On my right, Mom and Dr.
C looked almost as happy about me being kicked out of
wizard school as I was. Even if they were being nice and
gentle about it, there was no doubt I was being kicked out
of the Franklin Academy.

Draeden was as unreadable as ever, but I couldn't help
but think he had gotten what he wanted out of this whole
thing. Beside him, Master Polter overflowed his seat. He
was less than enthusiastic, judging by his expression.
Sentinel Dearborn sat to his left, clearly not happy.

"Mister Fortunato, you'll be happy to hear that several
of your teachers have included letters of recommendation
for you in your file."

"And the...other letters, Headmaster?" Polter asked
with a greasy smile.

"Which other letters, Master Polter?"

"The numerous reprimands, and the infraction reports
from the Sentinels? Do you think he will be happy to hear
about those? After all, he shot one of his instructors!"

"You shot someone?" Mom asked in shock.

"Just a little," I said. "Plus, he was the guy who
attacked Dee."

"Oh," Mom said with a smile. "Okay."

"All of Professor Talbot's entries in your son's file
have been removed, of course, and there is only one
infraction report from the Sentinels."

"Preposterous," Polter said. "I demand that he be censured for interfering with the Sentinels carrying out their duties! He carried out his own covert activities, there can be no doubting that. All of those supposedly anonymous messages could have come from no one else."

"Sir, we have no evidence of anything outside what we've documented," Dearborn said. "To censure him for what we *think* happened would go against our own code."

"And in spite of your feelings on the matter," Draeden said, "I know you're not about to issue a direct order to do so anyway."

"Of course not," Polter said. "So long as he does not graduate from this institution, I am content."

"And so am I," Mom said. I wasn't fast enough to stop my laugh, and it came out in a snort.

"You will…" Polter said, then stopped as when Mom turned her glare on him.

"I will what?" Mom hissed. "Go on, finish that sentence."

"This is the finest school in the nation," Polter said. "Show a little respect."

"I'm showing as little respect as I can," Mom said. "Or did you think I had forgotten that you voted to *kill* my son? If this is your alma mater, then I *certainly* don't want his name tainted with its stench. I was against sending him here in the first place."

"Your son blew up a nearly three-hundred-year old building, I'll have you know."

"Only one?" Mom asked. "I'd say he stopped too soon!"

"Miss Murathy, please," Caldecott said. "I understand your position, and we are truly grateful to your son for what he did."

"And the truth is," Draeden said, "there are several powerful families who feel a certain debt of gratitude to him as well. After all, he did save their children from a fate

282

that was truly worse than death. Even Andrew should be able to understand, however, that this is not the kind of thing the school wants to be known for."

"Well, if he wants discretion," Mom said, "he certainly doesn't know how to get it."

"Agreed," Draeden said. "Master Polter, please excuse yourself."

"Master Draeden, I have every right to be here."

"Your presence is not helping, Andrew. Now please go. While it is still a request."

Polter got to his feet and left the room, huffing and muttering.

"Now," Caldecott said. "Perhaps we can make some progress. Miss Murathy, Master Polter's sentiments aside, we do truly appreciate your son's efforts here. He is a good student, which would make him an exemplary student anywhere else. Letters of commendation and references from any instructor here carry a certain…authority that will help your son later in life. But…I am afraid Master Draeden is also correct. We would certainly appreciate your discretion regarding this whole matter. Especially regarding the fact that an instructor was involved, to say nothing of the eleven students he recruited."

"Eleven?" I asked. "There should have been twelve students. He had a full thirteen people in the circle."

"So we thought as well. But…we never did find any other sign of Miss Hart. The damage to her room was extensive, and we were unable to retrieve enough evidence from it to confirm her involvement. But back to the matter at hand. Your discretion in this matter…is of the utmost importance. If there is anything we can do to ensure that our students do not suffer unduly from the damage such information might do to this school's reputation, if it is within our power, you have only to ask."

"I can think of something," I said with a smile. Caldecott turned a shade of green before he nodded. "If he's willing, I want Ren's contract."

"Just one indentured sprite? You could have as many of them you wished, willing or not."

"Just the one, and that one in particular. And I want you to give Hoshi Nakamura and Kiya Marlin the same kind of commendations and references you're giving me. And…" I stopped, my throat suddenly too tight to speak for a moment. "And you have to do right by Desiree and her family. Make sure people remember what she did."

"The Council will see to her final arrangements," Draeden said. "Her family will not want for anything, I assure you."

"And…the students have already begun an impromptu shrine to her," Caldecott said, his own voice a little sad. "We will do something more…formal soon. Something befitting her sacrifice. We'll also take care of your friends. They're both welcome back here any time, as well."

"We've put my son through enough, I think," Mom said. "Chance, why don't you go on, and wait by the carriage."

I stood up and wiped my eyes. Caldecott came around from behind his desk and offered me his hand. After a moment's hesitation, I took it. The familiar tingle of contained power hit my palm, then I let go and headed for the door, letting the adults do the formal shit adults did. Mom put a hand on my arm, and I stopped for a second. I didn't have a smile for her. All I had was half of one, but it seemed to be enough.

Outside, I found myself face to round face with Desiree's Gram. Nearly a dozen other people were gathered in the waiting area as well, but Gram was the one who was right where she needed to be.

"I'm sorry," I whispered to her, unable to meet her gaze.

"Shush you," she said. "Look at me." She took my chin in her hand and turned me to face her. "Look in my eyes." I did, and did a double take. Her eyes were normal, not the solid black of a cambion. Her forehead was smooth, unmarred by horns.

"Your eyes," I said. "What happened to your... and your horns?"

"My Desiree," she said. "She redeemed us all."

"She saved a lot of lives, too."

"They told us that you...you were with her till the end. That you held her hand. And that you cried over her like she was your own blood." All I could do was nod. Hot tears slid down my cheeks as the wound opened anew. "Not many would do that for one of us. You're family, Chance Fortunato. The blood of the covenant runs thicker than the water of the womb." She wrapped her arms around me and held me tight for a moment, then pulled away and kissed my cheek. We both stood a little straighter, and she turned and walked out of the room, leaving me to face the parents of the other kids that we *did* save.

Most of them just sat there and watched me go, but one man stood and approached me. Sterling Lodge was a step behind him. "I'm Davis Lodge. Young man, if you ever need anything at all, you call me. Day or night." He pressed a business card into my left hand, then grabbed my right and shook it. Tears coursed down his cheeks. "Thank you," he said, his hand still gripping mine. "For saving my son. Thank you."

Sterling put his hand on my shoulder when his father stepped back and held his own right hand out. I took it. "Look, I don't know how to thank you, especially after...you know."

"I know. It's okay. Just...make your life...worth the sacrifice. That's all I can ask."

"I will." He stepped aside and let me past.

Junkyard was waiting in the carriage, and my luggage was loaded onto the back. I turned around a looked back at the Franklin Academy, and thought there were only a couple of times in my life that I was as glad to leave a place behind. For all that it was supposed to be this paragon of education, I couldn't help but think that it was so stuck in its traditions and standards that it had forgotten the most powerful thing about magick: the mystery. They had reduced it to formulas and recipes, into a tool for getting what you wanted. I had already learned from Dr. Corwin that it was much more than that. It was the bond between friends, the sound of your sister's laugh. The power of your mother's smile to make you move mountains just to be on the receiving end of it. It was the way the hair stood up on my arms when I heard my favorite musicians play, or how my lips tingled when Shade kissed me. It was in fire and lightning, wind and rain. That was where magick lived. But understanding it? That was a journey that took a lifetime. I sure as the Nine Hells wasn't going to figure it out here.

Another carriage pulled up behind ours, and the driver got down and opened the door. My heart froze in my chest as I saw the woman who got out. Silky white hair, the way she walked, the way she stood; I knew before she turned my way that her eyes would be silver. I knew this woman, even though I had never met her before. Just the memory of her was enough to make my breath come in short gasps and drop the bottom out of my stomach. Her gaze locked onto mine, and her lips moved ever so slightly, creating a smile that Dr. Corwin's memories replayed often.

"Kim," I whispered, finally saying her name out loud. The smile disappeared, and her head tilted to one side. Between heartbeats, she became a blur, then she was right in front of me. I felt something cold and thin at my throat, and her eyes filled my vision.

"Who are you?" she demanded. "How do you know me?"

286

"I'm Chance," I said. "I...remember you."

"We have never met, and only one man has ever said my name the way you just did."

"Dr. Corwyn," I whispered. "He's my mentor. We shared memories a year ago."

"Trevor," she breathed, and suddenly it was her turn to look gut punched. "Oh, sweet Inari." She took a step back, and I saw the blade she'd held to my throat. Almost as soon as I saw it, the blade disappeared with a flicker of movement, and her eyes came up to my face, never quite meeting mine.

"Is he here?" she asked, hope and fear in her voice. I nodded. "You must not tell him you saw me. He cannot know of this."

"Why the hell not?" I demanded. "He loves you!"

"And I, him," she said, her voice sad. "Please, promise me you will not tell my Trevor that you saw me. Please." *My Trevor.* He would have done anything to hear her say that to him again. Dr. Corwin loved her too much to ever say no to her, and so help me, I could see why. Even the memory of his feelings for her made me love her a little too.

"I promise," I said. The bond sealed between us, and she smiled as her hair ruffled in the ethereal breeze.

"I *will* make this right," she said before she turned away.

"You better," I said to her retreating back. She stopped and turned back to face me, her expression stern for a moment. Then her features softened and she inclined her head. A sudden warm rush hit me as she took on the burden of some unspoken promise of her own. She disappeared into the carriage, and moments later, Hoshi came out of the building and got in her carriage, then it sped off, leaving me with the puzzle pieces clicking in place. Kim was Hoshi's *kai ma,* his kitsune god mother. Another secret I couldn't tell anyone about. Great.

There's no place like home, I thought. And I couldn't wait to get back there.

The door to the hall opened, and Draden came out with his overcoat draped over his forearm. "None of this worked out as I'd hoped," he said as he walked toward me.

. "What did you think was going to happen?"

"I had hoped the Academy would be a positive influence on you."

"Surprise," I said. "It wasn't." I looked off toward the Blockhouse, where I knew Talbot was being kept, then turned away. My face burned in shame, and I was glad Desiree hadn't been there to see what I'd done to him. "I learned a lot of things here. But not how to be a good person. I need to be around my friends and my family to learn that. I need Dr. Corwin to show me the right way to be a mage."

"Perhaps you're right," Dreaden said. "I had hoped this place would take some of the rough edges off of you, but it appears as though that is your greatest strength."

"Hey, I'm a New Essex kid, not some blue blood," I said.

"I'm learning that perhaps it's best to leave well enough alone along those lines," Draeden said.

"Damn straight," I said. "I don't do normal worth a damn."

"Obviously," he said with a smile. "The offer to take the jet back home is still open."

"Sure, sounds good," I said. He owed me at least that much. I got into the carriage and leaned back into the seat. My goodbyes had already been said, and with Hoshi and Kiya already gone, I had no reason to want to stick around. I was leaving the Franklin Academy with a lot of new knowledge, but there was an aching wound on my soul as well. Wizards weren't supposed to be whiny. But we could hurt. And we could heal. It was time to go home.

Letter to the Reader

Dear Reader,

First of all, I want thank you for your patience with waiting for Charm School. I know this one has taken longer than the others. Between other contract obligations with a publisher and a lot of family business to deal with, I've faced more delays than usual. This was also a more subtle mystery than usual, and I had to be very careful not to give away too much, but also not to conceal too much as well. Here's hoping I got it right.

As always, your reviews are more than welcome, and in fact, necessary. Every book is driven by its reviews. They not only help me improve as a writer, but also help bring new fans to join your number. So, please, if you've made it this far, I'd appreciate reading your thoughts. Another way you can help not only self-published wirters like me, but any artist you like, is by posting links to their work on your social media. Just a quick word and a link is all it takes to help support your favorite authors, artists and musicians.

Independent authors like myself need your support. As always, you'll find some of my fellow indie authors suggested in the pages following. I've been friends with EM Ervin and JM Guillen for years, and I've only recently met RR Virdi, but the man is not only an amazing writer, he's a whirlwind of inspiration and support. What can I say? I have good taste in writer friends. If you enjoy the Demon's Apprentice series, the Nasaru Chronicles or the Dossiers of Asset 108, then I think you'll also like the Grave Report.

Thank you again for your patience and your continued support, dear reader. I appreciate all the kind words and encouragement. I remain

Yours truly,
Ben Reeder

Grave Beginnings by RR Virdi

Thirteen... As far as numbers go, it isn't a great one. Hell, it's not even a good one and Vincent Graves is going to find out just how unlucky of a number it can be. Because someone, or something, is killing people in the Empire state, and whatever it is, it gives people everything they ever desired and more. And it's the more that's the problem! Well...it's one of the problems. Vincent's investigation also seems to have drawn the attention of a relentless FBI agent and then there's the little bit where he has only thirteen hours to solve the case, or he dies. Talk about your literal deadlines... ...No pressure. By the end of this case Vincent will come to understand the meaning of an age old proverb: Be careful what you wish for - because you just might get it!

"I believe R.R. Virdi belongs with other Urban Fantasy greats like Jim Butcher. The Grave Report is sure to go far and only pick up more fans with each successful novel. I can't wait to see where R.R. Virdi will take us next." — A Drop Of Ink Reviews

"Fast paced, humorous, with action and drama on every page and paragraph, this paranormal thriller is reminiscent of one of my all-time favorite authors. This is like Jim Butcher's The Dresden Files but with a flavor all its own. RR Virdi is fame-bound with this series. If you like Jim Butcher, you'll enjoy this one. Highly Recommend." — CD Coffelt ~ Author of The Wilder Mage

Wake Up Call by EM Ervin

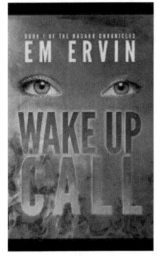

Jo is your average, everyday seventeen year old girl.

Wait, no she's not. Not by a longshot.

She is a girl with a secret. Possessed of powers no one would believe even if they knew that she had them. The ability to create illusions at thought is a dangerous weapon in the most responsible of hands, and Jo's aren't exactly squeaky clean.

Ever the trouble magnet, Jo is accustomed to finding more than her fair share of problems - most of which she brings on herself. The rebellious daughter of a senator and a diplomat, she has a rap sheet and has been kicked out of nearly every prestigious private school on the Eastern Seaboard.

This time, she's vowed to make an actual effort. Not to fit in - that'd be impossible - but to just not get kicked out.

Of course, this would be the school that turns out to be the favorite hunting grounds of a homicidal ghost.

What could possibly happen?

Aberrant Vectors (Dossiers of Asset 108) by JM Guillen

November 17, 1999
San Francisco, California

Few things are worse than a system undergoing a cold boot...

Michael Bishop is an Asset of the Facility, but tonight is his night off. His expectation is to have a few drinks with his friend Wyatt Guthrie, perhaps go out and have a night on the town.

But the Facility has made other arrangements.

Before he realizes what has happened, Asset 108 has been dispatched to a carnage-filled interior location, lit only with flickering and lurid light. As Michael drifts through the shadows, encountering stuttering and broken Facility technology, he attempts to figure out why he has been dispatched here and what his mission is.

Yet before he can, he is fighting for his life.

Soon, with his personal gear malfunctioning, Bishop is standing against foes familiar to him, foes that have been transformed into inhuman abominations. With time running out, he finds his way to his cadre, and they fight their way to the depths of the mysterious Spire. There, they discover remnants of a lost, broken, carnage-filled world.

As Michael and his cadre stands against the inhabitants of an entire world of bloody ruin, he is forced to face a painful truth.

It is possible that this dossier will be his last...

Made in the USA
San Bernardino, CA
11 February 2017